CANNERY ROAD

Book I of the Jinx Bay Series

Fret not thyself because of evildoers, neither be thou envious against the workers of iniquity. For they shall soon be cut down like the grass, and wither as the green herb. Psalm 37:7

Kay Chandler
A multi-award-winning author

Kay Chandler

This is a work of fiction. Characters, places, and incidents are the products of the author's imagination or are used fictitiously.

Scripture taken from the King James Version of the Holy Bible

Cover Design by Chase Chandler

Dedicated

To Betty Ayers, Betty Spann, Betty Yancey

I don't know the meaning of the name, Betty, but it must mean sugar and spice and everything nice, because that describes the Bettys in my life. They encourage me, make me laugh. and keep me straight. I need all three.

PROLOGUE

Eufaula, Alabama
Tuesday, February 1955

"Theodore Jones, either she goes, or I do, but don't expect me to go quietly."

"Don't threaten me, Gussie." He took a few puffs on his pipe, then laid it in the ash tray beside his chair. "I won't stop you from leaving. In fact, I'll pay you to go. Name your price."

With a toss of her head, she let out a sarcastic-sounding chuckle. Then touching her head to make sure she hadn't mussed her perfectly coiffed hair, she smirked,. "Remind me, Theo. How does that slogan on your desk, go? I believe it says, 'A good name is better to be chosen than great riches?' Trust me, dear husband, if you don't get that woman out of my house, I'll see to it that you have neither your good name nor your great riches. I can easily take both from you."

"Keep your voice down."

"You think I care if she hears me? I hope she does. What do you suppose your beloved grandson and the good townsfolk will say if I should make it known you were cavorting around with me before your saintly wife died?"

"That's ridiculous. You make it sound as if we were having an illicit relationship. No one would believe you."

"You think not? Try me. Besides, folks are probably already suspicious of a little hanky-panky going on between you and that shapely little daughter-in-law. After all, it was just the two of you, living here under the same roof for months. You're a handsome man for your age and the little gold-digger was raised in a reformatory school. It's not hard to imagine what went on." She looked up from painting her fingernails. "Adultery should guarantee me enough alimony to continue living in the manner to which I've become accustomed."

His jaw jutted forward. "You're an evil woman, Gussie, but I think that's even beneath you."

"Don't put me to the test."

The demonic gleam in her eyes frightened him. He pulled a tiny pill from his shirt pocket and tucked under his tongue, though he surmised the pain in his heart wasn't from an erratic heartbeat as the doctor suggested—but rather from a contentious, erratic wife.

Holding her hand in front of her, she blew on her wet nails. "If I left you, who could blame me?"

Theodore had always prided himself on being level-headed. He'd made a lot of important decisions in his lifetime, but marrying Gussie was not one of them. He wanted to believe if he hadn't been so devasted over losing Jenny, the love of his life, that he would never have fallen into Gussie's trap. How could he have been so blind? He stood, then stalked over to the window. His voice quaked. "What am I to do, Gussie? Deuce is Ronald's child. My only grandson. Ramona won't leave without the boy, and I can't just kick them out. Don't I owe it to my son to provide for his wife and child?"

"That's ridiculous. You owe him nothing. He's dead. I'm not. You owe it to me to get that woman out of my house. She acts as if she owns the place."

"Gussie, be reasonable. This was her house, long before it was yours. You knew Ramona and Deuce were living here, and you made no objections when I agreed to marry you."

"You're mistaken, but as usual, you weren't listening."

CHAPTER 1

Ramona Jones heard the disgusting lies spewed from the adjoining room, but what troubled her most was that her son heard them. There was one thing the woman was right about: Theodore Jones was indeed a handsome man for his age. But the suggestion that anything immoral went on between her and her father-in-law made Ramona sick on her stomach.

Seeing the distraught look on her fourteen-year-old son's face, she forced a smile. "Hey, why the long face, cowboy? We didn't like it here, anyway, did we?"

"Not since Granny died. I hate that woman."

"I'm sorry you heard that, Deuce, since it wasn't true. However, I don't like for you to use that word. We can hate Gussie's actions, but we don't hate her."

"I'm sorry, Mama, but I do. How can you not hate her? Where are we gonna live if she kicks us out?"

"Get that worried look off your face. Gussie is not kicking us out. We're leaving on our own. You and I are going on an adventure." She pulled a small suitcase from the top of the closet and laid it open on the bed. "One side is yours. We'll pack as much as we can, for our adventure."

"But what about the good luggage under the bed? It would hold more."

"I have my reasons. Just do as I say." After trying to stuff the taffeta and net crinoline in her side of the suitcase, she gave up and decided to wear it under the full, green cotton skirt with a starched white blouse.

If only Ronald were there to tell her what to do—where to go. When he left for the war, he made plans for her to live with his parents until he returned, but neither of them considered the dreadful possibility that he might not come back. After getting the devastating news, Ramona stayed at Rose Trellis because Granny, as she affectionately referred to her mother-in-law, insisted they needed one another. Looking back, she had no regrets. It was the only real home she'd ever had, and for the first thirteen years of Deuce's life, it was exactly where they needed to be. But everything changed when Granny lost her battle to cancer.

Ramona felt a wetness on her cheeks and turned her face toward the window to keep Deuce from knowing she was as frightened as he. It wasn't long after Deuce's grandmother's death that his grandfather brought Gussie into the house and announced they had just gotten married at the County Court House. Ramona knew Daddy Theo was lonely. But who gets *that* lonely? She volunteered at the time to find another place to live, but Ronald's father was adamant that Rose Trellis was her home, and it was ridiculous to even think of moving out.

In hindsight, she could see staying was a mistake. Every decision she ever made was based on what she thought Ronald would have wanted for his son. She stayed at Rose Trellis because Ronald would've wanted him to grow up knowing his grandfather. Now, it seemed he knew more than he needed to know about the man he called Daddy Theo.

"Mama, are you all right?"

"All right? Are you kidding? I'm excited. Hurry and finish packing." She looked at his side of the suitcase and said, "If you'll roll your clothes instead of folding them, you can pack more."

"How do I know what to carry if I don't even know where we're going?"

Attempting to sound cheerful, she quipped, "Don't you know half the fun of an adventure is in not knowing what comes next?" As convincing as she tried to sound, Deuce was bright for his years, and she didn't fool herself into thinking he couldn't see through her. She was scared and with plenty of reason.

When she picked up the packed suitcase, Deuce immediately took it from her hands. He was so much like his father. Tall, handsome, striking blue eyes and thick, dark hair that fell in ringlets. His one desire was to take care of her, and to make her life easier. It was a big job for a fourteen-year-old.

They strode through the parlor where her husband's father and his wife were sitting.

Gussie sneered. "If you think walking in here with a suitcase is gonna make us beg you to stay, you've got another think coming. It's about time you decided to take on some responsibility instead of depending on Theo to support you."

Theodore lowered his head. "That's enough, Gussie."

"I don't know why you want to act like it's all my fault. You know you're as glad they're leaving as I am."

He pushed back from the table and stood. Reaching for the suitcase, he said, "I'll take it to the car, Deuce."

Deuce held tightly. Tears glistened in his eyes. "No, Daddy Theo. We don't need you."

"I'm sorry you feel that way, son. You know how much your grandmother and I loved you."

"Granny, yes. I'm not sure you even know what love is."

Ramona said, "Deuce, that was rude. Apologize to your grandfather."

Daddy Theo shook his head slowly. "No apology called for. I understand. Son, could you please give your mother and me a few minutes alone?"

"Sure. The sooner I'm in the car ready to take off, the happier I'll be."

After he was out of earshot, Theodore said, "Ramona, you do understand, my hands are tied. If I had my way, Gussie would be the one leaving, but she has me over a barrel. She keeps reminding me that she can ruin me, but the truth is, she's already ruined me."

He reached in his pocket and pulled out a wad of bills. "Take this. It'll help get you on your feet."

"I don't want your money."

"But you and the boy will need money to get a start. Please take it."

If she could afford to turn it down, she would. But there was Deuce to consider. "I'll pay you back as soon as I land a job."

"Forget it. It's not a loan. His shoulders slumped. "This is not what Ronald would've wanted. You must hate me."

"I don't hate you, Theodore. I don't. I feel sorry for you."

"It hurts to hear you call me by my name. I know I don't always know how to show it, but I truly learned to love you, Ramona, and felt proud hearing you address me as Daddy Theo. In spite of what you think, I hate to see you go, but if you're determined to leave, I wish you'd wait until morning. It'll soon be dark, and I hate to think about you being on the road at night. Where do you plan to go?"

"Does it matter?"

"It matters more than you know. One day, I hope to make it up to you." He followed her to her car, leaned over and looked inside. "Goodbye, Deuce. Take good care of your mama and let me know when y'all get settled."

"Like you care what happens to us." Deuce turned his face in the opposite direction, which Ramona suspected was to keep them from seeing the tears in his eyes.

She cranked the car and backed out of the driveway. "Deuce,

that wasn't very respectful. He's still your grandfather."

"Yes'm. Sorry." A few miles down the road, Deuce said, "Mama, tell me again what my daddy was like?"

She flung her arm over the seat and patted his shoulder. "Honey, I can't think of anything to tell you that you haven't already heard dozens of times."

"But I want to hear it again."

Why not? Thinking about Ronald and describing his amazing attributes was her favorite pastime.

A couple of hours later, Deuce said, "It seems like there's been nothing but woods for a long time. Maybe we should pull off the side of the road and sleep until daylight."

"Are you sleepy?"

"No ma'am, but it's hard to see the road. How much further to a town?"

"I don't know. I thought we should be in Jinx Bay by now. I'm not sure where we are."

"What's in Jinx Bay?"

She glanced at him and winked. "Fish!"

His face lit up. "You don't mean—Mama, isn't that the name of the town in Florida where Daddy used to go every summer? It is, isn't it? Tell me that story again."

Ramona drew a deep breath, as if she were about to engage in a long narration. "You can probably tell it better than I. Your daddy said when he was a boy his uncle owned a fish house and cannery, and he and his friend, Joel, would go stay a couple of weeks every summer and work on the boats. He said catching fish didn't feel like work. He made it sound like a real adventure."

"So that's why you said we're going on an adventure. If we lived there, Mama, do you think we could get a job on the boats? What a life that would be to just fish all day and get paid for it."

"I'm not too keen on riding on a boat all day, but I thought it might be worth a try to see if they're hiring women to work in the cannery."

"A cannery? That stinks."

She snickered. "More than you know, I'm sure. But if it works out and they hire me, we'll see if they'll let you work on the boats during school holidays and in the summer."

"Oh, I'd want to do it year around."

"And what about school, young man?"

"Who needs school if you have a job you love? And I know I'd love fishing. I'd save my money to buy me a big boat, and maybe in time I could . . ."

Ramona found it hard to follow the conversation. According to the map, they should've been in Jinx Bay by now. Where did she go wrong? The gas gauge on her car was broken, and she had no idea how far she'd driven. There'd be no filling stations open until morning. The thought that they could be stranded in the middle of nowhere caused shivers down her spine. If only she knew how much further it would be to civilization.

Deuce said, "You aren't listening, are you? What's wrong, Mama?"

"Nothing. I hope. Just trying to figure out where we are."

Out of the darkness, something darted in front of the car.

Deuce screamed. "Mama, watch out!"

The warning came too late. There was a loud thud, screeching of brakes, and the car spun around, hitting a pine tree. Maybe she would've seen it in time if her mind had been on the road. Or if she had parked and waited for daylight, as her fourteen-year-old son had suggested.

Shaken, she said, "What was that?"

"We hit a deer. Are you okay?"

She bit her lip as her gaze locked with her son's. Okay? Would she ever be okay again? It seemed her whole life had been one disaster after another. "I think I'm alright. How about you?"

"I'm fine. That buck seemed to come out of nowhere. I should've been looking. I'm sorry, Mama."

Ramona laid her head on the steering wheel as the emotions fought within her. How blessed she was to have such a sweet kid, who always felt it his duty to watch out for her, but the intervening guilt overwhelmed her emotions. Was it his place to take care of her? He was only fourteen, for crying out loud.

The buck was still stretched out on the hood. "It's not your fault, son. But we aren't solving our problem by sitting here talking about it. Help me get him off the car."

"You're shaking. Sit here and I'll move it."

"You can't do it by yourself."

"Sure, I can. I'm stronger than you think. Stay put."

She pulled a handkerchief from her skirt pocket and wiped her face. He was right. He was strong, like his father. Not only in physical strength, but emotionally, as well. He had become her rock. Ronald would've been so proud of him.

CHAPTER 2

Everything was spiraling out of her control. Ramona placed her hands over her face and sobbed, uncontrollably.

"Don't cry, Mama. We're gonna be okay. We still have each other."

For fourteen years, she had thanked the Lord for that fact, more times than she could count.

Discovering the door was jammed, he crawled out the window. She watched as he tugged on the deer and saw the animal slide from the hood. Grabbing her car door, Deuce jerked it open, then yanked at her arm and yelled, "The car's on fire, get out!"

"Get my purse, Deuce." Sharp pains shot through her body when she tried to stand. Something wet and sticky trickled from her head, into her eye. She reached up and swiped blood from a cut on her forehead while watching giant flames lick the night sky. The world swirled around her, making her sick on her stomach.

Then, the next thing she knew, she was being carried by strong arms into a dimly-lit two-room log cabin by a tall, frightening-looking creature. Long bushy hair covered a large portion of his badly scarred face. She wanted to believe it was all a dreadful nightmare, but it was too real to dismiss. She screamed, "Where's Deuce? What have you done with my child?"

"I'm right behind you, Mama. We're gonna be okay." Her heart slowed at the sound of his voice. He said, "Lucky for us he happened to come along when he did."

She looked up into the face of the gruesome-looking character and shuddered. What were his intentions? "Put me down. I can walk." Recalling a movie that she once saw of a woman being carried away by a monster, she half-expected him to refuse her request. To her shock, he very gently eased her down until her feet touched the plank floor. She grimaced as she tried to stand, then braced herself by planting her hand on a nearby small porcelain kitchen table. Pain shot through her body. Would anyone ever find them in such a secluded place? She glanced around at the sparsely furnished room, while trying to plot their getaway. Never having seen such a frightening-looking specimen, she spoke very slowly and distinctly in case he didn't understand English. "Who . . . are . . . you and where . . . have . . . you . . . taken us?"

Raising a brow as if he hadn't understood, her fears intensified. "Please, don't hurt us. If it's money you want, look in my purse. You can have it all. Just let us go."

The creature turned to the boy, and in a hushed voice, said,

18

"Y'all hungry?"

Deuce glanced at his mama and read her expression. "No sir. Thank you, though, for asking."

Ramona reached down and rubbed her aching ankle. What was wrong with the ugly brute that he would direct his conversations to a kid and ignore her completely?

"I reckon you and your mama will need a place to stay until daylight. This ain't much, but it gets you out of the cold."

"You're very kind. We'd be obliged to stay, just long enough for her to get on her feet."

Ramona glared at her son. "No, Deuce. Tell him we're leaving. He doesn't appear to want to talk to me."

"Leaving? To go where, Mama?"

The man shrugged. "Y'all talk it out. I'll go outside and bring in some more wood."

She waited for him to close the front door, then whispered. "Son, I don't know where we'll go, but we aren't spending the night here. Did you see his face? He gives me the creeps. I've always been a good judge of character, and I'm telling you, I have a bad feeling about this. I don't trust him. I'm counting on you to get us away from here. I'll need your help."

"No, Mama. You aren't thinking straight. It's cold and dark outside and getting colder. We have nowhere to go and no way to get there, even if we had a destination in mind. I'm sorry, but he was nice enough to offer us food and shelter, and you're in no shape to leave."

19

She pressed her lips together in a tight line, when the front door opened.

Deuce paused and turned to the man who was now stoking the fire in the fireplace. "You've been very kind, sir. I'm sorry, I didn't catch your name."

"Didn't say it. Does it matter?"

Deuce shrugged. "No sir. I reckon not."

Ramona shot a glance toward her son, as if her fears had just been confirmed. It mattered. It mattered a lot. Who but a deranged criminal would have reason to refuse to identify himself? She swallowed hard. "You're wanted, aren't you?"

"Wanted?" For the first time, he looked her directly in the face, as if he could see straight through her. "By you, ma'am? You want me?"

She felt nauseous at the implication. "Are you crazy?" All she wanted was a way of escape.

The man stooped down and poked at the kindling, moving it around in the fireplace. Then turning to Deuce, he said, "Folks around here call me Skip."

"Nice to make your acquaintance, Mr. Skip. I'm Deuce and Mama's name is Ramona."

"Your mama doesn't look too good. There's a bed in yonder where she can rest. You can take the quilt off the foot of the bed and make you a pallet beside her tonight, if you like. I'll sleep in here. You want I should carry her into the bedroom?"

Ramona's frown deepened. How dare he talk *at* her and not *to* her. Planting her hands on her hips, she cringed. "Absolutely not."

Deuce looked at the fellow and nodded. "Thank you, sir. I apologize for my mama. She's not normally this contrary. I reckon she must've hit her head on the windshield, but I think she'll be able to walk to the bed, if she leans on me."

As much as she wanted to deny it, Deuce was right. How could she leave when she was in no shape to walk unaided into the next room? No way would she make it on foot to the next town, wherever that might be. She held onto the bedpost while Deuce pulled back the chenille spread. She whispered, "There are no sheets on the bed."

"Mama, having sheets is the least of our problems. Lay down and I'll get some ice to go on that ankle."

"Well, shut the door as you walk out, or I won't sleep a wink tonight."

Skip overheard her. "Ain't got no door, ma'am. Never needed one."

Deuce said, "Nor do we need one tonight. But could I please bother you for a rag and a little ice from your refrigerator?"

"Got no refrigerator." He reached up on a shelf above the sink. "I got this liniment that might help, and I could wrap that ankle for her, if she has no objections. It's beginning to swell."

"That's kind of you, Mr. Skip. We thank you."

Ramona yelled, "Deuce, tell him to give it to you. You can wrap it."

Skip handed him the jar and a strip of cloth, torn from an old bed sheet, then followed him into the bedroom. He took one look at Ramona's ankle and said, "Rub the liniment all around it, then start wrapping, just don't wrap it so tight that it cuts off the blood flow—but tight enough to bind it."

After several attempts, Deuce laid the cloth on the bed. "Mr. Skip, I've never done this before. Would you mind?"

"Drop the 'mister. It's just Skip."

"Yessir."

Ramona said, "Deuce, for crying out loud, it's not that complicated. You can do it."

"Sorry, Mama, but you can punish me all you want after you get back on your feet. But until then, I'll be making the decisions and you'll need to trust me." He picked up the cloth and handed it to the man.

She said, "I don't need you. My son is capable of doing this."

"Begging your pardon, ma'am, but I get my instructions from the man in the room."

"Man? Don't be ridiculous. He's fourteen years old."

"Some men grow up faster than others." Skip reached down and gently lifted her leg from the bed, just far enough to slide the bandage under. He motioned for Deuce. "Hold her leg until I can finish wrapping." As he wrapped, he said, "You got a daddy, boy?"

"No sir. He was killed in the war. Were you in the war, sir?"

He nodded.

"What outfit were you with? Maybe you knew my daddy."

"I don't talk about it. The war is over." His voice lowered to a whisper. "It's *all* over."

The pain was getting worse, and Ramona's imagination was at work constructing all sorts of frightening scenarios. There was only one reason why he'd be asking if Deuce had a daddy. He wanted to know if someone would come looking for them. They had to get away from there as soon as possible.

The gruesome-looking character trekked over to a small bureau, opened a drawer, and pulled out a cotton shirt. He threw it on the bed next to her. "This will be more comfortable to sleep in than that starched blouse. Sit up and I'll unzip the back, if you can't reach it."

She shivered. Her worse fears were about to be realized. The only thing that surprised her was that he asked her permission. "I don't need your help. Get out."

"Yes ma'am. Just thought I'd ask." He lumbered back into the front room, and Deuce watched him open a drawer and take out a spoon. Then, reaching on a top shelf, he grabbed a small medicine bottle. He said, "Take this to your mama, and put three or four drops on the spoon."

"What is it?"

"It's something called Paregoric. It'll ease the pain and put her to sleep."

"It's not dangerous, is it?"

"Not unless she drinks the whole bottle. I'd take it to her, but she'd spit it out if I gave it to her."

"She's stubborn, for sure, but she's all right when you get to know her." He lowered his voice to a near whisper. "Skip, did you mean it?"

"I don't know what you're referring to, but I'd say whatever it is, I meant it. I make a habit of not saying anything I don't believe."

"When you called me a man. You were just trying to make me feel good. Right?"

"I meant it."

"Thanks." Deuce approached his mother's bed, but she was already shaking her head. "No way. I'm not taking that."

"It's Paregoric, Mama. It's gonna help with the pain."

"I'm not taking it, Deuce. We don't really know what's in that bottle. He could be trying to knock me out."

"For crying out loud, Mama, the man has been more than kind, and I can't say the same for us."

"You mean me, don't you? Well, someone has to be the adult, and I happen to be the only one in the room, regardless of what he wants you to believe. Deuce, we've gotta get out of here."

"And how do we get there in the middle of the night, Mama? What's your plan?"

She buried her face in her hands. "I'll think of something as soon as we get away."

"Well, before I'm leaving, you've got to come up with a plan, because the way I see it, you won't be able to go ten feet on a badly sprained ankle. We're lucky that Skip has agreed to let us stay until you can walk." He put a few drops of Paregoric into the spoon, and to his surprise, she opened her mouth and swallowed it, without giving him trouble. "Good job. Now, try to get some sleep and I'm sure things will look better in the morning."

CHAPTER 3

The Paregoric apparently did what it was intended to do. Ramona Jones slept through the night. When she awoke the next morning, Deuce was standing at the window, looking out. She peered toward the door and whispered, "Have you seen him this morning?"

"He's not here."

"Where is he?"

"I don't know. I woke up when I heard his car crank."

"Good. I'm glad he's gone." She grimaced when she slung her legs off the side of the bed. "We need to hurry."

"Hurry?"

"Go outside and see if you can find a stick that I can use as a crutch. If we're lucky, we can be gone before he gets back."

"If we're lucky? No, Mama. I'm not going, and you aren't either. We're lucky he came along when he did last night."

"Deuce Jones, don't talk back to me. I said get me a stick and be quick about it."

"Mama, I promised my daddy that I'd take care of you, and that's all I'm trying to do."

Her voice softened. "Oh, son, come here." She sat on the side of the bed and patted the mattress. "Sit down." She stroked his cheek with the back of her hand. "How many times do I have to tell you, that was nothing more than a dream. Why do you insist on pretending it was real? You know your father died before he ever had a chance to see you. I am not your responsibility. You are mine."

"I know you don't believe me, and you can call it a dream if you want to. But it was real. I saw him. He looked just like his pictures, and when he spoke, I didn't have to ask who he was. I knew him, Mama. I wish you'd believe me. He said, "Deuce, you'll need to grow up fast. Take care of MoMo for me."

Her throat tightened. This wasn't the first time Deuce had insisted his father visited him in the middle of the night, but it was the first time he'd ever said the man in his dream called her MoMo. No one—not even Deuce knew that Momo was Ronald's pet name for her. It was a private joke, and certainly not something she would've shared with a child. She licked her dry lips. Surely she misunderstood. Almost afraid to ask, she simply rephrased his question. "Deuce, did you say the man in your dreams told you that you'd have to grow up fast, so you'd need to take care of your mama for him?"

"I'm sorry you don't believe me."

Her muscles relaxed when she was convinced she had heard what she wanted to hear. The memory of Ronald's pet name for her brought a heaviness to her heart, almost as weighty as the morning Daddy Theo entered her room, giving her the news that her precious husband had been killed. "Deuce, I've also had dreams that seemed very real. And the reason you recognized your father in your dream is because you've seen all of his pictures growing up."

"Believe what you will, Mama. Whether it was real or a dream, from the things you've told me about my father, you can't deny that he would've asked me to take care of you, if he could have."

At least he was right about that. It was exactly what Ronald would've said. Her voice quaked. "Honey, I know you don't agree, but if you really feel the need to take care of me, then get us away from here as quickly as possible. That man scares me."

"And what reason has he given you to be frightened?"

"It's not so much what he's said or done, but—"

His brow furrowed. "But, what, Mama? I can think of nothing he's done, other than to be exceptionally kind."

"But those horrid scars on his face. He looks—"

"Like he might have come back from the war? Is that how he looks to you? Tell me, Mama. Would you have wanted to run away if Daddy had returned home with the same scars?"

"Don't be silly. That's different."

Deuce turned at the sound of footsteps and saw Skip standing in the doorway.

Ramona's throat tightened. "I'm sorry you heard that."

He shrugged. "Forget it. I knew what you thought, so why not say it. You think I don't know that I look like a freak? I bought a block of ice from the icehouse. It's in the sink with a pick."

She felt her face flush. "Thank you."

He said, "Boy, there's a clean sock on the table."

"My name is Deuce." He picked up the large, woolen gray sock. "What am I supposed to do with it?"

"Put ice in it, so the ice doesn't touch her skin. Whenever you're ready, I'll take you and your mama to the bus station and get you tickets to wherever you want to go.. That is, if she's not afraid to ride in the same car with me."

Ramona swallowed hard. "I'm sorry for the way I've behaved. I'd be obliged if you could get us to the bus station, but it isn't necessary to buy our tickets. I have money."

"Really? Where?"

She bristled. How dare he question her. "It's in my purse. Where did you put it, Deuce?"

Deuce glanced at Skip. Then biting his lip, he said, "Mama, your purse was in the car."

Her eyes squinted. "Yes. But you got it out, didn't you?"

"I didn't have time. The car exploded."

She clutched her hand over her chest. "Are you saying—?"

"That we have no money? Yes ma'am, that's exactly what I'm saying."

She broke down in full-blown sobs.

Skip paced back and forth like a frightened animal. He yanked off his cap and threw it across the room. His voice was pleading, "Please, ma'am. Don't cry. Please, don't cry. I have money. As much as you need."

Touched that such a frightening creature could possess such empathy, Ramona nodded and sucked in a deep breath. "I'm sorry. I just needed to get it out. I'm okay." She pointed to her eyes. "See? No more tears."

He opened the door to the tiny closet, pulled out a crutch and handed to her. "I don't need this anymore. I'll saw off the end to shorten it for you. You and the boy will need a few clothes. I have a little money saved up and nowhere to spend it. If you aren't afraid, I'll take you to town to buy some duds, before putting you on the bus." Skip's sympathetic voice was almost enough to make her take down her guard, but she'd been lied to before from folks she trusted.

She looked up and for the first time, noticed that the greasy, matted hair was now clean and neatly combed. When their gaze locked, he quickly pulled his cap further down on his face, and turned in the opposite direction, which made her feel like an even worse heel. She said, "Why are you being so kind to us?"

"Why wouldn't I? Because that's not what you expect of freaks?" Before she could answer, he said, "Let me know when you're ready to go. I'll be waiting outside."

Deuce glared at his mama. "Are you happy, now?"

"Don't scold me. I feel badly enough."

"Where do we go from here? Back to Daddy Theo's?"

"We have no choice."

After Deuce finished wrapping her leg, Skip came back in with the shortened crutch. He said, "If you don't mind me asking, where were you headed when you hit the deer?"

"My late husband once talked about a fish cannery in Jinx Bay, Florida. Said folks from all around worked there, either on the boats or in the cannery. Since not many employers are keen on hiring someone who has spent time in a clink, I was hoping a cannery might be a good place for me to try to seek employment." She smirked. "You don't seem shocked. Do I look like an ex-con to you?"

"I haven't spent time thinking about your looks, ma'am."

She felt her face flush. Of course, he hadn't. Why would he?

"Well, I have a past, and therefore am not what you might consider 'employable.' I was hoping a fish cannery wouldn't be so choicy. If that doesn't work out, I'll try a mill town or maybe even go to South Florida to work in the groves. I'm afraid I got lost on the way and I have no idea where we are."

He rubbed his hand across his chin. "You weren't lost at all. In four miles, you would've been at your destination. Would you like for me to take you there?"

"You're very kind, but the wreck has thrown a kink in our plans. We need to go back home." She grimaced. "I don't know why I called it home. I have no home. But Deuce and I still have clothes and other things at my husband's father's house in Eufaula."

Deuce raised a brow. "You really think Gussie didn't throw our things out the back door as soon as we drove off?"

She didn't have to answer for him to understand he was to say no more.

Skip drove to the bus station and gave Deuce money to buy the tickets. He came back shaking his head. "Bad news, Mama. There's only one bus going to Eufaula, and it leaves every morning at eight-fifteen."

Not in a rush to face Gussie, the news didn't strike her as particularly bad, especially since she was no longer frightened. "Skip, I hate to ask, but—"

"You don't have to ask. You're welcome to stay as long as you like."

"Thank you, but we'll be out of your hair in the morning."

Deuce said, "Not so fast. That wasn't all I found out. According to the man at the ticket window, there's a fishing rodeo taking place tomorrow in Eufaula and there are no tickets left."

The news didn't seem to bother her. "I've done my share of fishing. I wouldn't be interested, anyway."

"I think you misunderstood. The bus seats to Eufaula are sold out for Thursday and the bus only runs from Monday through Thursday. We'll have to stay until next Monday."

Ramona glared out the car window. If she opened her mouth,

she was sure she'd start screaming. She was familiar with the annual fishing rodeo, but the date hadn't crossed her mind. Why was all this happening to her? Where was God?

Skip said, "It's not the end of the world. If you don't want to wait, I can drive you there. Eufaula is that little town north of Dothan. Right?"

Her voice cracked. "Thank you, but I can't ask you to do that."

"Then don't. I can have you there in about three hours."

Any thoughts she had about him having a job were now put to rest. Apparently she was correct in assuming he was living off of a pension.

Neither said anything more for the next hour, until Skip stopped for gas at a service station. "I'm sure you and the boy are hungry, since we didn't have breakfast. I'm gonna get a moon pie and a cola." He looked on the back seat, where Deuce was stretched out, sound asleep. "What would you and your son like?"

"Thank you. I'd like a soda and a pack of cheese crackers. Deuce likes chocolate milk and peanuts."

While the attendant pumped the gas, Skip went inside, and came out with their snacks and a book.

Ramona said, "Is that a Hardy Boys Mystery?"

"Yeah. It was on a shelf with other used books, but I thought the boy might enjoy it on the ride."

"That was kind. Thank you. I'll give it to him when he wakes up. I'm sure he didn't get a wink of sleep last night."

How it happened, Ramona wasn't at all sure, but she soon

33

found herself sharing parts of her life that she had never shared with anyone but her husband. Once she began, she couldn't seem to stop. Perhaps knowing she'd never see him again made it easier. She told him about her parents dying in a train wreck when she was ten years old, and the following four years spent in a foster home. "During tobacco season, I spent most of my waking hours in the fields. The remainder of my time was spent taking care of the younger children. I kept running away until the authorities sent me to a reformatory school."

"Didn't you have relatives who could've taken you in?"

"None who could or would accept the responsibility. I was labeled a 'bad seed.'"

"What was it like living in such a place?"

"I don't like to think about it." She glared out the window. "But I don't regret going. Not one bit."

"So, it reformed you?"

"No. I was headstrong and determined not to let them break me. But if I hadn't gone there, I would never have met my husband, Ronald."

"Are you saying the boys' reformatory school was nearby?"

"I beg your pardon?" When she realized he thought her sweet husband could've been incarcerated made her chuckle. "Ronald Jones never did a wrong thing in his life. He was the sweetest, kindest person I've ever known. His father, Theodore Jones was on the Board, and they lived in a lovely home that backed up to the school. Ronald was an only child, and—" She stopped when she

34

became aware that she was rambling. He couldn't possibly be interested in her life story.

CHAPTER 4

Ramona was surprised at how relaxed she had become in Skip's presence. Perhaps too relaxed. Was it good to let her guard down? Feeling ashamed at having such thoughts, she realized Deuce was right. The man had been nothing but obliging, yet she judged him entirely on his outward appearance. It wasn't hard to believe he must've suffered all his life because of the disfigurement.

The more they talked, the easier it became to see him as a human being and not as a freakish monster. She was glad he opened up and seemed more comfortable around her. Or was it the other way around?

He said, "I suppose your husband's parents must've thought a lot of you to permit their son to court one of the inmates." His already reddened face turned almost purple, and he quickly added, "Forgive me if that sounded harsh. Perhaps I should've used the word 'residents.'"

"You're wrong in assuming his father was pleased but correct in choosing the word 'inmate.' It was definitely a prison. I wanted out, from the first night I spent there."

Deuce raised up, and said, "I'm hungry. Could we stop somewhere and get something to eat?"

Ramona reached down and picked up a paper sack from the floorboard and handed to him.

He opened the bag and let out a 'whoopee!' "My favorites: chocolate milk and peanuts. And a book? Who is this for?"

Ramona said, "Skip bought it for you."

"Thanks, Skip. Mama must've told you I love to read."

"Nope, but I thought it might make the trip shorter."

Ramona glanced in the back. It was comforting to see her son curled up in the seat, looking so relaxed.

She lowered her voice. "Skip, I hope I didn't bore you. I don't normally talk so much."

"If you only knew how much I enjoy listening to you talk. Please, don't stop, Mona."

Her throat tightened. "You called me Mona."

"I'm sorry. I thought that's what your son said. Is that not your name?"

"It's what my husband called me years ago. It was just strange hearing you say it. It's short for Ramona."

"I suppose I should've called you Mrs. Jones."

There was something sad about the way he said it. Perhaps she had embarrassed him. "Mona is fine. I didn't mean to insinuate that I objected." She had been reluctant to look at him except when absolutely necessary, for fear she couldn't hide her pity. She was ashamed of having such appalling thoughts, but wouldn't any woman feel threatened by the sight of such a marred face? Yet she was no longer frightened. She said, "Your hair looks very nice." The moment she said it, she could tell she'd embarrassed him. Had he washed and combed it for her sake? The thought caused mixed feelings. A part of her felt flattered, yet her heart told her it could be dangerous to give him any hope that she could ever be interested in someone like him—regardless of the effort he put forth to be kind.

She couldn't deny the gentle sound of his voice was comforting, and if he desired for her to continue talking, didn't she owe it to him? It wasn't hard to believe he'd been lonely living alone in the cabin in the woods. She knew what it felt like to be lonely. Besides, it was the least she could do for him, after all that he'd done for her and Deuce. "What would you like to know?"

"How did you meet your husband?"

She knew he only asked because he sensed it was something she wouldn't mind discussing. "I call it fate. Do you believe in fate?"

"Not so much, but if you say it's real, maybe I'm wrong."

A shiver ran down her spine. He was being too kind. The last thing she needed was for him to get the wrong idea, just because she was no longer being combative. Perhaps if she could make him understand that there was, and never could be any other man for her, it would alleviate possible pain in the future.

"Well, whether or not fate is real, I won't debate, but all I know is that love is real, and I've never loved anyone the way I loved Ronald Jones. It all happened when the girls at the reformatory were playing baseball. The field backed up to the woods behind the Jones' mansion, known as Rose Trellis. I played left field, and one afternoon, I missed a ball, and it went over the fence. It looked as if the game was over, when the ball came flying back. I didn't see where it came from, but we assumed it was thrown by the groundskeeper. We all clapped, and our game continued." She laughed out loud, and it felt good. She couldn't remember the last time she had laughed. She glanced over at the same time Skip turned to look at her. Their gaze locked and for a moment, all she saw were two beautiful blue eyes and lovely dark curls hanging loosely around a deep scar on his neck.

He quickly turned away, looking straight ahead. His voice took on a somber tone. "Don't feel you need to entertain me with chit-chat. Why don't you lean back and rest?"

"Yeah. Sure. I think I will." Embarrassed that she had actually thought he could've been interested in hearing her life story, she sank down in the seat and crossed her arms over her chest. What had come over her to make her think he wanted to hear about her love life? But didn't he ask her to share it? She tried to remember. Maybe. But don't people often ask questions to be polite, when they aren't the least bit interested in the details? Does anyone really care 'how you are,' when they ask the question, 'How are you'? The only answer they're interested in hearing is 'Fine.'

Ramona tried to recall the question that led her to spill her guts. Her mind was blank. Maybe he hadn't asked at all.

Deuce leaned over from the backseat. "I need to go to the bathroom."

Skip immediately pulled off to the side of the road. "There's not a service station for miles, but the woods are thick."

"I'll hurry."

Skip and Ramona responded at the same time, "No rush."

Ramona knew why she said it. If she could, she'd make this trip last as long as possible, knowing what lay at the end.

Deuce practically had the door open by the time the car had stopped and went running through the dense forest.

Skip leaned his head against the steering wheel, as they waited. He mumbled, "I'm afraid I gave you the wrong impression."

"Not at all. I think I understood perfectly. I was boring you."

"No. You could never bore me."

Her heart raced. His attentive words frightened her more than the scars on his face. As much as she had dreaded going back to a place where she wasn't wanted, her goal now was to get there as quickly as possible. She leaned her head back on the seat and closed her eyes. "I was rambling. I don't know what came over me. I think I will take that nap."

"I wish you wouldn't."

"Really? You practically insisted that I stop talking. Chit-chat, I believe you called it."

40

"I'm sorry. I'm afraid I have trouble expressing myself at times. It's been a long time since I've had a real conversation with a woman. I love hearing you talk. Please don't stop."

She couldn't tell if he really meant it, or if he was trying to make up for offending her. It was easy for her to imagine he longed to have someone talk to him, since she could relate. He was the only adult who had shown an interest in anything she had to say since Grandmother died. Daddy Theo had been too busy trying to appease Gussie to think of anyone else.

Deuce came running back to the car and picked up his book. "This is a swell story, Skip. Thanks for giving it to me."

"Sure, kid. I loved The Hardy Boys, growing up. I thought you'd like it."

Skip drove back on the highway and said, "You left off where the groundskeeper threw the baseball back to you."

"Aww, yes. That was how it all began. I only saw him briefly and then the lunch bell rang, and we girls all started toward the lunchroom. That's when I heard him yell, 'Hey, you.' I turned around and he said, 'What's your name?' My seventeen-year-old heart almost leaped out of my chest. A tall, handsome fellow, no more than eighteen-years-old stood there staring at me. It must've been 95 degrees and he had his dungarees rolled up to his knees and he wasn't wearing a shirt." She giggled. "He was the best-looking gardener I'd ever seen." She paused, "I'm sure I'm boring you."

41

"Not at all. This is even better than The Old Man and the Sea."

"Who?"

"It's a novel I'm reading. So, what happened next?"

"Well, he had this big grin on his face. He stuck his hand over the top of the fence and said, 'I'm Ronald, what's your name?'" Her brow furrowed. "Did I hear you laugh? You did. You think it's silly, don't you?"

"Not at all. It's a beautiful story. Don't stop."

"Well, I turned to make sure the warden wasn't anywhere around, then reached for his hand. I felt a bolt of electricity shoot through me. I know you don't believe there is such a thing as love at first sight, but I'm here to tell you it's real."

"I said I didn't know if fate was real, since I'm not sure what it even means. But I can believe it's possible for one to fall in love on first encounter."

"You do? You're the first person I've ever found who believes me." She stopped and sucked in a heavy breath. Could he be referring to himself? She dared not ask for fear of stirring up painful memories. "To make a long story short, less than three weeks later, the matron came and told me the Jones family cook had been released and Mrs. Jones had requested me for the job. I didn't know the woman even knew who I was."

"Are you saying you'd never met her?"

"Not formally. She visited the different barracks a couple of times, but I have no idea how she would've remembered me."

"Why not? You remembered her, didn't you?"

"That's different. I remembered her because she was genuinely sweet. I wondered how she and old man Jones ever got together. I got the idea that if it were up to her, she'd free us all. That's how caring she appeared."

"Did you move into their home?"

"Oh no. A guard marched me over and unlocked the gate at six o'clock every morning, then I returned to my barracks, accompanied by a guard at six every evening."

"I can guess the ending. You and the gardener were able to see more of one another and eventually fell in love."

"You guessed wrong. My first night there, I stepped into the dining room and saw Ronald sitting at the dinner table. That's when it hit me that he wasn't the gardener, but the son."

"That must've been a shock! And I suppose a smart girl like you saw him as a ticket to a comfortable future."

She felt slightly offended that he could assume such of her, but why wouldn't he? "It might seem that way, but actually it was a bit frightening. Flirting with a gardener would've been safe, but flirting with the Jones's son would've added months to my sentence, and I wasn't about to chance it. I knew my boundaries, but Ronald was a daredevil. When I'd pour tea in his glass, he'd grab my hand and say, 'Let me help you.' I could see the displeasure in his father's eyes, but he never said anything to him. Not in front of me, anyway."

"I get it. Your fellow was a flirt."

"He was, at that, and I loved it." Ramona enjoyed reliving the most wonderful days of her life. No one other than Deuce had ever asked her to share her love story, but then she'd never come in contact with anyone who seemed so starved for conversation.

CHAPTER 5

It was not until she began sharing the most important aspects of her life that the muscles in Skip's face appeared to relax. He looked almost—normal. Though for fear of making him uncomfortable, she tried not to make a habit of looking too closely. She reasoned that if he enjoyed her story as much as she enjoyed reliving it, then there was no reason to hold back.

"I couldn't fathom why someone like Ronald Jones would've fallen for someone like me, and it still baffles me. But I never doubted his love, and he knew how crazy I was about him. He took every opportunity to sneak into the kitchen to be with me, although I pleaded with him not to take chances. I only had five months of my sentence left."

"What about parents? When they discovered you and their son were planning to marry, did they try to stop it?"

"Maybe they would have."

"Are you saying they didn't?"

"Ronald received his draft papers and was set to leave in two weeks. I was devastated but told myself it never could've worked out. Why would a man like him want to marry a girl like me?" She turned around to glance at her son, who was engrossed in the adventures of the Hardy Boys. She lowered her voice. "Ronald went to his father without my knowledge and told him I was pregnant with his baby."

Skip's brow formed a vee. "I see."

She giggled. "No, you don't. And neither did Mr. Jones."

"Pardon?"

"There was no way Ronald could've gotten me pregnant."

"Oh! So, it wasn't his child?"

"I could not have been pregnant with any man's baby. Ronald had only kissed me once, when I went out on the back porch to throw out the dish water."

"That must've been some kiss."

"Yes, it was." She snickered. "But it didn't get me pregnant."

"Then, why would he have made up such a story, knowing you'd soon be released and be free to marry as soon as he returned?"

"I had no idea he'd concocted such a tale. I was getting ready to walk back to my barracks one night when his father said, 'Ramona, there's no need in expressing my disappointment in you and Ronald, but what's done is done and now we have the baby to consider.'"

"I had no idea what he was talking about. I said, 'Baby?'"

"I glanced over at Ronald, who was sitting at the table, and he quickly said, 'Daddy, as I told you, it's all my fault. I took advantage of her, but I want to do the right thing and give our baby a name.' My head was spinning. I loved Ronald's quick wit and cute sense of humor, but that one caught me by surprise. I didn't know what kind of joke he was pulling on his father. I waited for the punch line. But I was confused when he kept a straight face. Then, his daddy looked at his watch and said, 'The minister will be here in ten minutes.' Ronald got out of his chair, approached me, and reaching for my hand, boldly announced, 'We're ready. Right, sweetheart?'"

"I was trying to take it all in. Me, pregnant and about to be married? Were they both crazy? I couldn't discern if I was having a dream or a nightmare. Whatever was taking place, couldn't possibly be real. I was still in shock when Mr. Jones informed me that he had made arrangements for me to serve the remainder of my time at the big house with him and Mrs. Jones. Ronald's mother rushed over and threw her arms around me, welcoming me into the family. Me? A part of the Jones family? I was too stunned to ask questions. She said she was thrilled that I'd be staying with them until Ronald came back from the war." Ramona choked back the tears. "But as you know, he didn't come back."

"I'm finding it hard to understand why your husband could've made up such a lie, knowing he was leaving you to deal with the consequences when it would become apparent that there was no baby. Surely, he realized that when his parents discovered you weren't pregnant, they'd think you made up the story to deceive their son into marrying you."

"That could've presented a problem, for sure. There was no baby at the time we married, but I was pregnant by the time Ronald left, eight days later. Deuce was born a couple of months after the war ended. Daddy Theo was so distraught, he never questioned the date. Granny admitted to me later that she and Ronald had concocted the plan together. She said she was afraid if Ronald had gone to his daddy and said he wanted to marry me before leaving for the war, that his daddy would've been angry and refused to allow me to stay there while he was gone. But if he thought I was carrying his grandchild, he wouldn't send me away."

"It sounds as if you loved your husband very much. I suppose it took a long time to get over your loss."

"I'll never get over him."

"How did the old man react toward the baby when he was born?"

"Oh, he loved him dearly, and because he knew we were a package deal, I think he learned to love me in his own way. And as for my sweet mother-in-law, she adored Deuce and treated me as if I were her own daughter. I don't know how I could've survived after getting news of my husband's death, if it hadn't been for the Jones's. Because of Deuce, I began to refer to them as Daddy Theo and Granny."

"So, what changed, that made you want to leave there?"

"Ronald's mother died, and I soon became in the way." She'd gone this far, she might as well explain. "After Granny died, Daddy Theo married Gussie, an old flame. She hated me from the beginning, which put pressure on Deuce's grandfather."

His lip curled. "Do you think it's possible that you might have resented the second wife because she was nothing like the boys' grandmother, whom you had learned to love?"

Ramona lowered her head. "Well, you're right in saying she wasn't like Granny. They were as different as sugar and vinegar. Gussie is mean as a snake and Daddy Theo goes along with her. She treats everyone, from the milkman to the grocer as if they're her servants. She acts like she's the Queen of Sheba, and everyone should bow down to her when she walks in a room. She sleeps half the morning, then gets all dolled up before she steps out of her *boudoir*."

"Her boudoir?"

"Yep! That's what she calls her bedroom. A boudoir. The woman is such a put-on. Even her night clothes are made of silk, and my guess is that they cost more than most women pay for an entire Easter outfit. She's quite beautiful to look at, I'll give her that. But she's a witch."

"I'm sorry to hear that. Living there must've been very hard for you."

"You can't imagine."

"Maybe, I can."

Of course, he could. How selfish of her to think her life with

Gussie could've been more difficult than his life, living alone with no hope of ever having a family of his own.

He said, "Do you mind if I roll down the window?"

"Please do. It does feel a bit stuffy." She watched the way his dark curls, highlighted by a few sun-streaked strands blew freely in the wind. What she'd give for such a beautiful head of hair. She quickly cut her eyes toward the road, for fear he'd think she was gawking at his face. It suddenly dawned on her that somewhere during the conversation she'd stopped noticing the scars and had begun to see positive attributes that she'd failed to see until now. He had beautiful blue eyes that squinted and twinkled when he smiled. What a handsome man he must've been before the war. She said, "What are you thinking?"

"I was wondering about your husband's mother. What was she like?"

"The very opposite of Gussie. She wore her hair in a bun, never wore makeup, and her clothes were rather dowdy-looking. Since Daddy Theo was well off financially, Granny could've had nice things, yet things didn't seem important to her. People did. She had a heart of gold. When a hobo knocked on her back door, asking for food, she didn't feed him on the steps. She'd invite him into the dining room, and if there was nothing left over from the previous meal, she'd have the cook fix something special just for him." The memory brought tears to her eyes.

"You say nice things were not important to your grandmother. Have you ever wondered what *was* important to her?"

"I don't have to wonder. I know. Her family."

"Are you sure?"

Her mouth gaped open. "Of course, I'm sure. Why would you question me?"

"It seems to me you're faulting Ronald's daddy for falling in love with a woman who was different from his first wife. Can you blame him for preferring a beautiful vixen to a frumpy-looking housewife? What man in his right mind wouldn't make the very same choice?"

Resentment rose within her at hearing this man she hardly knew, calling Granny frumpy-looking. How dare he! But wasn't that exactly how she described her?

For the next ten or fifteen miles, neither spoke. Mona sat with her arms crossed over her chest, staring blankly out the window as the car rolled along the paved road.

Skip was the first to break the silence. "Did I say something to upset you?"

The very question caused her to wince. Was he really so naïve? "No."

"Then what's wrong?"

"Nothing." She expected him to press her, but when he didn't, she blurted, "I can't believe you'd infer that Gussie's outward appearance would be more important than Granny's sweet, loving disposition."

He shrugged. "What's your point?"

"My point is—" She stopped. Then starting again, she said,

51

"My point is—"

"You seem to be having trouble expressing it. Let me help you. You find it incomprehensible that I could applaud the old man for choosing a beautiful woman whom you describe as 'mean as a snake,' over a frumpy-looking woman with a heart of gold. Did I get it right?"

She didn't exactly like the way he formed the sentence, but after considering it, she nodded. "As a matter-of-fact, I do find it quite annoying."

"But why?"

"You have to ask?"

"Is it that hard to explain?"

"Of course not. The Bible is plain in saying that a haughty look is an abomination to God."

"And you believe a haughty look refers to a beautiful woman's appearance?"

"Well, no, but it's a prideful thing and—" She stopped. "You're confusing me. There was much more to Granny than her physical appearance. Everyone loved her. Everyone!"

He raised a brow. "Apparently, not her husband, since he couldn't wait to replace her with someone with beauty. Why do you suppose that was?"

Now, she was more than irritated. She was angry. "I suppose the answer is because that's how most men think."

"I don't understand."

"It's a known fact that—" Ramona suddenly thought about

what she'd said. How *men* think*?*

How, in good conscience, could she fault Theodore for choosing Gussie's outward beauty over Granny's sweet soul? As much as she wanted to deny it, it was difficult for her to get past Skip's disfigurement, although her son didn't seem to have a problem. Sure, she felt like a hypocrite, but wouldn't any woman react the same way?

Ramona was relieved that Skip didn't choose to dwell on the subject. Instead, he wanted to give her money, when she had nothing but pity to give in return.

He reached over the sun visor, pulled down his wallet and handed to her.. "Take out what you need to help get you settled."

"I can't do that."

"Please! You know where I live. If you'd prefer to think of it as a loan, that's fine. I have no plans to leave any time soon, so after you get settled, you can come pay it back, if you choose."

"You're very kind, and I thank you." She placed the wallet back under the visor. "But I can't." The fact that she even considered it for a few short seconds made her feel cold and heartless. He had so little yet was willing to give what he had, in spite of the cruel way she'd responded to his kindness.

"I imagine you have close friends living in Eufaula. Anyone you can count on to help you?"

She was still thinking about his question, when Deuce popped up and said, "Mama, what about Joel?"

Skip said, "A beau?"

Ramona shook her head. "No. Just a family friend."

Deuce said, "He would be a beau if she'd let him."

Skip gave a hollow chuckle, "Tell me more, Deuce. What do you think about this fellow who is in love with your mama. Do you approve?"

"He's nice. And rich, too. Right, Mama?"

"I don't know about being rich, but you're right. He's nice." Sensing Skip was enjoying the conversation, she said, "Joel and my husband grew up together. He often came over for supper at the Jones's, and after Ronald died, he'd come by and check on Deuce and me any time he came home."

"Came home? I suppose he was in the war?"

"He was, but when it was over, he enrolled in college.. After getting a law degree, he came back to Eufaula and hung up his shingle."

Deuce said, "He asked her to marry him."

"Really? And how did you feel about that idea?"

"I begged her to, especially after Granny died and Gussie moved in."

"I see. So, why didn't you marry him, Mona?"

Ramona not only had relaxed and felt comfortable talking to Skip, she found herself wishing the trip could last longer. He acted as if he truly cared about what she had to say. "Joel is a wonderful man and he's good to Deuce, but it wouldn't be fair to deprive him of the love that another woman could give him. I know what true love feels like, and I don't love Joel."

"Maybe you'd learn to love him."

She found it amusing that this fellow she was so frightened of, now had her bearing her heart. She rattled on, as if she were wound up and couldn't stop. "Joel is one of the kindest men I've ever known. One day, some lucky lady will find him, and when she does, she'll have a prize."

"Sounds like you may be in love with the guy and are afraid to admit it."

"Trust me, I'd know it. As fond as I am of Joel, I'm not in love with him, nor he with me."

"I think you both may be in love and afraid to admit it. Your husband is gone, Mona. He'd want you and Deuce not only to be taken care of, but he'd want you to be happy. Don't you believe that?"

"You sound like quite the romantic. Instead of trying to marry me off, maybe you should be looking for Miss Right." When his eyes glassed over, she quickly apologized. What was she thinking to have made such a ridiculous statement.

For the next few miles, the silence was deafening.

CHAPTER 6

Wednesday morning, February 6

Joel Gunter was in his office alone when Frank Jinright showed up.

"Frank. Come in, man. Is it still raining outside?"

"You may find this peculiar, but outside is the only place that it *is* raining."

Joel feigned a smile, although Frank was never as funny as he seemed to think he was, and today he was not up for his corny jokes. "I wasn't expecting you."

Frank glanced around. "Where's that sweet secretary of yours?"

"She's late. It's getting to be a habit."

"I suppose she stopped for doughnuts. She does it for you, you know. Shucks, Joel, why don't you marry Peg and make an honest woman out of her? Maybe it's not for me to say, but someone needs to. She'd do anything for you, even against her better judgment, but you treat her like dirt."

Annoyed that Frank constantly showed up in the mornings, unannounced, led Joel to believe he either came for the doughnuts and coffee—or else Frank was sweet on Peggy. Joel's throat tightened. "You got one thing right, my friend. It's not for you to say. Suppose you state your reason for being here, Frank. I have work to do."

"Sorry. I didn't mean to hold you up. Connie and I plan to leave for Paris in the morning, to get Susan settled in school. I shudder at the thought of leaving my baby girl there, but she's wanted to study art in Paris since she was a kid. She's got a good head on her shoulders, but she'll always be my baby."

Joel attempted to hide his irritation. "What a wonderful opportunity for Susan. I'm sure she'll do well. I've been impressed with all the awards she's won, already."

The conversation ceased when Peggy darted in holding a cardboard box. She laid it on her desk. Her first remarks were directed toward Frank. "Good Morning, Mr. Jinright."

"Frank, to you, sweetheart. Whatcha got there?"

"The doughnuts smelled so good when I passed by, that I bought a dozen. Have a seat and I'll have a pot of coffee perked in a few minutes."

Joel pretended not to hear the conversation. "Peggy, get ready to take dictation. We've lots of letters to get out this morning."

Frank reached in the box and pulled out a chocolate doughnut. "I should go. I only stopped by to ask Joel to preside over the

Kiwanis Club meeting in my place."

Peggy rolled her eyes. "You came all the way here for that? Did you not pay your phone bill?"

"Would you think less of me if I admitted I needed an excuse to come gawk at Joel's gorgeous secretary?"

"If I were your wife, I'd be sending you out to secure the services of a reputable divorce lawyer."

He seemed to enjoy the banter. "Who are you trying to kid. You're just like Connie. Whenever you get that ring on your finger, there'll be no prying it off. It will be forever."

She wondered how some women could be so insecure that they'd put up with the likes of a man like Frank Jinright. She couldn't deny he was good-looking and kept her laughing with his foolishness, but she was sure it wouldn't be as funny to her if the big flirt were her husband.

Frank said, "So, Joel, can I count on you to fill in for me at the meeting?"

"Of course. I'll be there."

As he started out, Frank stopped and looked at a picture on the bookshelf. "That's you as a kid. Right?"

"Yep. Me and my best buddy, Ronald Jones. We were about twelve, and his uncle took a picture of us holding that string of fish we caught down at Jinx Bay."

"Ronald? Theodore's son?"

"Yeah."

"He was killed before we moved to Eufaula. I've heard a lot

58

about him, though. Theo still talks about him."

Joel strolled over and stood looking at the picture as if it were his first time seeing it. "We had some swell times together. I stayed over at his house almost as much as I stayed at my own. I won't ever get over missing him."

Peggy said, "Frank, are you sure you don't want to stay for coffee and doughnuts?"

"Thanks, beautiful, but I need to get back to the office."

After he left, Joel made a point to look at his watch. "Peggy, I'm delighted that you decided to come to work today."

"Don't be so ornery. It's not even nine o'clock, and I know how you love doughnuts." She pulled one from the bag and ran it under his nose.

He reached up and took it. "I appreciate the doughnuts, but I do wish you'd come to work on time or at least let me know when I can expect you."

"Who put that burr in your britches? This is not about me being late for work, is it?"

"Not entirely."

"So, what's wrong?"

"I'll tell you what's wrong. I don't like the way you flirt with Frank Jinright. I think you're giving him the wrong idea."

"Don't be ridiculous, Joel. There are a few unflattering names you might rightly call me, but flirt is not among them. Frank is a big tease, and I can't help laughing at his stupid jokes."

"Well, I don't like the way he looks at you."

"Then suppose you take it up with him. I have nothing to do with the way he looks at me, but I'll admit it's flattering to know you're jealous."

"That's ridiculous. I have no reason to be jealous."

"Exactly." She leaned over and with her thumb, lifted his chin and kissed him.

He jerked on the collar of his shirt. "I've told you before . . . not in the office. Someone could walk up."

It was cute the way any display of public affection embarrassed him. "And what if they should, honey? You're single. I'm single. There's no law against two single people kissing."

****

Skip drove into Eufaula, and followed Ramona's directions to Rose Trellis.

As they drove down the road, Ramona was surprised to see cars parked on either side of the road leading up to the house. People were standing around in the yard, and others sat in rockers on the wrap-around porch. Some she recognized as neighbors, others were complete strangers.

Skip said, "Looks like you might've gotten back in time for a party."

Deuce sneered. "Gussie having a party? That's a joke. She has no friends. I wonder what's going on."

"Would you mind getting the crutch and helping your mother walk up the steps? I'd rather not get out."

"Sure. I could pick her up and carry her inside if she'd let me.

I'm strong for my age."

"I can see that, but I think she can walk with a little help." He turned to look at Mona. "What's wrong? You're white as a ghost."

"I don't know."

"You weren't expecting the crowd, were you? You don't have to get out. We'll leave now, if you want to. Just say the word."

He had no idea how tempting it sounded. She supposed Deuce's grandfather was hosting the State Representatives and their wives, along with the school faculty. Granny had done it often in the past and Ramona always enjoyed helping. But not tonight. She had no desire to entertain or to be entertained. All she wanted was to get away.

"Mona, why don't we go back to the cabin and wait until tomorrow."

"You must be kidding. We've come too far to turn around and go back."

"We made it in less than four hours. I don't mind."

"You're very kind, but we're already here, and hopefully, I can get Daddy Theo alone, long enough to explain our circumstance, without Gussie trying to control the situation. He has a car and an old truck that he never drives. I plan to ask to borrow a few bucks and the truck until I find a job and can get on my feet."

"Do you think he'll give it to you?"

"I know he will. He'll do it for Deuce's sake. There's nothing he wouldn't have done for Ronald. He even accepted me into his home, knowing my past, but he did it because it was what Ronald wanted."

"What if his wife overhears what's going on before you have a chance to leave?"

"She'll pitch a fit, but when she learns without money and transportation we'll be forced to move back in, she won't stop him. She'll be as anxious to get us on our way, as we are eager to leave."

"I wish you both well. Deuce, your father would've been very proud of you. I'm sorry he didn't live to see what a fine young man you've become."

Deuce leaned over the seat and threw his arms around Skip's neck. "Thank you. I won't ever forget you, Skip. I wish we could stay with you."

Ramona's gaze met with Skip's. "You've made a huge impact on my son. I don't suppose our paths will ever cross again, but I agree with Deuce. We'll never forget you and what you did for us. I don't know what would've happened if you hadn't shown up when you did."

"I only wish I could've done more."

"You did more than you know." She leaned over and kissed him on the cheek. "Goodbye, Skip."

He didn't know which one was more surprised by the kiss—him or Mona. It was evident by the stunned look on her face that it was spontaneous and had happened before she had a chance to think about what she was doing. As she watched him drive away, guilt feelings of being so cold and suspicious of such a sweet guy, ate away at her. Was it true? Was she no different than Gussie?

CHAPTER 7

With Deuce's help and the crutch, Ramona made it up the tall steps leading to the palatial home. She spoke briefly to the guests on the porch and made her way through the crowd gathered in the parlor. She was taken aback when the first person she recognized was Gussie, who rushed toward her with open arms, crying.

"Oh, Ramona, dear, I'm so glad that someone knew where to locate you. I was devastated when I realized I had no way to contact you. I know Theodore would have wanted you and the boy to be here." Glaring at the crutch and wrapped ankle, she said, "Oh m'goodness, what happened, shug? Are you all right?"

Ramona choked. She'd gone through much worse than a sprained ankle while living at Rose Trellis. Gussie was putting on quite a show of concern in front of all the distinguished guests, but Ramona wasn't fooled by such a pitiful performance. But why was she going to such lengths to feign affection? "I'm fine, Gussie."

Her gaze traveled across the room. She could hardly hear herself think, with all the chatter around her. "What's going on, Gussie? Where is Daddy Theo?"

Gussie's jaw dropped. "Oh, dear. Oh, child, you mean . . . you don't know?"

"Know what?"

"Honey, my beloved Theodore passed away last night."

"What? Are you saying all these people are here for—"

"A wake. Yes, I'm afraid so, dear. The mortician just delivered the body about an hour ago. The Governor suggested as a longtime dignitary, known for his many contributions to Alabama, that Theodore lie in state at the Capitol in Montgomery. But I know how much Theodore hated recognition, so I insisted he be brought back to Rose Trellis, the place so dear to his heart. I've just come from viewing the body in the library. He looks real good and there's no one in there with him, now, if you and the boy wish to go in to say your final goodbyes."

Ramona's mind was reeling. She motioned for Deuce to go with her.

The open casket was gray with lots of silver pulls and a white, tufted satin lining. The lines on Theodore's forehead, which she had assumed were due to age, were no longer visible. Ramona hadn't seen him looking so peaceful since before Granny died. As she stood viewing the body, a sadness came over her. She knew how much Ronald loved his parents and how deep their love was for him. The thought of her sweet husband greeting his father into

Heaven brought a sudden sense of peace to her soul. But what now? Although Gussie acted as if she were glad they had come back, Ramona knew it was an act. But for whose benefit? It couldn't be because of a change of heart, since Gussie had no heart.

Deuce said, "Mama, I loved Daddy Theo. When we left, I was mad and told him we didn't need him, but I didn't mean it." He blinked hard, trying to stop the flow of tears. "I really loved him. I wish I could take back what I said."

"Oh, Deuce he knew you didn't mean it. He loved you, very much and he knew you loved him."

"I hope so."

"I think there are people waiting to come in to view the body. Shall we go?"

"Yes'm." She handed him a handkerchief to dry his tears.

As they turned to exit the room, two men holding their hats against their chest nodded slightly and strode toward the casket. She sucked in a lungful of air and exhaled slowly. All hopes of getting the truck died with Theodore's last breath. Gussie was too stingy to give up anything. She might even refuse to allow them to take their clothes from the house. But rather than ask her in private, wouldn't it be more difficult for Gussie to deny them in front of the people she was trying so hard to impress?

She walked back into the parlor and Gussie said, "Ramona, I hope you and Deuce won't rush away after the funeral, tomorrow. Come by the house and have lunch before you leave. The community has been bringing food in all day. There'll be plenty to eat."

Ramona understood it to be Gussie's way of saying, "If you came back thinking you'd stay, you have another think coming."

"Thank you. We had no idea Daddy Theo had died, so we didn't come intending to stay. We only returned, hoping to borrow his truck until I can purchase another vehicle. My car caught on fire, and we had to get a friend to bring us here. You don't have any objections to us driving the truck back do you?" She thought she'd worded it well. How could Gussie refuse in front of such a crowd?

"Honey, you know you don't even have to ask. Of course, you can drive it back. In fact, Theodore would have insisted. Consider it yours."

Hiding her surprise, she said, "Thank you, Gussie."

Deuce said, "Mama, tell her about your purse."

"It's okay, son."

"But it's not okay. Gussie, Mama was on the way to get a job when the car caught on fire and her purse burned up inside. We were gonna ask Daddy Theo to lend us his truck and for enough money for rent until she can make a paycheck. She doesn't even have money to put gas in the truck."

Gussie thrust her hand over her lips. "Oh, dear. How sad."

Ramona lowered her head. "It's okay, Deuce. We'll make out. We aren't Gussie's responsibility."

A tall lanky man was standing nearby. "You did the right

thing to come back. Theodore would have gladly helped you. I know how much he thought of his grandson, and seeing the boy now, I can understand why he was so proud of him." The man grabbed a hat from the nearby hat rack, then reached in his wallet and dropped a bill into the hat. "Here's for Theo." Then passing it to the next fellow who deposited a couple of bills, the hat kept circling around the room.

Gussie said, "Oh, dear, Ramona, I had no idea you were in such straights. Grover is right. Theodore would've insisted on helping you."

A short, stout lady took the hat after it had made the rounds, then marched across the room and handed to Gussie. "If you'll tell me which pocketbook is yours, I'll fetch it for you."

Gussie looked as if she'd been socked in the face. "It's the brown alligator bag, but I'm afraid I don't have any money in there, except a little change. I haven't been to the bank lately."

Undaunted, the woman said, "Grover could probably cash a check for you. Right, Grover?"

"I'd be happy to. Where do you keep your checkbook?"

Deuce said, "I know. It's on Daddy Theo's desk."

Grover said, "No need to get up, Gussie. We'll let the boy get it for you."

Deuce left the room, then came back holding a large checkbook and handed to Gussie, along with a pen.

Ramona sat stunned. She didn't know the man, but apparently he knew Gussie.

Gussie's hand shook as she held the pen. "How much do you think you can get by on, Ramona?"

Grover said, "Why don't you make it out to me for about three-hundred. That figure just came to mind." He reached for his billfold, and thumbed through the cash inside, then lifted a brow. "Yep, three-hundred is the exact amount left in my wallet. I think with your contribution and what was collected in the hat, she and the child might be able to get a decent start."

Her voice trembled. "Did you say three-hundred?"

"I think that sounds about right, don't you?"

Gussie wrote the check and handed the ledger back to Grover, who tore out the check and stuck it in his wallet. Then, pulling out three crisp one-hundred dollar bills, he deposited them into the hat. Giving the checkbook to Deuce, he said, "You can put it back where you found it, young man."

Deuce's eyes glassed over as he gazed into the man's kind face. "Thank you, sir. My mother and I thank you."

"All the thanks goes to your grandfather. We only did what we knew he would've done for any of us. I dare say there's a person in this room that Theodore Jones hasn't helped at one time or another."

CHAPTER 8

Joel Gunter picked up his coat and was ready to go to the Wake at Rose Trellis to pay his respects, when the phone rang. The voice on the other end said, "Hello, Joel. Are you alone?"

"Alone? Why do you ask? Who is this?"

"It's me. Ronald."

"Ronald who?"

"Jones."

"I don't know what kind of joke you're trying to pull, but I fail to see the humor."

"It's no joke. Listen to what I'm saying. I don't have much time. I'm alive and I need to see you."

Joel slammed the phone back on the cradle and stomped toward the door, when it rang again. Angry, he grabbed the phone and said, "I don't know who you are, but I do know you are not Ronald Jones."

"Don't hang up, Toe. I need to tell you something."

Joel's knees felt like jelly. Ronald had given him the nickname in high school when he kicked the final point in the game between Eufaula and Abbeville. Running his fingers through his hair, he yelled, "So you know he called me 'Toe.' Half the school knew."

"Meet me at the hideout in thirty minutes but never mind the Root Beer."

Why was he doing this? How could a stranger know these things? The hideout? The Root Beer?

"Remember? We'd meet at the hideout, and you'd bring the Root Beer and I'd grab a few cookies from the cookie jar."

Joel scratched his head. "I have no idea how you'd know these things, but in case you haven't heard, Ronald Jones was killed in the war over a decade ago. Besides, I'd know his voice anywhere, and you aren't him."

"I don't have time to argue with you, Toe. I was severely wounded in the war. My face was disfigured, and my vocal chords were damaged. I was in the hospital and couldn't speak at all for a long time. When I did get my voice back, it was much deeper, due to the damage. I suppose you've heard about my daddy by now."

Joel popped his palm against his forehead. "Now, I get it. You're telling me that you don't look like Ronald, and you don't talk like Ronald, but you've heard that his wealthy father just passed away, and you think if you can convince his best friend that you're an heir, everyone else will believe you and you'll be on Easy Street? Sorry, it won't work."

"Wait! Don't hang up. Remember how we wanted to sing bass in Glee Club, but ol' man Trugood said we were tenors? Well, I can sing bass now." He snorted when he laughed.

Joel's heart raced. Was he being played for a sucker? But who, other than Ronald, would know or even remember Trugood? "Your laughter sounds familiar. Ronald, is this really you?"

"It is. Now, please listen. I have a favor to ask. It's about Mona."

"Is she with you?"

"No. They're back at Rose Trellis. I suppose you've heard about Daddy."

"Yes, and I'm so sorry for your loss. I know you and your father were close. I guess you're here for the funeral?"

"No. No one knows I'm alive, and that's how it has to be."

Joel had an array of mixed feelings. "I have a million questions, Ronald, but I'll start by asking why you ran out on everyone who loves you."

"I had my reasons. I'll be at the hideout. Meet me in a few minutes."

"We don't have to go there. I'm living in the house I grew up in. I'm alone. Come on over."

"No. I can't. It has to be the hideout."

"I won't pretend to understand, but I'd meet you on the moon if you asked. I'll be waiting for you."

Joel thought of all the nights he and Ronald stayed at the hideout from the time they were kids until they were old enough to graduate. It was nothing but a dugout in the side of a clay bank, near the river and was barely large enough for two six-foot teenagers to sit up in. It was there they shared their deepest, darkest secrets. It was where Ronald broke the news to him that his grandmother had hired the cute left-fielder to become the cook at Rose Trellis. He and Ronald had admired the girl for months but couldn't figure out a way to get her attention without getting themselves in trouble with Ronald's father. They kept hoping a ball would get past her, and they'd have a perfect opportunity to draw her up to the fence, away from prying eyes, long enough to get acquainted.

Joel recalled his disappointment when he learned it happened on the day he was taking piano lessons. If only he'd been there, maybe he would've had a chance with her. But he wasn't, and Ronald won her heart.

Joel parked his car on the side of the dirt road, and looked for the path leading to the river, but it was overgrown with briars and dog fennels. He made his way through the brush to the hideout, but there was no one there. Belittling himself for being so naïve, he couldn't imagine who could've played such a nasty trick. Just as he was about to return to his car, he heard a voice. Looking down toward the river, he saw a man standing there, tossing pebbles into the water—the same way they did as youngsters. Joel flinched when the light of the moon outlined a horribly bloated, scarred face looking up at him. He waited as the creature made his way up the riverbank.

"I hope I didn't frighten you, Toe. I reckon I'm about as ugly as you, now. Ain't that a hoot?"

Joel's muscles relaxed. There was no question left in his mind. It was Ronald. It was the exact kind of thing he would say. In their teens, they constantly teased over which one was the best looking. He rushed toward his buddy with open arms. "Where have you been? Why didn't you let me know you were alive? I know Ramona was shocked to see you." He winced at his own words. "I didn't mean shocked, I meant surprised."

"No offense taken. Shocked was right, but she didn't recognize me, so she still doesn't know that I'm alive. I plan to keep it that way. As far as she knows, her husband is dead and an ugly brute who goes by the name of Skip befriended her." His throat tightened. "I met my son, Joel."

"Yeah? How about that son of yours? Handsome devil. Looks just like you, doesn't he."

"You mean how I looked the last time you saw me. By the way, I'm leaving Eufaula tonight, but I hope you have a happy birthday tomorrow."

"Knowing you're alive is the best birthday present I could ever hope for." Joel paused and his voice softened. "What happened to you, buddy?"

"I'll try to have all the answers for you one day, but I'm here to ask a favor of you."

"Anything. All you have to do is ask."

"Joel. I want you to marry Mona and be the dad to Deuce that I can't be. He's growing up so fast."

"What? Are you insane?" Biting his lip, he turned away and paced back and forth. "No. No way. Ramona loves you, Ronald. She's never gotten over you. I could never take your place."

"I'm not asking you to take my place. I want you to make your own place in her life."

"That's the craziest thing I've ever heard of. Why?"

"Why not?"

"I'm sorry. I can't."

"Don't tell me you don't love her. You've loved her from the first time we saw her playing softball in that cute little blue gym suit, and she had her hair in a ponytail. Remember?"

"Aww, that was a long time ago. We were all kids, and I fell in love with every girl with a pretty face back then."

"You might fool some people, but you don't fool me."

Joel ran his hand over the back of his neck. Since you've seen her, I don't have to tell you that she's still the same sweet, beautiful girl you fell in love with." He paused. "So, why don't you want her?"

"Are you kidding? I want her and my son more than I've ever wanted anything in my life but take a good look at me. However, there's no reason for her to be lonely, because of me."

"Ronald, man, I never thought I'd have to confess this, but the truth is, I've already asked Ramona to marry me—not that either of us is in love with the other, you understand—but I thought we could benefit from what the other has to offer." He groaned. "I know how that must've sounded, but she's been miserable at Rose Trellis since your mother died. I tried to convince her that it would be a chance for her to move out and allow me to provide for her and Deuce. And I could use a woman around to keep house."

Ronald's lip curled. "So, you need a maid, do you?"

"No, that's not what I meant, either. I just thought—"

"I'm teasing you. I don't care what your reason for asking her was, I want you to be persistent. Convince her that you not only need her, but that you love her."

"That's crazy. I can't believe you're saying this. You were always the romantic. And now, you want your best friend and your wife to settle for companionship without love?"

"Only because I know the reason you've never found the girl of your dreams is because I found her first. Whether you'll admit it or not, I know you're still in love with her. And I'm not convinced that she doesn't love you."

"Oh, you're wrong. You are so wrong. She's been faithful to you for fifteen years."

"I'm sure of it. And I don't think she knows she's in love with you, but even if she weren't, I know once you two are married, she'll learn to love you. Mona needs to love and to be loved. Will you do it? You'll have to act quickly, since I'm sure she's planning to leave town again after Daddy's funeral tomorrow afternoon. But when you see her tonight, tell her you'll take her and Deuce to the funeral. Then, when it's over, tell her you'd like to drop Deuce off at the theatre and to take her out to dinner to help celebrate your birthday."

"This is crazy. Then what?"

"Pour your heart out. I think you've held back, feeling as if you'd be betraying me. Now, you have my blessings. Convince her that you two need one another. Take her to Briar Point, overlooking the river. Hold her in your arms and tell her that you love her. Do it for me, Joel. She needs to be held."

Joel ran his fingers through his hair. "Man, this is crazy."

"I'll never ask you to do anything else for me, but you, Mona and Deuce mean more to me than life itself. I wouldn't ask it of you if I didn't believe with all my heart that all three of you would be happier for it."

"Hold on, Ron. I'm sure you have your reasons for conjuring up such a crazy scheme, but I have a better idea. I'll invite her over to my place for a dinner for two, where you'll be waiting for her. Then, I'll leave the house and let you two get reacquainted over a nice dinner."

Ronald laughed. "If you're doing the cooking, I'll pass."

"Hey, I can't cook much, but I can grill a mean steak. Besides, once you have her alone, eating will be the last thing on your mind. She loves you, Ron. She'd never forgive either of us if she should discover you're alive and we conned her into marrying me."

Holding his head back for the moon to reflect on his face, Ronald pushed a finger under his chin. "Look at me man! Take a good look. This is not the man she fell in love with."

"You're wrong, Ronnie. You are still the same man. I'll admit when I first saw you, I didn't recognize you. But it only took listening to you for a couple of minutes, before I began to see you—the real you—and the scars on your face suddenly became less visible."

"I can't do it to her. I won't. Joel, we've always leaned on one other. I'm counting on you to do this one thing for me, and don't ever tell her you've seen me or know that I'm alive. It's all I'll ever ask. She needs you. Deuce needs you. And you need them. Goodbye, my friend."

"Where are you going?"

"Out of their life and out of yours. That's all you need to know."

"Ronald, it was hard losing you the first time, but saying goodbye this way is even harder."

"But you'll do it, won't you? Do it for me, for Mona, for Deuce, and for yourself."

Joel nodded, then threw his arms around his best friend. Both shed tears that came from saying a final goodbye, then Joel watched through blurred eyes as Ronald disappeared into the darkness.

CHAPTER 9

Mr. Grover's Stetson hat was brimming over with loose bills. There were lots of fives, tens, and twenties. Deuce could hardly wait to get alone to count it.

Mr. Grover said, "Young fellow, you seem to know where everything is located here. Do you think you could find me a paper sack to put the money in? This bald head of mine will get cold if I should have to leave my hat behind."

"Yessir. I know exactly where to find one."

Ramona's voice cracked when she tried to speak to the crowd. "I am in awe at the generosity you all have shown. I know many of you have given above your means, and if it were just me, I would give it all back and not accept such a charitable gesture. But I have my child to think about. Your gift will allow me to move on. I'll be leaving Rose Trellis after the funeral in search of a job and a place to live."

Although she couldn't see him for the crowd, she recognized

Joel's voice, coming from the back of the room. "Why should you leave? Rose Trellis is your home. If you want a job, I'll hire you to work in the office."

Ramona was about to speak, when Gussie jumped up and yelled, "I smell smoke. It's coming from the kitchen."

Sissy, the maid, yelled back, "It's alright, Miz Gussie. Just a little grease fire. It's done put out."

Ramona was glad for the distraction, for fear she might've said more than was necessary if she had spoken too swiftly. But there was no way she could stay at Rose Trellis. Gussie wanted her gone when Theodore was alive. Staying there now that he was gone was out of the question. Even if Gussie were to agree, Ramona had no desire to live in the same house with the woman. She'd rather live in a little cabin in the woods and eat wild game than to stay there. Not only could she envision such a place, but the occupant seemed to fair just fine.

Joel stepped inside Rose Trellis and made his way to the front of the room. He approached Deuce and attempted to make small talk with the teenager. "I suppose you like to play football?"

"I don't know."

"What do you mean?"

"Never played. There was no team at my school."

Joel rubbed his hand across the back of his neck. "I knew you went away to school, but I didn't realize they didn't have a team. When will you be going back?"

"I won't. Going to the Harrington School for Boys was Daddy Theo's idea, but I hated it, so when I came home for Christmas, Mama said I could stay and go to school here."

"How do you like it?"

"I like being with Mama."

"Eufaula has a great football team. They'll begin Spring practice soon. Do you think you might like to play?"

He shrugged. "Dunno how."

"Well, I could fix that, if you think it's something you'd be interested in."

"Yessir. I'd like that. Mama said you and my daddy were great football players."

"We loved the game, that's for sure. What about movies? You like going to the theatre?"

"I love picture shows. The Titanic starring Barbara Stanwyck is on at the Avon and I've been wanting to see it."

"Then, I think you should."

"I can't. We'll be leaving tomorrow after my granddaddy's funeral. Maybe it'll be showing wherever we're going."

"And where would that be?"

Lifting a shoulder, he said, "Dunno. Mama calls it being on an adventure. She says we'll know it's right when we get there."

"Where did you go when you left here?"

"Mama said don't tell anyone where we've been or where we're going, but I don't really think she'd mind if you knew."

Ramona overheard a portion of the conversation. "Mind if he

knew what, Deuce?"

"Mr. Joel asked me where we went before coming back here, but I didn't tell him. Did I, Mr. Joel?"

He raised his hand as if to promise. "His lips were sealed."

Ramona said, "Deuce, please go upstairs and look under my bed, where you'll find a three piece set of luggage. You take the larger suitcase and leave the smaller one and the train case for me. Pack all you want to take with you and try to find something appropriate to wear to the funeral. We need to be ready to leave after the service tomorrow."

"Yes'm. I reckon it's good you didn't take the nice blue luggage when we left here, since it would've burned up. But why didn't we take it, Mama, instead of that old brown one that looked like it was made out of cardboard?"

"Don't stand there asking questions. You have a job to do."

"Sorry." He held out his hand to Joel. "Nice talking to you, Mr. Joel."

"You, too, Deuce."

When he scampered off, Joel said, "He's a fine boy, Ramona. You have every reason to be proud of him. He's his father made over."

"Thank you. I think so, too."

"Deuce mentioned the blue luggage. Is that the same set of Samsonite that I gave you and Ronald to take with you on your Honeymoon?"

She nodded. "Exactly. I hated to leave it, but I knew I'd break down in tears every time I opened it. For almost fifteen years, it has been stuck away, with nothing in it but the white gown and negligee that Granny gave me to wear on my wedding night. I couldn't bear to look at it. I'll never forget the look in Ronald's eyes the night—" Her jaw dropped. "Oh, dear. I'm so sorry. I had no right to talk about something so personal. I hope I didn't embarrass you."

"Not at all. But there's something I need to ask of you."

"Shoot."

"Tomorrow is my birthday."

"Aww, Happy Birthday, Joel."

"I heard you say your plans were to leave after the funeral. But as a special favor for me, would you consider delaying your departure an extra day, in order to go to dinner with me tomorrow night to celebrate?"

She bit her lip and stammered. "I really need to get away, Joel."

"I understand. It's just that there's no one—"

She reached over and placed her hand on his shoulder. "Of course, we'll stay and celebrate with you. You only turn thirty once. What time would you like to pick us up?"

"Deuce said there's a movie on at the Avon that he'd like to see, so I thought we could drop him off there, and you and I will go to Andy's Steak House for a Prime Rib."

"The Titanic."

"Pardon?"

"The movie he's been talking about. The Titanic."

"Yes. That's the one."

Ramona had held mixed feelings about going out with Joel. It seemed too much like a date. But knowing how pleased Deuce would be to see the movie, relaxed her.

"Great. Everyone appears to be leaving, so I should go, but I'll see you both tomorrow about five-thirty. The main feature generally starts at six o'clock, so he'll have a chance to get his popcorn and drink, find a good place to sit and see all the previews."

"You're a good man, Joel. It's rather sad that you feel you have no one but me to spend your birthday with. I wish you could find a woman you could love and could love you the way you deserve to be loved."

"Maybe I have."

Her eyes lit up. "Oh m'goodness, why haven't you told me before now? Who is she?"

"The time wasn't right. But telling you will be part of the birthday celebration."

"I'm looking forward to it. I can tell already that she's very special to you."

"Indeed, she is. Goodnight, Ramona. See you tomorrow evening."

"Won't you be at the funeral?"

"Funeral? Oh! Yes, of course. I wasn't thinking. I'll see you there."

"I don't know who this woman is, but I can tell she has you tied in knots. I'm happy for you, Joel. Goodnight."

Deuce came running back downstairs. "Finished packing. Where's Mr. Joel?"

"He just left. But he's invited me to have dinner with him tomorrow night to celebrate his birthday. He's offered to drop you off at the theatre to see Titanic. Would you like that?"

"Would I? That would be swell, Mama. Thank you. I like Mr. Joel. He's all right, isn't he?"

"Yes, sweetheart. Joel is one of the finest. He reminds me so much of your father. I suppose that's why I enjoy his company so much."

"You always say that I'm like my daddy, but I don't think I look anything like Mr. Joel."

"It's not that Joel looks like Ronald. It's his mannerisms that reminds me so much of him. You, on the other hand are your father's spitting image. But everyone is leaving, so why don't you go upstairs, get your bath, and get ready for bed. We have a long day ahead of us tomorrow. I'll be up shortly."

CHAPTER 10

After the last guest had left, Ramona went into the kitchen to clean up and wash all the cups and saucers lying around.

Gussie stomped in, holding a few plates she gathered from the parlor. "I declare, some folks act like they were born in a barn. How hard could it be to take a dish or two back to the kitchen instead of leaving it for us?"

"Mrs. Teuton offered to help."

"I wasn't about to let her stay. She never knows when to stop talking. She drives me crazy. But I can't excuse the rest of them. They could all see that you have a bum leg, and I'm in mourning. I shouldn't be expected to clean up after them."

"I know you're tired, Gussie. Why don't you go on to bed and I'll take care of this."

"I am tired, but there's something we need to get straight."

"Oh? Like what?"

"I'd think it would be obvious. For nigh fifteen years, you and the kid have had free reign of Rose Trellis. You lived here rent-free, and my husband—may he rest in peace, made sure you always had money in your pocket. As Theo told me so many times, he did it because you were kin. Well, I don't know how you found out he was gone, or why you felt the need to come, but let me remind you that you and I are in no way, shape, or form, related. You owe me nothing, and I owe you nothing. Is that clear?"

Ramona lifted her hands from the dishwater and picked up a towel. "Gussie, you've resented me from the first day you married Deuce's grandfather. Why?"

"We've had our differences, that's for sure, and I won't deny that it bothered me the way Theo coddled you and your boy. Sometimes I thought he cared more about you than he did me. But just so you'll know, I plan to sell this place and move back to Satsuma, where I have kinfolk."

"You're selling Rose Trellis?"

"That's right. I thought you should know, in case you had some cockeyed idea of trying to get what's not yours. I'd hate for you to go to the trouble for nothing."

Every muscle in her body tightened. "If that's what's worrying you, you can relax. I don't want anything that belongs to you, Gussie."

"Well, in case you aren't aware, I put three-hundred dollars in the hat when Grover took up a collection for you and the boy. It must've been very humiliating for you to take charity."

"Perhaps it should've been, but for Deuce's sake, I felt obliged to accept. However, I'll be happy to return your money to you. I'm sure you felt forced into signing the check."

"That's ridiculous. I gave of my own free will. But I was appalled that Mr. High and Mighty made it appear as if I didn't plan to donate."

"In that case, I appreciate your generosity. Deuce and I thank you."

"Well, of course. Uh . . . Ramona, when did you say you'd be leaving?"

"Friday morning, if that's agreeable to you. I had intended to leave tomorrow, but it's Joel's birthday and he's invited me to have dinner with him tomorrow night to celebrate. I hope you don't mind if we stay over one more night."

"Don't mind at all. So, it's Joel's birthday? That's nice. I like him. He's a fine young man and comes from means. You could do worse."

"What does that mean?"

"I think you know. I certainly don't blame you for setting your cap for him. I'm sure I'd do the same if I were in your shoes. He's single, well-off, and certainly not bad to look at. You're single, attractive, and need someone who can afford to take on a ready-made family. That's all I'm saying. But what do you plan to do with the boy while you two are having a romantic dinner? You don't plan to leave him here, do you?"

"No, we plan to take him to a movie."

"That's good. I may be conducting business with the prospective buyer, and it would be best if you take him with you. That's all I was saying. Well, goodnight, shug."

Shug? What brought about the sudden change? "Goodnight!"

Gussie yelled from the Master bedroom. "Ramona, if you still want that old truck, the keys are hanging on the wall beside the back door."

"You mean it?"

"Of course, I mean it. It's what Theo would've wanted."

Ramona put her hands back in the sudsy dishwater and attempted to second guess Gussie's motive. When she put on the friendly act in front of the guests, Ramona knew it was solely to impress them. But now that everyone was gone, why the uncharacteristic pleasantries? Did it matter? Deuce would be thrilled to learn he would get Daddy Theo's old truck.

She found it amusing that Gussie assumed there was something romantic going on between her and Joel. Not that he wasn't everything she'd alluded to, and more. Ramona had never been able to understand how he'd stayed single so long.

Thursday, February 7, 1955

Ramona spent the following morning repacking the clothes that Deuce had chosen to take. She took his blue sports coat off the hanger, and with a clothes brush, gave it a thorough brushing. The sleeves would be a little short on him, but after being on her leg more than she should have the day before, she decided short sleeves or not, she wasn't going shopping.

The money collected was to be used for necessities, and buying new clothes didn't fit into that category. If only she hadn't packed her best dresses when they left. There were only a few garments remaining in her closet and all should've been donated to the church rummage sale: A floral house dress, a faded green skirt, a cotton blouse, and the navy blue suit, which was a favorite a few years ago, but now looked dated. Yet, it would have to do. She pulled it down and threw it across the bed. She'd wear the floral to dinner with Joel. Everyone else in the restaurant might gawk at a house dress being worn in such a swanky place, but she was sure Joel wouldn't care what she wore. They'd been friends forever—or at least as long as she wanted to remember.

She was washing out a pair of stockings when she heard Gussie call. "I'm in the bathroom, Gussie. I'll be down in a minute."

"Well, hurry, dear. I have something to show you."

She hung the stockings over the shower bar and hobbled down the stairs, grimacing with every step. Gussie stood at the foot of the stairs, holding up a beautiful black dress with a scooped neck and tiny pearl buttons up the front. "I went shopping this morning. How do you like it?"

"It's gorgeous. It will look beautiful on you."

"On me? Don't be silly. It's for you to wear to the funeral." She reached in a bag lying on the stairs and pulled out a beautiful tea-length dress. "While I was in the store, I couldn't resist this beautiful red chintz for you to wear on your date."

The word date made Ramona flinch, but that was the least of her concerns. Why was Gussie doing this? What was her motive?

"If you don't like it, just say so."

"They're both beautiful, but you didn't need to buy me clothes."

"Didn't you lose your best dresses in the fire?"

"Yes, but I could've bought a dress. You shouldn't have."

"Ramona, I've done a lot of things in my life that I shouldn't have, but this is not one of them. Tomorrow, you'll be leaving and I don't want us to part with ill feelings between us."

"I don't know what to say, Gussie."

"Thank you will do. But that isn't all." She opened a shoe box and held up a black ballerina-style shoe. "These are a half-size larger than you normally wear, because of the swelling in your left foot. We'll stuff the other with something to keep it from slipping off. You can't wear that old sock with your pretty new clothes, and since you can't wear high-heels, these soft little shoes will go nicely."

"They're lovely. Thank you." If only Gussie could've been half as kind during the eight months she was married to Theodore, how much easier life would've been for all concerned.

At a quarter past nine, Ramona had finished dressing for the funeral and knocked on Deuce's door. "It's about time, honey. I hope you're ready."

"Yes'm." He opened the door and took one look at his mother. "You look beautiful, Mama. That's a new dress, isn't it? It looks expensive. Where did you get it?"

"Gussie bought it for me. Like it?"

His nose crinkled. "Not so much, now that I know where it came from."

"Deuce, I think Gussie has had a change of heart. She's being very kind."

He raised a brow. "When Gussie is nice to anyone, she's up to something."

"You're becoming much too cynical, son, and it doesn't become you. I believe it's her way of apologizing."

"Mama, I'm not sure what you mean by being cynical, but if it means I don't trust the old biddy, then you're right."

"Deuce! What has come over you? I didn't teach you to disrespect your elders. I blame Skip for putting thoughts into your head that you're grown. Well, you aren't."

"I don't know why you're saying mean things about Skip and taking Gussie's side."

She put her arms around him. "I'm not taking sides, sweetheart. I'm just saying that sometimes people say and do bad things they later regret. I don't know what caused Gussie to mellow, but I'm willing to forgive her, and I'd like for you to do the same."

"I hope you'll forgive me if I don't. Daddy Theo once told me that a leopard can't change its spots. I don't know what she's up to, but she's got you fooled. Gussie won't ever change."

Holding him tightly, she said, "Honey, if I can forgive Gussie after all she put us through, I can certainly forgive you. But it doesn't mean I think you're right to hold onto a grudge. We should go downstairs. It'll soon be time to leave."

Gussie was in the parlor with the limousine driver. Taking a last look in the hall mirror, she grumbled, "I don't know why Max at the Funeral Parlor couldn't switch Theodore's service to two o'clock as I requested. Who ever heard of having a funeral in the morning?"

"Ma'am, he explained that Mr. Bozeman's service was already scheduled for two o'clock."

"They could've switched it. I doubt that bunch of Bozeman's can tell time. It'll likely be the first time the heathen's have been inside a church."

Ramona and Deuce stood listening. Deuce glanced at his mother and grinned. "Told you."

Gussie looked him over from head to foot and scowled. "Young man, don't you own a suit?"

Ramona whispered. "Sorry. The sleeves were too short. I think he looks nice in the vee-neck sweater."

Making it plain she didn't approve, Gussie said, "It's too late to do anything about it now. I hope you found the keys to the truck. I'll meet you at the church."

The chauffeur said, "Begging your pardon, ma'am, but there's plenty of room for all three of you in the limo. There's no need in them taking a truck."

She muttered, "I wasn't thinking. Well, hurry and get in. I don't want to be late."

Deuce said, "Don't let us hold you up. We'll take our truck."

Ramona nodded. "Deuce is right. We'll follow you."

On the way to the church, Deuce said, "Do you still want to believe she's changed? Mama, we can't get away from here fast enough to suit her or me. Let's leave as soon as the funeral is over. We have a vehicle and money. There's no need for us to hang around."

"Deuce, we can't leave until tomorrow."

"Why not?"

"I promised Joel, I'd go with him to dinner tonight to celebrate his birthday."

"I hope you don't plan to leave me at Rose Trellis with fussy Gussy, because I won't stay there." He wailed, "I mean it, Mama."

"Calm down. You aren't staying there. Joel said you mentioned the Titanic is on at the movies, and he suggested you might prefer going to see it, instead of going to dinner with us."

"Boy, would I? That would be swell. I reckon I could stay one more day. Like you said, it wouldn't be right to let Joel down on his birthday."

She winked. "I thought you'd see it my way, once you had time to think about it."

When they entered the church, Grover, and another fellow she saw at Rose Trellis last evening were serving as ushers. They led her and Deuce all the way to the front of the large church and sat them on the front pew alongside Gussie, who muttered between heavy sobs, "He's gone. My precious Theo is gone. What am I gonna do? What am I gonna do?"

Deuce did nothing to hide his disgust. After the funeral, everyone moved outside to the church cemetery. Joel escorted Ramona to the truck and whispered. "Five-thirty?"

Gussie could be heard squalling as she was helped into the waiting limousine, yet as soon as she stepped into the house, her tears dried like an unprimed pump. "Ramona, dear, what time do you plan to leave in the morning? I hope you can have your things out by eight o'clock so the maid can give those two rooms a thorough cleaning. Do you think that might be possible?"

"I'm sure of it, Gussie."

Deuce mumbled out of the corner of his mouth. "Didn't I tell you? Now that's it's just the three of us, I think all that sugar is turning to vinegar."

Gussie turned around and scowled. "What's that, young man?"

Puckering his lips, he said, "I asked if you'd like a little sugar."

"I heard what you said the first time. If you were mine—"

Ramona wanted to make excuses for him, but she had none to offer. "We'll be gone before daylight, Gussie."

CHAPTER 11

Deuce was waiting at the door at five-thirty when Joel came calling. "Thank you, Joel. I've been so excited ever since Mama told me that I'll finally get to see Titanic."

"I'm glad to know you're excited, because I'm rather excited myself."

"I read the book. I can't wait to see the movie." Deuce led him down the long hall.

Seeing Ramona holding onto the railing as she attempted the stairs, Joel rushed to her aid. "Oh, my stars. You look amazing."

Deuce did most of the talking on the way to the theatre, giving a detailed synopsis of the book.

Joel pulled up in front of the Avon, reached in his pocket, pulled out a ticket and handed it over the back seat. "I picked it up earlier to make sure you could get in. I didn't want to chance it being sold out."

"Gee, thanks. That would've been a bummer, for sure."

As they drove away, Joel reached his arm over the back of the seat and ran his hand under her hair. "I have a feeling this is going to be a birthday I'll never forget."

"You're very thoughtful, Joel. You certainly know how to make a girl feel special."

"But you are special. You always have been, from the first day that Ronald and I spotted you playing softball."

"Goodness, that was a long time ago, wasn't it?"

"Not so long that I've forgotten anything about you. How you wore your hair, the sound of your voice, how you'd give your left foot a little kick when you threw the ball to home plate."

"You're so funny. I'm certainly not kicking very high, nowadays with this bum ankle."

"I remember how well that little gym suit fit you. You were a beauty then, Mona, and you've only grown more beautiful with the passing of years." He pulled up in front of the restaurant and parked.

"You're very sweet to say so, Joel. But . . . but you called me Mona."

He didn't react but reached into the back seat for her shawl. "It may be cool inside the restaurant."

"That's what Ronald called me."

"I beg your pardon?"

"Mona. No one else has ever called me that."

"No one?" He chuckled. "Seriously? Then it makes me happy

to know that it's now my very own affectionate name for you." He jumped out, ran around the car, and opened her door. "Have you ever eaten here?"

"Are you kidding? This whole night is a first for me. I think I'm beginning to understand how Cinderella must've felt."

They strolled into the dining room and the hostess greeted Joel by name and showed them to a little table in the far corner of the room. He ordered for them both, and although she wasn't sure it was ladylike to finish off such a huge meal, it was too delicious to leave anything on her plate.

After dinner, he escorted her back to the car, then reached for her hand, and pulling it to his lips, he kissed it. "Thank you, Mona."

She attempted to dismiss her objection as being silly. "Oh, Joel, it's I who should be thanking you. I've done nothing, but you've given me and Deuce a night to remember. I knew the boy, Joel, but I feel tonight I've gotten to know the man, Joel. I can truthfully say I'm very fond of them both."

"It thrills me to hear that. It's too early for the movie to be over, so I'd like to take you somewhere while we wait for Deuce." He turned down a little dirt road that ran beside the lake.

Ramona commented on the gorgeous way the moon reflected on the water.

"Gorgeous is right." He drove up a hill and parked the car overlooking the glistening waters, then took the top off the convertible. "I hope it isn't too chilly for you." He slid over in the seat next to her and rubbed his warm hand across her shoulder. "Does this feel better?"

"Actually, the breeze feels good." Leaning her head back and resting it on top of the seat, she gazed up at the stars. "I can't imagine a more beautiful setting to end a perfect night."

Joel slid his arm around her. "Neither can I." Then pulling her close, he leaned over and kissed her.

Stunned, she jerked back. "No, Joel. This isn't right."

Holding his lips to her ear, he whispered, "You're wrong, Mona. I'm right for you, and you're right for me. We've been afraid to admit the truth."

With both hands planted on his chest, she shoved him away. "Joel, months ago when you suggested we should marry, we admitted that we weren't in love, and nothing has changed. Pretending won't make it so. Please, let's leave."

"Don't you see, Mona? The only reason we haven't wanted to admit it is because of our devotion to Ronald. But I realize now, he'd choose this for us if he could."

"Oh, Joel, if I gave you the wrong impression tonight, I apologize. We've been friends too long to let a moonlit night make us say or do things we'll regret in the morning."

He slid so close, she was jammed against the door. He brushed her hair back and his breath warmed her neck. "Say you don't feel the same thing I feel, Mona. Tell me you don't."

Her heart hammered. Was he right? She couldn't deny she felt something the moment he first touched her shoulder. Then the feeling intensified when he leaned over and kissed her. Something inside her wanted the feeling to linger. It had been so long since she had felt a man's lips on hers or felt strong arms pulling her so close she could hardly breath. How could it be so wrong if it felt so right?

"Joel, we should go."

"I've offended you."

"No. You've been nothing but wonderful. But I'm not ready for this."

"But you are, Mona. I can feel the beating of your heart. You feel the same thing I feel, and if we'll be truthful we'll admit it didn't just begin tonight. When I proposed and denied that I loved you, I lied. I love you so much I can't sleep at night." He gently lifted her chin with his thumb and placed his lips on hers.

Confused, she didn't push him away. He kissed her, then brushed a strand of hair from her temple and smiled. "Now, that wasn't so bad, was it?"

To admit the truth would make her feel disloyal to Ronald. "Joel, I've wondered for years why you weren't married. A girl would be crazy not to want a man like you in her life."

He slid down with his head resting against the back of the seat. "Any girl but you. Is that what you're telling me?"

"Yes. Uh, I mean no. I don't know, Joel. Besides, nothing can become of it, since Deuce and I are leaving early in the morning."

"But you don't have to. Stay, Mona. Please stay. Marry me and let me take care of you both. It's what I want, it would be what

Ronald would want, and although you're afraid to admit it, I believe it's what you want."

"Oh, sweet Joel. I won't deny it sounds very appealing, but this concerns more than you and me. I'd need to discuss it with Deuce."

"Then we'll talk to him tonight."

"Not we. This needs to be between my son and me, and I want him to have time to absorb the idea without feeling he has no say-so in the matter."

"But you will talk to him about it tonight. Right? And if he has no objections?"

"No. I've promised Gussie we'd be out of Rose Trellis by tomorrow."

"But you don't have to leave town. I'll get you a room at the hotel until we can make arrangements to get married."

"No, Joel. Deuce and I are leaving in the morning, but if you and I are meant to be together, God will work out the details."

"I don't suppose there's anything I can say to keep you here. Where were you headed when your car caught fire?"

"Jinx Bay."

"Jinx Bay? Why?"

"To look for work."

"But there's nothing there but a cannery."

"I've always been fascinated by the stories Ronald told of the summers you and he worked at the Fish Camp and how much you enjoyed it."

"But you aren't a fisherman, and we didn't work in the cannery."

"Deuce has heard the stories of the fish camp so many times, he thought he'd like to go there. If I'm lucky, I'll get a job in the cannery, and maybe he can go out on one of the boats during Spring Break. He'd love it."

"You? Working in a cannery? That's not a life for you or Deuce, Mona."

Her muscles tightened. "You and Ronald seemed to like it."

"That was different. We were kids, and since his Uncle Walter owned it, we weren't held to the same rigorous standards as the men who fished for a living. It's hard work and minimal pay."

"I don't doubt it. But the stories aren't my only reason for considering the cannery. My choices for employment are limited. Daddy Theo didn't believe in women working, therefore my resume is not very impressive. As you know, I received what little education I have at the State Reformatory for Girls, and I've never held a job." She chuckled. "Be truthful. If you were an employer, would you hire me?"

"I'd do better than that. I'd marry you." He looked at his watch. "The movie should be over in ten minutes. We'd better go."

When Joel pulled up in front of Rose Trellis Deuce opened the back door and jumped out. "Thanks, Mr. Joel. The movie was even better than I expected. Goodnight."

"'Nite, Deuce. I'm glad you enjoyed it, but I hope you'll learn to call me Joel. I have hopes of us becoming very close friends, real soon."

"That would be swell, but didn't Mama tell you? We're leaving tomorrow."

Ramona said, "I'll be inside shortly, hon. Go ahead and get your bath. We'll need to be up early in the morning."

After Deuce went inside, Joel reached for Mona's hand. "There's nothing I can say to make you want to stay?"

"Joel, do you really think that I don't want to stay? Don't you realize that being your wife sounds much more appealing than going to work in a stinky cannery or digging potatoes or pulling fruit? Those are my choices for employment."

"Then, that settles it."

"No. I have Deuce to consider and he's counting on going to Jinx Bay. I promise not to keep you waiting long. Tonight was very special, but it would be foolish to make such an important lifelong decision based on fifteen minutes of passion in the moonlight."

"I love you, Mona. I believe if you'd be honest with yourself, you'd admit that you're in love with me, too?"

"I won't keep you waiting long, but I have to be sure. Give me three months. If after that time, I find myself constantly thinking of you and the life we could have together, then I'll know it's real and not based on a couple of kisses under the stars, and it will give Deuce time to get accustomed to the idea of having a man around. He likes to think I need him to take care of me. He could resent someone taking his place unless it's handled right."

Joel couldn't allow himself to be deterred by a mere three-months timeline. She loved him. He knew it, even if she didn't. Besides, it would take that long to plan a wedding. His heart felt as if it would burst wide open with so much joy inside. "Okay, three months! I'm thinking a Spring wedding would be a perfect time for a honeymoon. Do you think you'd enjoy a South Sea Island Cruise?"

Without answering, she said, "It's been a lovely evening, Joel. Thank you."

"If I don't hear from you at the end of three months, I'll know you decided working in a cannery is better than being married to me and proof that I'm a worse kisser than I thought."

The comment made her smile. She loved the way Joel could take a serious, uncomfortable situation and turn it into a light moment. It felt good to laugh. She recalled how the three of them could always find something to laugh about as long as Ronald was alive.

He walked her to the door. "You've given me a reason to hope, and for that I am grateful."

"Goodnight, Joel, and I hope it's been a Happy Birthday."

"It's been beyond my expectations. I just wish I could talk you into staying. What time do you plan to leave in the morning?"

"Eight o'clock."

"Then there's still time for you to change your mind." He planted a kiss on her forehead and left more determined than ever to change her name to Mrs. Joel Gunter.

CHAPTER 12

Ramona woke up in the middle of the night in a cold sweat. The dream seemed real. So very real. Ronald's arms were wrapped around her, his lips caressing hers. Her heart raced, wishing she could go back to sleep and make it last. Or was it Joel's arms she felt? Joel's lips? How could she not see his face, when the feelings were so strong heart was still pounding like a jackhammer?

Had she made a mistake by not accepting the proposal? Joel loved her. It felt good to be loved. Did she really want to work in a fish cannery? She shuddered. Joel was right. Working in a cannery sounded dreadful. But didn't she owe it to Deuce to at least take him to Jinx Bay to let him see the boats his father worked on as a boy? Hadn't she much rather pick fruit in the open air? She found it difficult to go back to sleep with so many questions and so few answers.

At the crack of dawn, Ramona was up and dressed. She knocked on Deuce's door and told him to get on his clothes, they were leaving.

"It's eight o'clock, already?"

"No, but there's no need to wait. Be quiet. We don't want to wake Gussie."

On the way out, she grabbed a couple of apples from the bin, packed a sleeve of saltine crackers and a wedge of cheese.

Deuce ran and jumped in the truck. "I was shocked when Gussie said we could have the truck. Weren't you surprised?"

"Not really. It's old, and Gussie fussed about it being parked in front of Rose Trellis. She wanted your grandfather to get rid of it as soon as they married, but he refused."

"I'm glad. I've always loved it. Daddy Theo once told me that as soon as I was old enough to drive, I could have it. He said he bought it for my daddy when he graduated from Military School."

"Yes, he did."

"I don't care that it's old. I never want to sell it. We won't, will we, Mama?"

"No, darling. It's your truck, just as your grandfather promised."

****

Joel tossed and turned in the bed, all night. He couldn't let her leave without trying one last time to convince her she was making a huge mistake by leaving. He glanced over at the clock. Six-thirty. He jumped up, dressed, and drove over to Rose Trellis.

His heart sank when he realized the truck was gone. Jumping out of the car, he ran up the steps and rang the doorbell.

Gussie came to the door. "Oh, it's you. Well, I'm sure you aren't here to see me, but you're too late if you came to see Ramona. They left before I was up this morning."

"But she said eight o'clock."

"Well, I reckon she changed her mind."

He turned and meandered back to his car.

****

As they headed to Florida, Ramona was surprised at how things appeared much differently in the daylight. Attempting to hide her anxiety, she made up road games to play with Deuce as they traveled.

"Mama, what's wrong?"

"Who said anything was wrong. We're finally continuing our adventure. And this time in your very own truck. What could be more fun?"

"Then why do you look so worried?"

"I can't fool you, can I? Honey, I do have something weighing on my mind. I'm beginning to believe that I may have made a big mistake."

"Like what?"

"By allowing you to fantasize what it would be like to live in Jinx Bay. That's no life for you. For either of us."

His mouth gaped open. "Why are you saying this?"

"Honey, Joel has asked me to marry him. I know how much

you like him, and he could give us a good life. You know what? It's not too late." She stopped the truck and put it in reverse.

"What are you doing?"

"We're going back."

Tears welled in his eyes. He screamed. "No. No, Mama, we're not. If you go back, I won't stay there. I'll run away."

"You're getting riled over nothing, son. We're going back to Eufaula, but not to live with Gussie. Joel has asked me to marry him. I think I shall. He'll be good to us. We'll all go to a Justice of the Peace, get married, then you and I can move in with him. He lives in that big house, all by himself."

"Count me out." He burst into tears.

"But I thought you'd be pleased. He has a lot to offer us. You said you really like him."

"I do like him. But not for you. He's a nice man and I like hearing him tell stories about the things he and my father did growing up, but you don't love him, Mama. You know you don't."

"That's the thing, sweetheart. I *don't* know. I'm confused."

"Since when?"

"Since last night."

"What changed your mind?"

Ramona swallowed hard. How could she explain to her fourteen-year-old son? "You wouldn't understand."

"Oh, I think I do."

"No, you don't."

"You weren't even thinking of marrying him when you left

home last night. What did y'all do? It must've been some kind of date for you to suddenly decide to get married. Did he wine and dine you at an expensive restaurant, then take you to a fancy hotel? Or did you skip the meal, entirely?"

Before she had time to think, Ramona's palm slapped across her son's jaw. Then bursting into tears, she embraced his face with both her hands, crying, "I'm sorry, Deuce. I don't know why I did that. I'm so sorry. I've never slapped you before."

He glared into her eyes. "Seems I hit a nerve." He reached for the door handle and opened the door.

"What are you doing?"

"You go back to your lover. I'll hitch-hike the rest of the way to Jinx Bay."

"Deuce, you have it all wrong. Joel did kiss me, but that was all. I promise you. Please, shut the door, and I'll explain everything to you while we ride."

He sucked in a heavy breath. "Okay, but don't treat me like a kid. Mama, I know you're lonely and it's not that I object to you getting married, but when you do, I want it to be because you love the man. Not because of the lifestyle he can offer. If you did that, you'd be no different than Gussie. I resented her for marrying Daddy Theo when everyone knew she didn't really love him. She wanted Rose Trellis and all the trimmings. She ruined his life in order to get what she wanted. I like Joel. I like him too much to see you ruin his life the way Gussie ruined my granddaddy's. It's up to you, Mama. You can turn around and head back alone, or you can keep going and we'll continue our adventure."

Startled that her son was issuing an ultimatum, she quipped, "Goodness! Where was I when you grew up? I didn't see it coming." Knowing he'd resent the marriage if she rushed into it, she had to keep her promise and take him to Jinx Bay. At first, Ramona found it awkward sharing her intimate feelings with her son, but once they began to talk, she realized he was much more mature than she had given him credit for. It seemed he was much wiser than she had been. Everything he said made sense.

"Mama, I didn't really believe you went to a hotel. But I wanted to shock you into admitting the truth. I wanted you to think about why you'd suddenly want to marry him this morning, when it was the last thing on your mind when you left the house to go out with him last night. I hope one day you *will* fall in love, but when you do, I want it to be for the right reason. So, now, be honest with yourself and with me—are you in love with Joel?"

She pressed her lips together before answering. "No."

"I didn't think so." He grinned. "But he must be a powerful kisser. Maybe he'll give me a few tips."

"You're embarrassing me. I think it's time to change the subject."

CHAPTER 13

Ramona drove into Jinx Bay and stopped at the City Café for lunch. Deuce ordered a hamburger and milkshake, and asked for a large glass of sweet, iced tea.

"Mama, aren't you gonna eat something?"

"Not hungry."

"You're worried, aren't you?"

"Worried? No, son, I'm fine."

"Well, I'm kinda worried."

"What do you have to be worried about? We're together. Remember? You have nothing to fear."

"I'm scared the cannery might not be hiring and I really want to live near the water and be able to see the boats come in. I'll bet it's a sight to see when they unload their nets. I sure hope they don't think I'm too young to go out. Do you think I have a chance?"

She might as well break the news to him now. Prolonging it could only make it harder. "Deuce, I wanted you to see the Fish Camp that you've heard so much about, but we aren't staying here."

His brow furrowed. "What do you mean? You're going to get a job in the cannery. Aren't you?"

"I was, but that was before. After talking with Joel, he helped me realize this is not where I need to be."

His lip quivered. "I thought we had this straight. Fifteen minutes ago, you said you were going to wait three months before giving him his answer."

"And I plan to. But Joel says the cannery is hot, smelly, and I'd be on my feet all day with sweat pouring in my eyes. He says I can do better."

"You can't do this to me. You promised. I hate Joel Gunter."

"Stop it! I won't have you talking like that."

"So, if we aren't staying, why did you even bring me here? Was it just to taunt me?"

"You know better. I promised to bring you here and show you the boats, but I never promised to stay."

He pouted the remainder of the way to the fish camp. But once he looked out over the water and saw the boats unloading fish, he jumped out of the truck and ran across the yard, past the cannery, and didn't stop until he reached the end of the dock.

Ramona got out of the truck and looked around. Everything was just the way Ronald had described it. She advanced toward the dock when a fellow stopped her. "Are you the one who called about the bookkeeping job?"

"No. Sorry. My husband worked here when he was a kid, and my son has always wanted to come see the place he's heard so much about."

"That's too bad. I was hoping you were looking for a job."

Ramona bit her bottom lip. What would it hurt to at least give it a shot? She said, "As a matter of fact, I am unemployed at the present."

"Excellent. Would you like to fill out an application? It's merely a formality. If you want the job, it's yours. It pays a hundred dollars a week."

"Are you serious? To work in a cannery?"

"Those dear souls deserve a hundred dollars for what they do, but I'm afraid they work for much less."

She followed him into an office, where he offered her a seat, an application, and a pen. After signing her name and former address, she looked at the next line: Former places of employment. She laid down the pen and looked up. "I'm sorry. To be honest, I've never made a paycheck in my life. I married young, had a child, and became a widow, all in the same year. For fifteen years, I've stayed home to raise my boy."

"I'm sorry."

She stood and picked up her purse. "Me too. I was beginning to feel I was in the right place."

"I believe you are. When I said I was sorry, I meant I was

sorry that you lost your husband. I need a bookkeeper and I need one bad. Past employment is not a requirement. I'm Boyd, by the way."

"Nice to meet you, Mr. Boyd."

"Just Boyd, and if you want the job, it's yours."

"I wish I could say yes."

"Why can't you?"

"I know nothing about keeping books."

"Can you add and subtract?"

Her brow lifted. "Math was my best subject in school."

"Then why don't we say it's a temporary position, and after two weeks if you feel it's not what you want or if I feel you aren't capable of doing the job, then I'll pay you a month's salary and we'll shake hands and part ways. You're the most promising looking person who has shown up here."

Ramona glared out the window at her son standing on the wharf. He looked so much like Ronald standing there. *A bookkeeper?* It was an opportunity she hadn't dared to consider.

"If I didn't think you could do it, I wouldn't waste your time or mine."

"But you don't know me." She wasn't sure why she blurted it out, but the words came tumbling out before she had time to stop them. "I didn't finish high school. I was incarcerated at a School for Girls from the time I was thirteen. I made good grades—as long as I attended school, but the truth is, I left before graduating." She lowered her head, unwilling to see the shock on his face.

"Information duly noted." He put the application in his desk. "You're hired."

"You're serious?" She clamped her lips shut. What was she doing? Trying to talk him out of it? Drawing a long breath, she said, "Thank you. We've just come into town, so I need to make a phone call. I saw a house listed in the paper for rent that said it was only a couple of blocks from the fish camp on Cannery Road. That would certainly be convenient if it's still available."

"It's available."

"I hope you're right."

"I am. The company owns it. There are twelve houses on the strip, which are rented to fishermen. The turnover is small. The only reason there is one available now, is because the fellow who rented it moved up north to take care of his elderly parents. I can look at you and tell it's not what you've been accustomed to. It's a small, two-room cabin that was built in the 1920's."

"Sounds perfect. I'll take it."

"But don't you want to look at it first?"

"You're taking a chance on me. Why shouldn't I be willing to take a chance on a place to stay?"

"I'd feel better if you'd ride over there and check it out. I'm afraid you may change your mind once you look at it. However, I must warn you that there have been very few houses for rent in Jinx Bay since the war ended. When our soldiers came home, there were barely enough houses, since they went away boys, living with their parents and came back men, ready to start a family. They left inexperienced in the workplace, so when they returned, the chance of fishing for a living appealed to them. And once they get a taste of the salty air, they stay."

"I'll take it. When should I show up for work?"

"How does eight o'clock Monday morning sound?"

"Could we make it nine? I'll need to get my son registered in school."

"Take all the time you need to get him settled." He shook his head when she reached into her purse. "Pay at the end of the month."

"But I can pay now."

"I'm sure you can. But let's wait and see how things work out. I'd drive you over there, but I was on my way out when you showed up. My wife's mother is in the hospital in Panama City, and I promised to take her to see her this afternoon. I should've left an hour ago."

"What about a key?"

"There's no key. Never needed one. Take a left out of the parking lot, then turn right. It's on a dead-end dirt road. There are six cabins on both sides of the road, and they're all alike."

"I don't mean to hold you up, but just curious. My deceased husband's uncle once owned the Fish Camp. His name was Tobe Alberson. Does he still own it?"

"No, Mr. Tobe died several years ago. He ran a tough ship, but if you did your job, he was a good man to work for." He followed her outside, then got into his car and drove away.

Ramona couldn't wait to tell Deuce the good news. She approached the wharf and looked around. Failing to find him, she inquired of two fishermen, who remembered seeing a tall, lanky kid hanging around, but paid no attention to where he went.

Ramona ran inside the cannery, but it only took a couple of minutes to know he wouldn't be there.

After a desperate search of the premises, she jumped in the truck and drove slowly down the road, searching both sides of the woods, when she spotted him. "Deuce Jones, get in this truck, this instant. You scared me. I didn't know where you were. Where do you think you were going?"

Crawlin in, he slid down in the seat. "What do you care?"

Ramona pulled off the side of the road and parked. "What do mean? You're my son. I care what happens to you."

"Then why did you let Joel talk you out of staying here? You were good with it until you talked to him."

"Well, I have something to tell you, but first, I want you to tell me something. Did it not register with you that I would be worried out of my mind when I couldn't find you? Where were you planning to go? No money. No car. No job. Answer me, Deuce. What were you thinking?"

Tears welled in his eyes. "I dunno. Sorry, Mama."

"Well, don't ever scare me like that again. I have something to tell you, but I'm so angry with you right now, I don't know if I should."

"I said I'm sorry."

Unable to keep it in, she said, "I have a job."

"How? I mean, where?"

"Working in the office at the fish camp."

"Are you serious, Mama?" Whether the gleam in her son's eyes was from the wetness, or sheer happiness, she couldn't discern. "Doing what?"

"I'll be keeping the books."

He twisted to the edge of his seat. "You're jousting with me, aren't you? You're no bookkeeper."

"You're right, I'm not. But if you'll help me, maybe I can be before Monday. That's when I'm supposed to report for work."

"Aww, Mama, don't kid about something like that. You *are* kidding, aren't you?"

"Nope. I'm serious."

"So, what are you gonna do when they discover you've never done it before?"

"I told the fellow who hired me. But I plan to be a bookkeeper by the time I report for work."

Deuce laughed. "And how did you pull that off? Lie on your job application?"

"You know me better than that. I told him the truth, but he seems to have confidence that I can do it. He's almost convinced me."

"Sure, you can. You're smart, Mama. I know you can do it. So where are we going, now?"

"To find a library."

"For what?"

"To find a book on accounting. I plan to be a top-notch accountant before I report to work, Monday morning."

CHAPTER 14

Friday night, February 8

Joel knew Mona didn't love him, but she would. He'd see to it that she forgot she was ever married to Ronald Jones. Deuce was a good kid, as good kids go, but Joel figured he'd be doing him a favor by sending him off to a military school. The boy worshipped the father he'd never met, so how hard could it be to convince him that it's what Ronnie would've wanted for him?

Glancing at his watch, it was a quarter 'til eight. He barely had enough time to make it to the poker game. He racked up last week and had a gut-feeling his luck had just begun. He couldn't deny he'd always been a bit jealous, knowing Ronald would inherit his father's enormous estate, while his own family was left practically penniless after the Great Depression, with nothing left but the old homeplace. It hadn't seemed fair. But that was then.

Never could he have imagined that in a few short years, things could've turned out in his favor. He had built up a decent law practice and would go home after the game tonight with enough money to buy Rose Trellis from Gussie, if Mona should choose to live there.

He pulled up to the Blue Willow Motel and knocked three times on the door. Lomax opened it, and said, "Hey, fellows, make room at the table. We weren't sure you'd make it, Joe-Joe."

Joel cringed at the childish sounding nickname. "Wouldn't have missed it." He glanced around the table. "It's a little early, but why don't we get started? Looks as if we're all here."

Jerry made a point to look at his watch, "It's still early and we've got one more coming."

Glancing from left to right, Joel's brow shot up. "Who?"

"A guy from Birmingham. They call him Big Ed."

"I don't think I like his moniker. Who invited him?"

"I did. If you've got a problem with it, maybe you'd like to bow out."

Joel rubbed the back of his neck. "Forget it. I'm sure he's fine, if you say he is."

The game went on for hours. Joel was winning in the beginning, but his luck changed. At two o'clock in the morning, he not only had lost the five-hundred bucks he'd brought with him, but he had lost sixteen-hundred more than he had in the bank. Sweat gathered on his upper lip. He jumped up and yelled, "It's not fair. You brought in a card shark. I didn't have a chance."

Big Ed pushed back in his chair and roared, as if it were the funniest thing he'd ever heard. "How does that saying go— 'All is well in love and poker?'" He chuckled at his own words, while lighting a cigar. He took a few puffs, and the smile quickly gave way to a scowl. "Pay up, Joe Joe, or should I bring in someone to coerce you?"

Joel's hand shook as he pulled a pen and pad from his pocket. He wrote a check for two-thousand dollars and handed it to Big Ed.

Ed pulled a pair of spectacles from his coat pocket, and holding the note at arm's length, he read it and frowned. "What are you trying to pull?"

"It's all I have." He jerked out the small, leather bank balance book he kept in his shirt pocket, opened it, and shoved it in Big Ed's face. He pointed to the balance. "I only kept the thirteen dollars and thirty-five cents to keep from closing out the account, which could draw attention. Ol' man Drummond—he's our bank president—would likely find out if I closed the account and he'd want to know if I was in trouble."

Jerry slapped his hand against his thigh and howled. "Well, aren't you?"

"Shut up, Jerry. This doesn't concern you."

"Oh, but I think it does."

Big Ed said, "Boys, boys . . . be nice." He gathered the money from the table and counted it once more. Then shaking his head, he said, "This won't do, padre. Maybe you should check your pockets to see if you've forgotten something. I'll wait while you decide how you plan to come up with sixteen-hundred bucks."

"That's all I have. I'm not a magician. I can't make money appear in thin air."

Ed took the cigar from his lips and grinned. "Maybe you should've thought of that before deciding poker was your game. Thick or thin air, it makes no difference to me where it comes from. Throw in that shiny new Cadillac convertible you drove up in, and I'll knock off the remaining sixteen-hundred."

"You can't be serious. It just rolled off the lot last week. I paid $3,800 cash for that car." He shook his head. "Nothing doing."

His answer appeared to anger Ed. "Frankly, my boy, I didn't realize you were in a bargaining position."

"Have a heart, man. I can't afford to do without my car. I have to have a way to get back and forth to work."

"From the way I see it, you can't afford to *keep* your car. However, I'm not into automobile sales. So, my advice would be for you to sell it or come up with another way to get the dough. What else do you have?"

"Nothing. Nothing except the house I live in. It's old. It's been in the family for five generations."

Ed's brow formed a vee. "Did you say, 'nothing?'" He pursed his lips. "That's too bad. Would you boys like to own a spanking new Cadillac convertible or an old Victorian house?"

Joel's Adam's apple bobbed. He'd ordered the convertible the day after he won the windfall in the last game. It had only arrived last Monday. "Have a heart, man. I beg of you, give me a couple of months. Please! I can get the money. It'll just take a little time."

Big Ed stood and faced him, nose to nose. "Aww, I hate to hear a grown man grovel. Now, you know how these fellows felt when you showed no mercy at your last game."

"I'm sorry. I was wrong. I'll make it up to them. I promise."

The four-hundred-plus pound man gave a chuckle. "I think you just did with that last hand." He glanced around at the men sitting at the table. "So, how did I do?"

Jerry appeared to speak for the group. "You did just fine, Ed." Heads nodded.

Joel pulled out a handkerchief and swiped the sweat from his brow. "If you'll take an IOU and give me sixty days to come up with the money, I'll pay the balance."

Big Ed gave a hearty laugh. "You're too kind."

"I'll collect from a few clients who owe me, but I can't get it overnight."

"Well, now that sounds reasonable. I'm not a hard man to deal with." He looked at the men sitting around the table. "Am I hard to deal with, fellows?"

Jimbo pursed his lips. "I have found you to be most cooperative, Big Ed."

"See? I tell you what I'll do." Ed galloped over and gazed at the calendar on the wall. Then tracing the days with his fingers, he said, "Give Jerry an IOU for the remaining sixteen hundred bucks and come up with the cash within the next thirty days." He smirked. "And then, I'd advise you to find another hobby."

"Thirty days? That's too soon."

"Thirty!"

His chin quivered. "Where can I reach you?"

"Don't worry about me. I have what I came after—retribution for my friends." He gathered the cash on the table and divided the spoil evenly among the players. Then he handed Joel fifty dollars.

Joel shrugged. "What's this for?"

"I don't believe in leaving a fellow stone-broke, and I believe that's what you are."

Joel wanted to throw it back in his face, and he would have if he could've afforded to. But knowing this was all he had, he'd need it until he could call in some debts. He pounded his fist on the desk. "This is against the law."

Big Ed seemed to find the situation humorous. "Yeah, we thought of that. Gambling is illegal in Alabama. But we happen to know a good lawyer. You *will* represent us, won't you, Joel?"

"I'll see that every one of you pay for what you've done. You'd better hope you never come up against me in court."

He heard the grating laughter as he slammed the door behind him. He drove home, then sat in his beautiful convertible with tears welling in his eyes.

****

Joel paced the floor at work Monday morning, waiting for the bookkeeper to get to the office.

When Peggy arrived, she pulled off her galoshes, shook the water from her raincoat and hung it on the hat rack. "Goodness, it's really coming down out there, now, but we needed a good rain."

Joel stomped from his office and stood in front of her desk. "Did you finally decide to come to work?"

"I beg your pardon?"

"It's almost ten minutes past eight. I need you sitting in your desk at eight o'clock sharp every morning. If you don't like this job, maybe you should quit and allow someone have it who wants to work."

Her lips parted. "If you have a problem with me or my work, Joel, perhaps you should tell me what it is, instead of screaming at me."

"I've been going through the books, and I've come across several accounts who are delinquent in settling their debts. I've counted on you to see that everyone pays in a timely manner."

"I am well aware of the accounts you're referring to, but if you will recall, it was you who told me to—"

"I don't need excuses, I need action. Whatever you had planned for today, I want you to put on hold and spend your time going after these outstanding debts."

"And how do you propose I do that?"

"That's for you to figure out, not me."

She picked up her purse from the desk, traipsed over to shake water from her raincoat, then sat down to put on the wet galoshes.

His brow shot up. "Hold on. I didn't mean you have to contact them personally. Not this early, anyway. Just call and put the squeeze on them. After that, if they don't appear to want to cooperate, then you can go to their places of business to let them know we're serious. Threaten to turn them over to a collection agency. That should expedite things."

She raised a brow. "Is that where you think I was headed? To collect your debts?"

"Then why are you putting on—" He bit his lip. "Uh, maybe I got a little overwrought. Take off that garb and sit down at your desk."

"My desk? But I no longer have a desk, Joel. It belongs to the girl who wants the job." And with that, she scooted toward the door. She turned around and stared. "Goodbye, Joel. I'm finally realizing how foolish I've been to think you'd ever marry me. I'm easy and cheap, and someone you can order around to do your dirty work. What a chump I've been."

Joel followed her out to the hall, wanting to stop her. But he knew Peggy. She wasn't about to come back unless he promised to set a wedding date. For years, he kept promising to get around to it, and only a month ago, he almost committed. But that was before he thought he'd have a real chance to marry the only woman he had ever loved.

Peggy had been with him from the first day he hung his shingle, and he couldn't imagine a more efficient employee. He turned around, stomped back into the office, and slammed the door behind him. She might as well leave. There was no reason to believe she'd stick around, once she discovered that she was only a convenience, since Ramona Jones owned his heart.

Plopping down in his chair, he folded his arms on the table, and laid his head down. He'd told Mona she had three months to make up her mind, but only because he knew it wouldn't take that long for her to discover she wasn't cut out for manual labor. If she lasted three weeks at a sweat shop, he'd be surprised. But what if she should come back and discover he had lost everything in a poker game and there was no money, even for a honeymoon? He knew how she'd react. She'd leave him. For good. And why not? He'd only kidded himself into believing Mona loved him as anything more than a friend. Her only reason for even considering marriage would be because she needed someone to take care of her and the kid, but he had hoped that once they were married, she'd learn to love him. But he didn't stand a chance with her if she ever found out he had gambled away his last dollar.

He scribbled numbers on paper for forty-five minutes. Then, tossing the pencil across the room, he groaned through his teeth when he realized that even if he could collect everything from the clients who owed him, he still wouldn't be able to afford to send Deuce to military school. The kid would be constantly underfoot. It would take a couple of years or longer before he could be in a position to send him away. The longer he thought about being set up in the game—and without question, he was definitely set up—the angrier he became. How could he even think of marrying Mona. It would never work. He had no money and neither did she. The last thing he needed now was a wife with a kid under foot, when he couldn't even afford to provide for himself.

Peggy would've taken him, debts, and all. Why she loved him, he'd never understand. He certainly hadn't been very lovable. She had looks—although admittedly nothing remotely close to as beautiful as Mona—but he was aware of the way men's heads turned when she passed by. Especially Frank Jinright's. The thought of Frank made him bristle. Peggy was quick-witted, fun to be around, and smart. Not only that, there was nothing she wouldn't do for him, and he'd taken full advantage of it. He couldn't deny he'd enjoyed the numerous "business trips," they'd taken together. There were few men in the world who wouldn't want to be in his shoes. But Peggy wasn't the one Joel wanted to go home to every night. *Home?* If he didn't come up with a way to finish paying off his debt, he'd soon have no home.

Thirty days! There was no way he could meet such a large obligation in such a short length of time. He was ruined. Despicable thoughts shot through his head. Dark, frightening thoughts, which he'd never considered before. But never had he been placed in such a no-way-out situation. Why did he allow himself to get entangled with a bunch of dangerous crooks? Even if Big Ed had given him the sixty days he requested and he'd given him the bill of sale for the Cadillac, he'd still have nothing left except an old house in need of repairs and no money with which to do it with. He didn't even own his office.

CHAPTER 15

Deuce could hardly contain his excitement as they headed toward the Jinx Bay Library, Friday evening. Holding out his arm, he said, "Pinch me, Mama."

"What?"

"Pinch me. I want to make sure I'm not dreaming. This is far better than anything I could've imagined. Why don't we go tell Skip, we're back? I think we can find his place from here, don't you? I'm sure he wouldn't mind us staying with him, until we can find a place to live."

Ramona's nose crinkled. "You really took a liking to him, didn't you?"

"He was nice."

"Yes, he was. But we won't have to rely on his good nature. We have a place to stay."

"We do? Where?"

Ramona drove over to the cottage and parked in front of #7. She had hoped Boyd was exaggerating. He wasn't. "Well, looks like this is it. It isn't much, but—"

Deuce squealed. "Oh, Mama. It's perfect."

"You haven't seen the inside."

"I don't care. I love it. I've dreamed about working on the boats for as long as I can remember. This is my chance."

"Hold on, young man. You won't be going out on the boats. Not yet, anyway. Maybe Spring Break. We'll see."

"That's okay. I'll just hang out on the wharf when the boats come in. I'll get to know the fishermen and maybe they'll let me help out. I may even find some who remember my daddy."

"Well, let's go inside and see if we think we can turn this little shanty into a home."

"Of course, we can. Didn't you tell me all it takes to make a house a home is love? And we've got plenty of that. Right?"

She reached up and tousled his curls. Her throat tightened. In a few days he'd turn fifteen and already he was almost as tall as his father. How she wished Ronald could've lived long enough to know they had a son who looked more like him every day.

Ramona thought she was prepared when she opened the door, but nothing or no one could've prepared her for the shabby furnishings. A wood stove? She'd never cooked until she took a Homemakers' class at the reform school, and then it was on a modern gas stove. At Rose Trellis, she cooked on an electric stove. But even if she could figure out how to work the old iron monstrosity, where would she get wood to put into it?

She winced seeing the filthy old couch with straw poking through holes in the cover, a rocker with a broken arm. The only thing Deuce seemed to notice was the large console radio in the corner. "Hey, look. A radio." After several minutes of turning the dials, he said, "So, it doesn't work. Who cares? I'd rather read, anyway, and you and I have a lot of accounting to study up on, and what better place than the kitchen table?"

If not for his positive attitude, Ramona knew exactly what she would've done. She would've been back in the truck and headed south to the orange groves, as fast as she could go. What gave her the crazy notion she could become a bookkeeper overnight, anyway?

She could only hope that after a few weeks, he'd realize the vision of working on a fishing vessel was nothing more than a pipe dream. An old cast iron radiator sat under the window. She walked over and turned the valve. Nothing happened. She turned to zero, waited, then turned it again and waited. "I don't think it works."

"No big deal, Mama. We're in Florida. How cold can it get?"

"I'm chilly now, or I wouldn't have tried to turn it on. It may not reach the freezing point, but if you'll remember, it was cold the night we spent at Skip's."

He chuckled. "So, what if it does. We're on an adventure, right? We'll buy a couple of blankets."

His happy-go-lucky nature was his father made over. Wasn't it exactly the way Ronald would've reacted? Ramona stopped and stared out the window, when she realized how many times in the past twenty-four hours that Ronald had entered her thoughts. What about Joel? She recalled the kiss, the sweet words, the look in his eyes when he looked at her, the rekindling of romantic feelings that she hadn't had in a very long time? It was real. Wasn't it? Love? Or lust? She shuddered at the thought that she could be 'that kind of woman.' She sucked in a heavy breath. "Love," she whispered as she exhaled.

Deuce chuckled. "What was that?"

"Just thinking about what I need to do, son."

"Sounded like you said, 'love.'"

"Did I?"

"Yes'm. I love you, too, Mama."

She sat down in one of the cane-bottom chairs at the kitchen table and buried her face in her hands and lamented not accepting Joel's proposal. She was confident she no longer needed three months to come to a decision.

Deuce called out, "Hey, don't you want to see the bedroom? It's perfect."

Ramona pushed back from the table and ambled into the next room.

"Look, Mama, a chifforobe. The mirror is cracked, but at least it has a mirror." He sat down on the bed and bounced a couple of times. "Good springs, but a little squeaky."

Ramona's eyes searched the room. "Oh, honey, there's no way we can do this."

"But we can, Mama. It's an adventure. Remember?"

How she wished she had never used that word. Deuce didn't seem to understand the difference in an adventure and a nightmare.

His face reddened, and his voice cracked when he blurted, "What's wrong with it, Mama? Why can't you be happy?"

"Honey, don't you know how much I wanted this to work, for your sake? But when the fellow told me it had two rooms, I thought he meant two bedrooms. I didn't know it was literally *two rooms*." She groaned, then wrapped her arm around her son's waist. "I know how much you wanted this to work, sweetheart, but this will never do."

"Of course, it will. It's a big room. We'll hang a sheet between the bed and the wall, and I'll sleep on the other side."

"On what? The floor?"

"I wouldn't mind. I've camped out on the ground with Daddy Theo, and it was fun. But we can go to the Army surplus store and buy a cot if it will make you feel better. Let's go now before they close."

She didn't want to burst his bubble when he seemed to be so excited, but it didn't make sense to buy furniture for a dump they'd be leaving in less than three months. This was a much bigger challenge than she anticipated. *Me? A bookkeeper?* Who did she think she was fooling? Maybe she fooled Boyd, but if holding down such an important a position was as easy as she tried to make it sound, there'd be a line of applicants standing outside the office door. The best thing for her to do would be to get in the truck and drive on to South Florida. "Deuce, I'm sorry. I wanted this to work for your sake. But this is an impossible situation. I'm no bookkeeper and this is no place for us to live."

"So, you're a quitter? Just like that, you're giving up? Is that the kind of advice you give me when I'm faced with a problem?"

"Deuce, maybe I'd consider staying, if the bedroom was the only problem. But I was told the cottages have bathrooms. Do you see one, because I don't."

"I've already been out there."

Her brow shot up. "Out there? Do you honestly think I'm going to get up in the middle of the night to walk to an outdoor toilet, that's probably shared with eleven other family's on the strip?"

"See? You keep trying to find something wrong with it. There is a bathroom and it's on the back porch. I agree, it's not as nice as the one at Rose Trellis, but it has all the essentials." He opened a door that led to a back porch that had been converted into a crude bathroom.

Ramona peeked out and grimaced. "I thought that was a closet door. So, there's no closet?"

Deuce threw up his hands. "I give up. It has a nice, big chifforobe for your clothes, but you keep wanting to find reasons to leave."

Ramona choked back the tears as she weighed her choices. She could make life easier with one phone call to Joel. But in doing so, she'd break her son's heart. Or she could make the best of the situation and let him be the one to conclude that Jinx Bay was not the place for them. She glanced at her watch. "If we're gonna find the Army Surplus store before it closes, we'd better hurry or you won't have a place to sleep tonight."

With tears in his eyes, he grabbed her around the neck. "Are you serious, Mama? We're staying?"

"Of course, we're staying. I have a job, remember? But I'll need your help. We have three books to read before Monday morning."

She drove up to the service station to inquire about an Army Surplus store and was told there wasn't one in town. After finding out her reason for needing one, the owner of the station said, "Hold on. I'll be right back." He came back minutes later holding a folded, canvas-lined cot. "I've kept this for years, thinking one day I'd have a use for it, but it's been in the shed out back, collecting dust. I hope you can use it."

Deuce jumped out of the car, ran around, and put it in the back of the truck. "It's perfect. Thank you, sir."

Ramona tried to pay him for it, but he refused. "Don't want no pay. Welcome to Jinx Bay. Just stop by here whenever you need a fill-up."

Ramona reached out and shook his hand. "Thank you. Everyone we've met has been more than kind."

His leathery face brightened "We're all just common folks, but you'll find it to be a nice place to live. In fact, Jinx Bay should've been named Niceville, but the town down the road beat us to it." An elderly woman with her hair all knotted up in a bun came walking across the road, carrying an armload of quilts. "Got something you folks might could use. Me and my sisters spend hours making quilts and to tell the truth, I'm running out of space to store them. Could you take a few off my hands?"

Ramona's quizzical expression must've given her away.

The woman chuckled. "You're wondering how I knew? Abner called me on the phone and told me you were at the station. We live across the road."

"I still don't understand. How did you know we'd need cover?"

Abner put his arm around his wife. "That bunch of women know everything that's gonna happen in Jinx Bay, two days before it's even thought up."

Ramona said, "These are beautiful. How much do you sell them for?"

"Aw, pshaw, child. They ain't for sale. The good Lord tells us to do the quilting and then He tells us who to give 'em to."

"Are you sure I can't pay you?"

"Well, there is one thing you could do. How about you and the boy sitting with me and Abner in church, Sunday morning and joining us for dinner, afterward?"

"We'd be delighted. Which church?"

"The little white clapboard one on the other side of the fish camp."

When Abner proceeded to give better directions, Ramona

recalled seeing it on the way in. "Thank you. I know the one."

****

Sunday, February 10th

Deuce was up and dressed for church Sunday morning before Ramona put her feet on the floor. He even had the coffee made and toast in the toaster. "Those sure were nice folks to invite us to church and to have Sunday dinner with them. I think we're gonna like Jinx Bay just fine, don't you, Mama?"

Ramona knew her son well enough to know that it wasn't church or dinner that had Deuce so excited, but the thought that it could possibly be a sign they were about to make Jinx Bay home.

Abner and Sara Guthrie were waiting at the front door of the church when they arrived, and from their surprised expressions, Ramona guessed they weren't very confident that she and Deuce would come. She might've changed her mind, had it not been for Deuce, but now she was glad she hadn't disappointed the sweet, elderly couple. There were no more than thirty-five people at the most, but she was sure all thirty-five introduced themselves. Never had she felt so welcome in a church. The preacher wasn't the most eloquent that she'd ever heard, but the simple message pricked her heart. His text was from Psalms, and before church was over, she had the verse memorized. "I shall teach thee and instruct thee in the way thou shalt go. I will guide thee with mine eye." The pastor ended his sermon with the words, "When you don't know where to turn, turn to Jesus."

Ramona hadn't known how to put her desire into words, but

what could be better than divine direction? She wondered if God could really read her thoughts. She hoped so. But even if God could *know* her thoughts, how could she be sure she wouldn't miss *His* thoughts for her? When she was forced to leave Rose Trellis, she felt unwanted and unprepared to take care of her son. But things had changed, and she now had options. She no longer felt unwanted, since learning Joel wanted to marry her, nor did she feel unprepared to provide for Deuce. He wanted to stay in Jinx Bay, and with the bookkeeping position, she now felt confident that she could care for them both, at least for the time being. But could she afford to send him to college? Joel could. But if she married Joel, wouldn't Deuce resent him for taking them away from Jinx Bay? On the other hand, wouldn't it be irresponsible of her to allow a child to direct her path? That's exactly what she'd be doing if she allowed Deuce to decide their future? He was a kid. She had hoped to hear God's voice, but all she was hearing was confusion.

Sara had a delicious dinner of fried chicken, creamed potatoes, gravy, butterbeans, homemade biscuits, and sweet-iced tea. Abner said grace and thanked the Lord for their guests.

After dinner, Sara threw a clean cloth over the food on the table, and insisted they go sit on the porch, saying that she'd wash dishes later.

Abner pulled out a pack of papers and tobacco and proceeded to roll a cigarette. "So, you say you're gonna be working in the cannery?"

Deuce quickly added, "Not the cannery. Mama is the new

bookkeeper. She'll have an office job."

"Well, that's mighty impressive. I can see you're proud of your Mama."

"Yes'm. She's real smart."

Ramona took in every word, wondering if somehow God was attempting to tell her the way that she should go, but the conversation quickly changed, and she was no closer to knowing if she was making the right decision. What would Ronald advise her to do? The answer was obvious. He'd want her to remarry—to have a man who would love and protect her. Someone who would teach Deuce the things every young man should know.

CHAPTER 16

Ramona poured over the accounting books all weekend, and Deuce turned out to be more help than she could've imagined. If he could be satisfied living in such cramped quarters, why couldn't she? He studied with her, and even made up accounting tests and graded her. By Sunday night, she had confidence that she'd be as competent as any bookkeeper the Seafarer's Fish Camp had ever had in their employ.

Monday morning at breakfast she said, "I can hardly believe I'll soon have a fifteen-year-old son. I'm so proud of the man you're becoming, Deuce."

"Thanks, Mama. Whenever I'd tell someone I was fourteen, they'd say I looked at least fifteen. Maybe when I turn fifteen, they'll think I'm sixteen."

"There's plenty of time to grow up, son. Don't rush it."

After breakfast, Ramona drove over to enroll Deuce in school.

He had the door partially opened before the truck came to a stop.

"My goodness, Deuce, don't be in such a hurry. Where's your lunch money?"

"In my pocket, where I put it when you gave it to me this morning. I wish you'd stop worrying about me. I'm not a kid."

"You're right. I'm sorry." Ramona waited for him to walk inside, before she went into the office to register him. Impressed with the congenial office staff, she felt good about enrolling her son at such a fine school. Things were turning out much better than she could've imagined. She had a decent job, a place to live within walking distance of both her work, and her son's school. But most importantly, Deuce was happy. As long as Deuce was happy, she could live anywhere. Even on a dirt road in a two-room shanty.

When she arrived at the fish camp, Boyd ran out, opened her car door, and escorted her into the building. He led her to her desk, handed her a ledger, then pointed to the filing cabinets. "Our last girl apparently had trouble with the alphabet, since the files are a mess. Filing will be your biggest challenge for a while."

If filing was the most difficult task she'd have, the job would be a breeze. "I'm sure it won't be a problem."

At the sound of the dinner bell, Ramona walked to the edge of the pier, sat down with her sack lunch, and dangled her feet in the water. She could see the fishing vessels in the far distance. The water looked like a sea of glass. All the stories Ronald had shared about his experiences became real to her. Until now, she hadn't fully understood his fascination. He was right. Even with the smells, the flies, the heat, there seemed to be something magical about the place that trumped any obstacles and made you feel all was well with the world. That's exactly how she felt.

Ramona finished her lunch, then went back to pulling files. She was almost glad the files were a mess, since once she finished straightening them out, it would help prove her efficiency. Besides, filing allowed her time to think about things that were important to her.

She considered writing Joel to let him know there'd be no wedding. Wasn't it wrong to allow him to continue to live with hope? On second thought, although things seemed perfect at the moment, shouldn't she wait to see how Deuce would feel about his new school? The fish camp had been a dream of his, but dreams don't always turn out the way they begin. And what if Boyd decided her work was not up to par? No, it was too soon to turn down a life with a good man who loved her and who could provide a great life for her and her son. She said three months, and three months it should be.

****

The first day of school, the teacher sat Deuce directly across the aisle from the prettiest girl he'd ever seen. She had the blackest hair and the biggest brown eyes and when she smiled, deep dimples sank into her rosy cheeks. With full lips shaped like a Valentine, he felt God must've been so pleased at creating such a gorgeous creature. Not only was she beautiful, but she was about the sweetest girl he'd ever met. When the other students went to the lunchroom, Deuce was thrilled to see she had brought her lunch, too.

She said, "I like to sit under the pines back of the school to eat. Would you like to sit with me?"

His throat was too dry to swallow. He murmured, "I guess." What a stupid answer. Why did he say such a dumb thing? He didn't have to guess. He knew even before she asked him that he wanted to be wherever she was, whether he was eating or just admiring her beauty.

As she pulled out a sandwich, she said, "I've never known anyone named Deuce. I like it."

"I've never known anyone named Margo."

"My father is Mexican, and it's a family name, meaning Pearl. I was named after my grandma. It's spelled with a 't' on the end, but after I started to school, I dropped the 't', since people would call me Mar Got, although the 't' is silent."

"Well, I think Margo suits you."

"What do you mean?"

"It's a beautiful name and you are very—" He stopped and felt his face grow hot. "What I mean is—" He coughed in his hand, attempting to think of a way to get out of what was running through his head when he said such a stupid thing.

"I'm glad you think I'm beautiful, Deuce."

Relieved that she wasn't offended that he was practically gushing over her, his tense muscles relaxed. He lowered his eyes to keep from looking at her when he said, "Anyone who wouldn't think you're beautiful would be crazy." Then quickly changing the subject, he said, "Whatcha got for lunch?"

"Cheese biscuit. And you?"

"Peanut butter and jelly. I made it myself since Mama was running late for work." He pointed to the jelly oozing out the sides. "It's not as messy when she makes it."

"Maybe that's because you put more jelly in it than she does."

They both laughed, although after he thought about it, he wondered why they thought it was so funny.

Lunch lasted thirty minutes, but he learned a lot about her in such a short length of time. They discovered they both lived in the village, and she had lived in #5 since she was four-years-old, when her family moved to Florida from Mexico City. Her daddy was a fisherman, she had never gone to another school, her mother died two years ago, when she was twelve, and she stayed by herself when her daddy was out on the boat.

Deuce said, "But he comes home every night. Right?"

She pressed her lips together.

"What's wrong?"

"I'm not supposed to tell anyone."

"What?"

"That I'm alone when he's on the water. Papa is afraid the authorities will take me away if they find out, even though I'm capable of taking care of myself. I've been doing it for two years. You won't tell, will you, Deuce?" Tears muddled her eyes. "I shouldn't have told you. I've never told anyone, although I know

145

the fishermen and their families know, but they'd never tell. But I don't know your parents. If you should tell them, how do I know they wouldn't report me to the authorities?"

Seeing the tears, he reached for her hand. "Hey, stop worrying. First of all, it's just me and Mama. My daddy is dead."

She wiped her damp cheeks on her sleeve. "I'm sorry."

He shrugged. "Thanks, but he died before I was born."

"That's sad. So, you never knew him."

"Not really, but I feel as though I did. Mama has told me so much about him, I almost feel as if I knew him."

"I suppose he was a fisherman?"

"Only in the summers. He lived in Alabama, but his uncle owned the Fish Camp at the time, and they'd come stay with him and go out on the boats when they were in high school. Mama told me all the stories that he told her, and for years, I've known I wanted to do the same thing."

"If you're father is not a fisherman, then how did you get one of the cabins on Cannery Road? I thought they were reserved for the Seafarer Fish Camp employees."

"My mama works in the office at the cannery. She's a bookkeeper."

Margo slapped her hand over her lips. "Oh, no. She works in the office with Mr. Boyd?"

"I think that's what she called him."

"Deuce, please promise you won't tell her what I told you. I'd just die if they came and took me away from Papa."

"They who?"

"The authorities."

"I know you said the authorities, but who are they? The Jinx Bay Police? The State Welfare Department?"

With her forefinger planted on her cheek, she said, "Gee, I've never really thought about it. That's just what Papa calls them, and the word has always terrified me."

"Well, you don't have to worry about me. I don't want anyone to ever take you away. And if they did, I'd go after you." He was surprised how brave he'd gotten since finding out she trusted him with her deepest secret that she'd never told anyone else.

The bell rang, and Deuce realized he was still holding her hand. When school let out, he carried her books and walked her home. And every day after that, he stopped at her cabin and sat on the steps, while she ran inside, put up her books and came back out with two glasses of lemonade. They never seemed to run out of things to talk about, and he had to make himself leave in time to finish his homework before his mama came home.

****

Boyd stepped into the office and told Ramona she was the best worker he'd ever had. She always put in more hours than required, but she'd caught up with the backlog and she should go home.

She could hardly believe it was five o'clock, already. "Thanks, I still have lots to do, but I'll take your advice and leave since it's my son's birthday."

She drove by the dry goods store and bought a red corduroy

shirt and had it wrapped. She could hardly wait to see it on him. Red always looked so good on Ronald and Deuce was becoming his spitting image.

Then, on to the grocery store where she picked up a chocolate cake and a little package of birthday candles and a pack of playing cards.

The moment she turned down the road on Cannery Road the truck lights flashed on two people sitting on an old stump. The man jumped off, then with his hands reaching for a girl's waist, he helped her down. Ramona's throat tightened as she got a closer look. *Man?* It was no man. *Deuce!* It couldn't be. She squinted, then felt her heart sink.

Holding to the girl's hand, the two figures, now quite distinguishable, ran to the center of the road. Deuce's smile stretched across his face as he waved her down. Ramona pulled over and rolled down the window. "What's going on?"

"Hi, Mama."

She watched as he put his arm around the girl. "This is Margo. Uh . . . Margo, meet my mama."

"How do you do, Mrs. Jones?"

Glaring at the kids standing there arm-in-arm, took her breath away. "Deuce, you need to get to the house. Now."

"OK, Mama. I'll be there in a few minutes."

"You heard me. I said now." She drove away and parked in front of the cottage and waited. All sorts of frightening thoughts ran through her head. Staring into the rear view mirror of the truck, she watched the girl go into the house, two doors down. Deuce ran up to the truck and shouted, "I hope you know you embarrassed me. I told Margo what a great sport you are. I guess she thinks I lied to her. There was nothing sporty about the way you acted. I can only imagine that you must've had a bad day at work, but even that doesn't give you an excuse to be so rude."

"Get in the house. We'll finish this conversation inside."

He swung his right foot, kicking up dust. "As far as I'm concerned, it's finished, already." He turned and took off running into the woods back of the house.

Ramona parked, picked up the cake, went inside and put it on the table. Then falling across the worn sofa, she burst into sobs. "Oh, Ronald, why did you have to die? I can't do this." Her first thought was to drive over to the drugstore and use the pay phone to call Joel. What she needed was a man to help her raise a teenage boy.

Just as she was about to drive away, she saw Deuce coming from the woods. She stepped out and waited as he lumbered toward her. With his head down, he muttered, "Sorry, Mama."

She held open her arms. "Perhaps we both were wrong." She opened the door to the truck, took out the gift and handed it to him. "Happy Birthday, son. I'm sorry it got off to a rocky start."

"Forget it." He wrapped his arm around her and shook the package. "Wonder what it is."

They agreed he should wait until after supper to open it. Ramona cooked hamburgers, his favorite meal, then lit the candles and sang Happy Birthday.

Deuce opened his present and after trying it on, seemed quite pleased when he saw himself in the mirror. "I love it, Mama."

She clutched her hands over her heart. "I love it, too. You look so handsome." She pulled out the pack of cards. "Are you ready for me to beat you in a game of Hearts?"

"We can play Hearts later."

"Why later?"

"Mama, I appreciate all you've done to make my birthday special, but I think we need to talk about what happened earlier."

Shaking her head, she said, "It's over, Deuce. Let's just move on."

"But it's not over. To ignore it will only cause it to fester. I'd like for you to explain your actions, and for you to give me an opportunity to explain mine."

"I don't want to talk about it."

"I'm sorry, but I do, Mama. I met Margo at lunch. She was sitting in front of me during History, and we chatted for a few minutes before class. I was glad to see that she had brought her lunch. I was hoping it would give me a chance to be with her." He waited for a response. When there was none forthcoming, he continued. "All she had was a cheese biscuit, but she tried to share it with me. She's sweet like that. Then we discovered we were neighbors. She was excited when she found out we lived on the strip." He prattled on, hardly taking a breath. "I found out that's what everyone calls Cannery Road—the strip. Margo told me that when I walked into class, she assumed I was rich. It was funny to me when she said she was glad to find out that I'm not. Isn't that a hoot?"

"I'm afraid I fail to see the humor in someone gloating because of our financial situation. What's funny about that?"

"But don't you see? She likes me. She said when she thought I was rich, she felt I could never be interested in a girl from the strip. I told her that was crazy. Even if I were rich, where a girl lives wouldn't matter to me."

A tinge of shame swept over Ramona, as she reflected on the way she met Deuce's father. Ronald didn't mind where she came from either. But times were different then. Weren't they? Girls were much more promiscuous nowadays and Deuce had been sheltered. He didn't have a father to warn him of the kinds of girls to watch out for. Her thoughts had taken her away from the conversation, but Deuce didn't seem to notice.

"Mama, it all happened so fast. Thirty minutes with her, and it was as if we had known one another forever. She understands me. Her daddy is a fisherman, and she's lived in the same cottage most of her life."

"Deuce, how old is this girl?"

"She's fifteen—like me."

"You're barely fifteen. When is her birthday?"

"Geez, Mama. I thought you'd be happy that I've made a friend already. What's with the third degree?"

"I'm sorry. I suppose it does sound as if I'm condemning her without really knowing her. I just want you to be careful, son."

"Of what? She's not an ax murderer. She's a sweet, beautiful girl with a great personality. She makes me feel good."

"What do you mean, she makes you feel good?"

"You know. Like it's good to be around her."

"Deuce, I'd like to meet her parents before you become too chummy with this girl."

"Chummy?" That's hilarious. Is that what they called it when you were young? We're fifteen, Mama."

"Meaning what?"

"Meaning that I can see me falling in love with her. And why not? She's everything a guy could want."

Ramona's throat felt dry. Was he insinuating that he and that girl— Licking her dry lips, she said, "Deuce, girls tend to mature much faster than boys, and I want you to be very careful. When you fall in love, make sure she's been brought up with high morals." She could tell she hit a nerve, the way his chin quivered. It frightened her.

He blurted, "Like your high morals when my daddy fell in love with you, Mama? He didn't find you on Cannery Road. No sir, buddy. You were more refined than that. He found you at a reformatory school. I'm sure all the genteel young ladies there were of the highest caliber." Before waiting for her response, he rushed out of the house and slammed the door.

When she heard the truck crank up, she ran outside to see the dust flying from behind the wheels. She was glad Theodore taught him to drive, but in his frame of mind, how could she be sure he wouldn't do something stupid? Deuce had always been so level-headed. Why was he doing this to her now? It was Margo's fault. Ramona could only imagine the scandalous thoughts the girl had put into his head.

After pacing the floor for almost thirty minutes, she kept watching out the window for the truck to pull up at Cabin #5. Grabbing a brush and running it through her hair, she decided it might be a good time to meet her new neighbors. When she knocked, Margo opened the door, dressed in a faded chenille robe.

"Mrs. Jones? What do you want?" Lowering her head, she mumbled, "I suppose that sounded rude. I'm sorry. I just meant is something wrong? Where's Deuce?"

"That's what I'd like to know. He was angry and took off on the truck."

"Well, he isn't here."

"I'm aware of that, since the truck is not here. Would you please tell your mother I'd like to speak with her."

"My mother?"

"Yes. I think it's time we met, don't you?"

"Why?"

"Never you mind why. Just tell her I'm here, please."

"But she's not here."

"Will she be gone long?"

"She didn't say when she'd be back."

"From the way you're fidgeting, I don't think you want us to meet."

"No ma'am. It's not that. It's just—"

Ramona heard the truck pulling up and saw car lights shine through the window. Seconds later, Deuce pounded on the front door. Ramona looked at Margo. "I'll get it. We both know who it is, and you aren't dressed."

His wide-eyed expression was evidence of his surprise. "Mama! What are you doing here?"

"I might ask the same of you, young man. Get back in the truck and I'll see you at the house."

"I came to talk to Margo." Looking past his mother, his gaze locked with the beautiful brown eyed girl.

"You can talk to her at school tomorrow. Her mother isn't here, and I need you to go home."

Margo pulled her robe together. "Deuce, I think you should do as your mother says. I'll see you tomorrow."

Ramona saw him get into the truck and drive in the opposite direction from their house.

Ramona paced the floor until she heard the truck pulling into the yard. She met him at the door with, "Deuce, I don't know why you suddenly feel you can do as you please, but we need to get a few things straight. I've been worried sick. Where did you go?"

Ignoring her question, he pushed past her and asked one of his own. "What were you doing over at Margo's?"

"I thought she might know where you went."

"Yeah? And what did you plan to do if you found out?"

"I wasn't thinking, Deuce."

"Seems that's becoming your pat excuse. You never seem to be thinking, Mama."

"Just tell me why you left."

"Because you're smothering me. I had to get away to get some air."

"I'm sorry you feel smothered, but that's what mothers do. And as long as I feel you could be heading for trouble, then expect to be smothered."

"Heading for trouble? What kind of trouble do you anticipate me getting in, Mama? It's Margo, isn't it? You don't like her, and you don't even know her."

"Calm down, Deuce. This is not like you to become so combative. I thought it would be a good idea to meet her mother, so that we could . . . well, we could see that—"

"You're making it up as you go along, aren't you?"

"No, and I don't like your attitude. I was hoping her mother and I could agree on setting boundaries. Son, it's not that I mind you having a little girlfriend, but the fact that she lives so close, and I work late sometimes. . . well, it could lead to temptations that neither of you are mature enough to handle.. That's why I want you to promise that you won't go inside her cottage or invite her into ours, unless there is an adult in the house. That sounds reasonable, doesn't it?"

"What about if you trust me, Mama? That sounds reasonable,

too, doesn't it?"

"Honey, I do trust you."

"Fine. So, we can end this conversation. How about a game of Hearts? Where are the cards?"

CHAPTER 17

Monday, February 11th

Joel Gunter was looking through the ledger on his secretary's desk, searching for phone numbers of delinquent accounts, when the door opened, and Peggy strode in.

He looked up briefly, then continued to shuffle through papers. "I suppose you came back for last week's pay. Well, you'll have to stand in line. I don't have it."

She stood looking down at him. "I figured as much."

Looking up, he studied her expression. "What do you mean?"

"You're broke."

"Who said?"

"I know you, Joel. I know you better than you know yourself. I'll admit I was bumfuzzled whenever I left here. Those outstanding balances that last week you instructed me not to bother with, suddenly became top priority, and you were demanding that they be paid immediately."

He couldn't look at her. "I can't explain. I have to figure this out, myself. Just go and leave me alone."

"That's an impossible request. I love you, Joel. I want to help you."

"I'm sorry, Peg. I'm sunk and there's nothing you can do to help me."

"So, you lost it all in a poker game. It was stupid, but it isn't the end of the world, Joel."

He jumped up with his mouth gaped open. "Who told you?"

"No one had to tell me. I finally figured it out. It hadn't made sense to me that you suddenly acquired a pile of money—enough to pay cash for a new Cadillac. Then two weeks later, you start yelling at me, insisting I collect from delinquent accounts, when only days earlier, you'd agreed to be lenient with them. None of it made sense, until lying in bed last night, I recalled you telling me that when you were a teen, you got into trouble with your father when he discovered you had lost the new motorcycle he bought you in a poker game. I saw the gleam in your eye when you said, 'I had the bug. I didn't care whether I won or lost, I just enjoyed the thrill.' The bug never left you, did it?"

His chin trembled. "Whatever you think of me won't be nearly as awful as what I think of myself. I'm ruined, Peggy. I have no money left in the bank, and a sixteen-hundred-dollar debt. I'll have to come up with the money, somehow. I was so stupid."

"Stand up."

"What?"

"I said stand up."

He stood, and she threw her arms around him. "I think you need a hug."

"You're too good for me, Peg, but I need a lot more than a hug."

"Grab your hat and come with me. I'll drive."

"I'm not very hungry, but I'll go with you. I've poured over these books until my eyes are crossing."

When she passed their favorite restaurant, he said, "Are we going to the Catfish House?"

"Better than that." She pulled up in front of the Court House and stopped. Then taking his hand, she said, "Joel, I know you love me, but for some reason you've been afraid to commit to marriage. I think it's because your parents didn't have a good relationship. But baby, we aren't your parents. I haven't spent much of my money for the past four years, since we do everything together, and you've footed the bills. But now, it's my turn. Let's get married, and what's mine will be yours. We'll pay off your debt, then take a honeymoon to South Florida. I've always wanted to see the Everglades." She reached for the door handle.

He bit his bottom lip. "I don't know, hon. I haven't had time to think—"

"Joel Gunter, you've had four years to think. It's time to stop thinking and start acting." She opened her door and stepped out.

He couldn't deny it would solve his immediate problem,

although it would end all hopes of ever being with the one he loved. He had to face reality. That dream came to an end the moment he left the poker game. No way would Ramona marry him, now that he couldn't provide for her and her son, which was the only reason she ever considered it in the first place.

A few minutes later, Peggy Druthers had become Mrs. Joel Gunter. She drove to the bank and insisted Joel sign his name beside hers, making it a joint account. She then drew out the amount of money her husband owed, plus enough cash for them to take a honeymoon.

Driving back to the office, she said, "I'll call and cancel all our appointments for the next two weeks while you call Jimbo to let him know we'll take the money to him before leaving town. After that, we'll put a sign on the door, lock the office and go home to pack."

"What's so funny?"

"When I said we'll go home, we both understood it to mean you'd go to your house, and I'd go to my apartment. But after today, when we go home, we'll be going together. I don't suppose it's funny. I'm just so happy, I can't keep a straight face. My rent is paid through the end of the month, but I'll notify Mrs. Manasco that I'll have my things out as soon as we return from the honeymoon."

Joel swallowed hard. Everything had happened so fast, the fact that she'd be moving into his house had not even crossed his mind. He enjoyed a little weekend rendezvous ever so often. But being tied down with her for twenty-four hours a day? What was he thinking?

"We're leaving this evening. I'll pick you up. I'll leave my old clunker at the depot, and we'll take a train."

Forty-five minutes later, Joel heard her old '49 Ford pulling into the yard. He met her at the door. "Come on in, Peg. We need to talk."

She reached up and kissed him. "We can talk on the way. I don't want to miss the train." Then looking around, she said, "Where's your bag?"

"That's what I wanted to talk to you about. I can't possibly leave now. We'll go on a honeymoon later. I promise."

"I've heard your promises before, sweetheart. Nothing doing."

He rubbed his hand across his chin. Her mind was made up, and didn't he owe her? She had just possibly saved his life. "You win. It won't take long to pack. Have a seat and make yourself comfortable. I'll only be a minute." His eyes squinted. "What's so funny?"

"I'm no longer a guest here, my sweet husband. I'm home. No need to offer me a seat." She pulled a small notepad from her purse. "I have our itinerary all mapped out. We'll spend the first night at the beach. Oh, Joel, I am so excited. We're gonna have so much fun. Our first stop will be at our beach cottage."

"Our what?" He looked up as he crammed a few clothes into a knapsack.

"I inherited it when my parents died, but I turned it over to a realtor, who has been renting it out for me."

"Are you joking? Where?"

"Gulf Shores.

"You never mentioned it. Do you have any idea how much it's worth?"

"No, but it doesn't matter, since I have no plans to sell it. I thought it would be fun to spend our first night there."

The right corner of his lip slightly lifted. "Our *first* night?"

"You know what I mean. Our first night as husband and wife. It's just across the road from the Gulf, and it's where my parents spent their honeymoon in 1931. It's nothing fancy, but I loved going there as a child."

"What else do you have that you haven't told me about?"

"I wasn't trying to keep it from you." Then with a shrug, she added, "That's not exactly true."

"I don't get it."

"I didn't want to go there with a man I wasn't married to, and I was afraid if I mentioned the cottage, you'd insist that we go there. You know how difficult it is for me to say 'no' to you."

"That doesn't make sense."

"It does to me. I felt it would be disrespectful to my parents for me to go to the romantic place that meant so much to them, while disregarding the morals they tried to instill in me."

"That's just plain silly. Times have changed since your parents' day, Peggy."

"Maybe. Joel, I have something to confess."

"More good news, I hope."

"You might not think so. But I'm glad you lost everything in the poker game."

"What?"

"It's true. I have felt like a kept woman, far too long, and the guilt has been eating away at me. Every time you planned another trip for us to go out of town, I wanted to say no. But I was weak, and I was afraid if I refused, you might take someone else. If you hadn't lost your money, I'm afraid you would never have married me, and we would've continued to live in sin."

"Hey, what have I told you about preaching to me? Good grief, Peggy, if I want to hear a sermon, it won't be coming from someone who enjoys the same vices as I do." He winked at her and chuckled.

Peggy's lip quivered. "I guess I deserved that."

"Aww, I didn't mean to hurt your feelings. I'm just saying don't try to pretend to be something that you're not. Not with someone who knows you as well as I do. It's like this . . . If a person tells me that eating strawberries is sinful, yet continues to eat them for breakfast, dinner, and supper every day, I'm gonna know they love strawberries more than they hate sin, and it sure won't have an effect on my strawberry cravings. Talk is cheap."

Hearing the train whistle, he jumped up from the bench and grabbed both pieces of luggage. "I hear it coming around the bend."

The train was not on schedule, but Joel was thankful it arrived when it did. He didn't want Peggy getting all religious on him, now that they were married.

At six-thirty, Joel and Peggy disembarked at the train depot in Mobile, Alabama, where they rented an automobile and drove to Gulf Shores. After spending the first three nights at the beach cottage, swimming, fishing, and touring the ruins of a colonial fort, they took a train to Miami, where Peggy's life-long dream of riding through the Everglades on a tour boat became a reality. She said, "This is just the way I imagined it. It seems as if Tarzan should come swinging from one of these vines."

Joel could've thought of things more fun than watching eight-foot gators swimming up to the small craft, but he couldn't deny he enjoyed seeing Peggy so happy. It had been a long time since he'd seen her having so much fun. In the beginning, he found his thoughts centering on Ramona Jones and what might've been. But those thoughts were becoming less and less frequent, which was a good thing, since it was never to be.

The last night of their honeymoon was spent back in Gulf Shores at the beach cottage. That night in bed, Peggy said, "Joel, are you glad you married me?"

He rolled over and wrapped his arms around her. "That's a silly question."

"Do you love me?"

"Yes, Peggy. I love you. How many times do I have to say it?"

"I'm glad. I'm real glad, because I have something to tell you."

"What? You love me, too. Right?"

"I do, but that's not what I was gonna say. Joel, we're gonna have a baby."

"A what?"

"You heard me. I'm pregnant."

"That's impossible."

"I suspected it three weeks ago, but I went to see a doctor in Montgomery to confirm it. The day before we left, I got a call that the rabbit died."

He sat straight up in bed.

She said, "Say something."

"I can't think straight. A baby?"

"You aren't upset, are you? We're married, and I'm not so far along that it should raise questions. I was hoping you could be happy."

"Oh, honey, why wouldn't I be happy. That's wonderful news. But why wait until now to tell me?"

"Don't you see? I didn't want you to marry me because you felt trapped. That's why I'm glad things worked out as they did. I know it will sound silly, but for years, I've felt there was someone else who owned your heart, and that I was just a convenience for you."

"Well, you won't have to worry about that any longer." He held up third finger, left hand. "I'm an old married man who will

165

soon be someone's daddy. Think of that—me with a son. I'd like for him to have my name. Joel Jamison Gunter, Jr."

"It's a lovely name, but a mouthful." She snuggled up under his arm. "But what if it's a girl?"

"Sheesh! I know nothing about little girls."

"Would you not want her?"

"That's a silly question. What do you think about the name, Ramona?"

"Isn't that your friend's widow? The one you said you grew up with?"

"Yeah, when we were kids, the three of us were inseparable, and if it hadn't been for the war—" He got a faraway look in his eyes.

"Finish."

"Ronald married her on a whim, just before being shipped out."

"What do you mean—on a whim?"

"You know. Soldiers did it all the time. That's why there were so many divorces after the war ended. Marriages weren't based on love, but on having a last hurrah before leaving. Ronald, Ramona, and I were like The Three Musketeers. If I'd been drafted first, there's the chance she would've been my wife. We were all that close. She would've done anything for Ronald or me. I truly think she loved us both."

When he stopped short, Peggy wanted to pry, yet her instincts told her it was better off leaving some things unsaid.

"I think Ramona is a pretty name for a girl, don't you? We'll call her Mona. Now that I think about it, I'd love to have my own little girl."

Peggy repeated the name a couple of times. "It's certainly worth considering, but we have plenty of time to think about it."

CHAPTER 18

Deuce hurried home from school, finished his homework, then went to his Mom's office to let her know that he'd be late for supper. "Margo's dad's boat is expected to dock around sunset, and Margo wants me to go with her to meet him."

After all the normal questions concerning school, his homework and test scores, she told him to come straight home after making Mr. Lopez's acquaintance. Wearing a broad grin, he scampered out of the office, where Margo was waiting on the outside.

"What did she say?"

"No problem. At least not as far as Mama is concerned."

"What d'ya mean?"

"Just saying Mama didn't care if I go to meet your father, but to tell the truth, I'm a little nervous."

"Don't be ridiculous. You'll love my papa. Everyone loves

him. He's funny and very sweet."

"Have you ever introduced a boy to him before?"

"No, but I've told him about you. I think he approves."

Deuce swallowed hard. "You think?"

She grabbed him by the hand and swung his arm. "I know he will. You two will get along great." They strolled out to the pier to wait.

Deuce had never known anyone he could talk to the way he could talk to Margo. He shared things that he'd never told anyone. She knew more about him than his mama. But she had revealed very little about herself. He thought it a bit peculiar, but decided girls weren't as open with their feelings as guys, who didn't care whether people liked them or not.

They were sitting on the edge of the pier, when she jumped up and pointed to a boat in the distance. "Here it comes. That's it. That's the MoMo."

"MoMo?" He tried to think where he'd heard that word. "What does it mean?"

She shrugged. "I have no idea. Funny name, isn't it?" She started waving toward the boat, then threw her arms around Deuce. "I get so excited when I see it coming toward the dock. I miss Papa terribly, when he's gone."

The boat docked, just as the sun began to go down. Deuce had never gotten accustomed to the beauty of the brilliant colors as the sun set over the waters. A big guy with dark skin, long hair, a shaggy beard and smelling like dead fish, stepped off the boat and didn't seem to notice Deuce standing there.

He rushed toward Margo with open arms and swung her in the air. "I told the fellows you'd be on the pier, waiting for your papa. Did you miss your ol' man?"

"You know I did, Papa. I always miss you when you're gone." She thrust her hand over her mouth and giggled. "Oh! I almost forgot. Papa, this is my friend, Deuce."

Deuce licked his dry lips, then extended his hand. "Nice to make your acquaintance, sir."

The fisherman cocked his head to the side and seemed to be studying him. "Deuce?"

"Yessir."

"You French, boy?"

"French, sir?"

"Yeah. Deuce is French, meaning the second."

"Oh. Yessir. Mama told me that."

"So, who was Uno?"

Deuce felt his face burning. "Uno, sir?"

"Yeah, the first one. The one you're named after."

"That would've been my father."

"But if you were named after your papa, you'd be Junior."

Deuce looked past Mr. Lopez at a man standing near the wharf. The man turned around, then reached up and pulled his cap further down on his forehead. Although it was getting dark, Deuce was almost sure it was his friend Skip. He yelled his name, but the man didn't respond. Instead, he reached down, picked up a duffle bag, threw it over his shoulder and as if he hadn't heard, he proceeded to briskly walk past them, taking long strides.

Deuce's gaze followed the tall, lanky fisherman. He said, "Bye, Margo. See you at school tomorrow," then ran after the mysterious fellow to get a better look. But if it was Skip, what reason would he have for ignoring him? Just as Deuce convinced himself he was wrong, Margo's father yelled, "Skipper, you know this kid? Because if he's gonna be hanging around my daughter, I need to know he's okay."

The man slowed down, pushed the cap away from his forehead and mumbled. "He's okay."

Confusing thoughts ran through Deuce's head. "So, it is you. It's getting dark and with your cap pulled down, I couldn't see you very well. Boy, will Mama be surprised when I tell her you're a fisherman and that I just happened to see you. If I hadn't come with Margo, I reckon I could've missed you."

Skip's broad chest rose when he sucked in a deep breath. "I'd like it if you wouldn't mention seeing me to your mama, Deuce."

"But why? You could have supper with us. She'd love it. I know she would."

"I have a reason for asking you to let it be our secret. But what are y'all doing here? I left you in Eufaula."

"It's a long story."

"Did your mother marry that fellow? I believe you called him Joel?"

"No, but he hasn't given up. We came here because Mama needed a job, and she promised me that she'd check here first. When we were staying with you, did I mention that when my daddy was my age, he came to this Fish Camp in the summers and sometimes got to go out on the fishing boats?"

He covered his lips. "I believe you mentioned it a time or two. But you were talking about your mama's boyfriend. What makes you say he hasn't given up?"

"Because just before time to leave, he asked her to marry him. I was afraid she was gonna take him up on it."

"But she didn't?"

"Not yet."

"You say, not yet. Do you anticipate it happening?"

"Yeah. He's given her three months to make up her mind. Or maybe it was the other way around. Maybe she gave him three months, but either way, I think she's gonna marry him."

"How do you feel about it?"

"I don't like it."

"Any particular reason?"

"Actually, there are a couple of reasons. Number one, I love it here. I don't want to leave. My granddaddy told me so many stories about how much my daddy loved coming here every summer. I've known since I was a kid that I wanted to come and do the things he got to do. I loved this place as soon as we drove up and I saw the boats coming in."

"And the second reason that you're leery about Joel?"

172

"I don't trust him."

"That surprises me. I thought you liked him."

"I did at first. But now, I think he's only being nice to me because he wants my mama. There's something fake about him."

Skip rubbed his brow. "I'm sorry to hear that. I hope you're wrong."

"Why would you care?"

"Why? Because I like you, Deuce. I like you a lot."

"I like you, too, Skip. More than I've ever liked any grown man, besides my granddaddy. That's why I wish you'd go home with me and see Mama. I know she was rude to you in the beginning, but that was only because you were—" He bit his lip. "You know, don't you?"

"I do know, and I understood."

"But after she got to know you, she really liked you. I could tell. That's why I think you should go see her."

"I have my reasons, Deuce. Trust me?"

"Sure, Skip. If you have reasons, I'm sure they're good ones."

"Get on home now, before she gets worried about you."

"I'm sure I'm already in trouble for staying out after dark. Mama still thinks I'm a kid."

Skip ran his fingers through the boy's hair. "I think that's what mother's do. Get on home but remember your promise."

Deuce pretended to zip his mouth shut. "It's our secret."

On the way to #7, Deuce dreamed up all sorts of possible scenarios to explain why Skip was being so mysterious. Had he committed a nefarious crime in his youth, and the cops have been looking for him for years? Was he hiding from a wicked woman who was trying to trick him into marrying her? Was he a stowaway from another country? Could he be a CIA agent? Whatever his reason for wanting to hide, Deuce was sure it was a good one. And no one would get it out of him, even if they stuck thorns in his fingernails.

He marched into the house and announced, "Fried chicken. Thanks, Mama. I'm starving."

She turned a golden-brown chicken breast with a pair of tongs. "I suppose you met Margo's daddy? What's he like?"

"Huge. We're talking really, really big." Deuce picked up an apple from the basket on the table and took a bite. "He reminded me of the Giant in my old Jack and the Beanstalk book. And he talks kinda funny."

"Are you saying he doesn't speak English?"

"Oh, he speaks English, but he doesn't sound like us. I had to listen closely to understand him. Margo said he has a sense of humor, so I didn't know if he didn't believe me when I told him I was named after my daddy, or if he was trying to be funny."

"For goodness sake, why wouldn't he believe you?"

"He said my name should be Junior and not Deuce."

"What sparked that conversation?"

"According to him, if I had my daddy's same name, I'd be called Junior. He said Deuce means the second person down the generational line to have the same name as the first. That's not right. Is it?"

"Deuce, when your father learned we were having a baby, he wrote that if you were a boy, he'd like to name you Theodore Alexander Jones, after your granddaddy. You would've been Theodore Alexander Jones II, so Ronald said we'd call you Deuce, meaning the second one with the same name. I loved the thought of having a little boy called Deuce."

"But my name is not the same as Daddy Theo's."

"You're right. It isn't. That was the original plan. But when your daddy died before you were born, I wanted you to carry your father's name. However, since Ronald wished for you to have his father's name, I didn't feel right going against his wishes. So, I came up with a compromise. I settled on Ronald, after your daddy, and Alexander after your granddaddy. I combined two beautiful names but nicknamed you Deuce, which is what your father wanted his son to be called."

"So, are you saying Mr. Lopez was right? I should be called Junior?"

"You'd only be Junior if I had named you Ronald Maxwell Jones, which was your daddy's full name."

"I reckon that makes sense. Deuce means two, and my names came from two people."

"Exactly. But I'm sure Mr. Lopez was only attempting to make conversation for Margo's sake."

That night, after lights were out, Deuce said, "Mama?"

"What sweetheart?"

"I had the most wonderful day today."

"Oh? And what made it so great?" When he didn't answer, she repeated the question. "Honey, I'm glad you had a good day. What happened?"

"Can't tell. Goodnight, Mama."

"What do you mean you can't tell?"

"I made a promise. But I hope it's not the last time."

Ramona lay awake wondering what could've made her son's day so wonderful, but even more curious was the peculiar statement that he couldn't tell because he'd promised someone. Her heart pounded. *It's that girl. There's no other explanation.*

He was only fifteen, for crying out loud. The girl seemed sweet, but she didn't have proper supervision. The longer Ramona thought about it, the more she realized that Deuce was left alone far too often. What he needed was a man's guidance. Someone who could talk to him about those things. Maybe it was time to give Joel her answer.

CHAPTER 19

Monday, February 25ᵗʰ

After a whirlwind ten days, Joel and Peggy arrived home Thursday night and were back in the office Monday morning, as husband and wife.

She brought over a cup of coffee and sat it on Joel's desk. "Frank called a few minutes ago and said he needs to see you. It sounded urgent, so I told him to come on."

"I thought he and Connie were in Paris."

"They were, for two weeks. They got in Thursday night."

"How can that be? We were only gone ten days, and we got back Thursday night, also."

"But they left a few days before we did."

He shrugged. "Those ten days flew by. It certainly didn't seem that long."

She walked over and standing back of her husband with her hands planted on his shoulders, gave a gentle massage. "It didn't seem nearly long enough for me either, sweetheart. Time flies when you're having fun."

Frank Jinright strutted in and headed straight for Peggy. "Aww, the beautiful blushing bride. I couldn't believe it when Joel gave me the news on the phone. I hope the groom will allow me to kiss the bride." Before she saw it coming, he wrapped his arms around her, pulled her close and kissed her forehead.

Joel felt his blood boil. "Peggy, why don't you run down the street and pick up some doughnuts."

"But I thought you said earlier, that—"

"Forget what I said. I've changed my mind."

Frank held out his hand, but Joel pretended not to see. "Have a seat. What's this urgent business that needs my attention?"

"I'm getting to it. It's Gussie Jones. She's been driving me crazy all weekend. She's mad because I left for Paris, the night before Theodore died, as if I should've hung around in case the old man kicked the bucket."

"If you think being the executor of the estate is a job, try being her attorney. She left a message with Peggy before we left for Florida, to tell me that it's urgent that I get in touch with her."

"Everything is urgent with Gussie Jones. She thinks there's no one on the planet but her. Are you saying you haven't talked with her in person since the funeral?"

"That's right. I took the day off, Friday, since Peg and I got in late Thursday night. We were both exhausted, and I don't do weekends. Not even for ol' lady Jones."

Frank chuckled. "They tell me honeymoons tend to wear you out. I wouldn't know."

"I believe we were discussing Gussie."

"Of course. I'd like to get the woman out of my hair as soon as possible and she wants to see you and me together. Could we set up an appointment with her for tomorrow?"

Joel flipped through Peggy's calendar, then nodded. "Sure. Say around nine o'clock?"

"Fine. The sooner the better. I'm ready to get it over with, but it's not gonna be pretty." He strode over to the window and looked out. "I was sorry to hear about Theodore's death. I hear the whole town turned out for the funeral. I'm not surprised. He was a good man, but how he ever got mixed up with that woman, I'll never figure out."

Joel stood and shook his hand. "I'll see you in the morning."

Frank was halfway out the door when Joel said, "Wait! What did you mean when you said that you're ready to get it over with, but that it's not gonna be pretty? Were you implying you don't think Gussie will get as much for the estate as she's anticipating?"

Frank whirled around on his heels. "What do you mean she won't get as much? Haven't you even looked at the Will?"

"Not lately. Why?"

Frank gave a sardonic chuckle. "I'm afraid Gussie is going to be in for a wide awakening."

"What do you mean?"

"A couple of weeks before we left for Paris, Theodore came to see me to make sure his Will was in order. We went over it. It clearly states that at his death, everything he owns will go to his daughter-in-law, and at her demise, everything will go to his grandson."

Joel slapped his palm against his forehead. "What? No. That can't be."

"I'm afraid it is."

"Oh, this is gonna be a mess. She'll contest it, for sure. When did he change it?"

"Change it? That would've been about fourteen or fifteen years ago. Theodore looked it over, but just wanted assurance all the i's were dotted and the t's crossed. The original Will listed Theodore's first wife, Jenny, as his beneficiary, and in lieu of her death it would go to their son, Ronald, and at his death would go to his wife. The grandson was added later. If I remember correctly, the kid wasn't even born when we drew up the will and Ronald died shortly after the will was executed. Then, Miz Jenny died, which leaves Ronald's widow as the heir. You should have a copy in your files." Frank looked out the window. "It's taking Peggy a long time to get back. Didn't she just go around the corner for doughnuts?"

"Don't worry about Peggy. So, you're telling me that Gussie isn't even mentioned?"

"That's exactly what I'm saying. Look it up, if you don't believe me. It's never been in her name. Ever. But she doesn't know that."

Joel went to the file cabinet and shuffled through papers until he found a copy. Walking back to his desk, his eyes scanned the pages. "Well, I'll be dog. You're right. When I got out of law school, Theodore hired me to represent him. I was thrilled to have him as one of my first clients. He brought a copy of the Will that Lawyer Smithers had drawn up before he died, and Mr. Theo asked me to look over. Everything seemed fine, but of course at that time, Miz Jenny was alive. When he turned around and married Gussie only months after his wife died, I guess I was thinking he added her. I suppose I should've checked, but I've had a lot on my mind."

Joel's thoughts went in a dozen different directions. Could it be true? His heart pounded. Of course, it was true! With Miz Jenny gone and Ronald declared dead, Frank was right. Ramona was the beneficiary of the Jones' Estate. She'd get the whole shebang. His voice quivered when he asked, "Has Theodore's daughter-in-law been contacted?"

"No, and I'm sure she has no idea, else she would never have left here. I heard from the grapevine that the community took up a collection for her the night of the wake, since it appeared Gussie was kicking her out of Rose Trellis. Everyone assumed the estate would go to Gussie—including Gussie. I don't know Theo's daughter-in-law that well, but I've heard nothing but nice things about her."

Joel rubbed the back of his neck. "I still can't believe it."

"Why would you question it?"

"Oh, I don't question it. I'm just dumbfounded."

Frank said, "You seem stressed over the situation. Aren't you proud for the girl? Or are you disappointed that Gussie is being left out in the cold?"

Joel nodded. "Of course, I'm proud. That's great news. But we need Ramona present when we have the reading of the Will. I'll get in touch with her."

"Then you know where to find her?"

"No, but I have a couple of ideas where to look. Why don't you and I go to Rose Trellis tomorrow and convince Gussie that it's impossible to have a reading of the Will until we contact an interested party who might voice objections. She'll immediately figure that Theodore must've left something for his grandson."

"Sounds fine to me, but Gussie is gonna blow a gasket if she thinks anyone is getting a dime out of what she believes to be her inheritance."

Joel's brow lifted. "Maybe not. I think she'll assume it's an old truck Theodore promised Deuce, and it's already in his possession."

"Well, let's get this finalized as soon as possible. Where do you plan to look for the girl?"

"Not sure, but I have a pretty good idea. If she's not there, I have a couple of other thoughts. Don't worry, I won't stop looking until I find her." He could tell he convinced Frank. If only it would be as easy as he made it sound.

Joel watched out the window until he saw Frank get in his car and drive off, then gave out a loud, gleeful, "Whoopee." Deuce had never lived anywhere but Eufaula. He'd be glad to come back. Now, that they'd be coming home to Rose Trellis, Joel could . . . he could . . .? His mouth suddenly felt as if he'd swallowed cotton. Just exactly what could he do? Nothing. Nothing at all. He was a married man. Tears welled in his eyes. For over a decade, he had waited, hoped, dreamed, prayed, but never thought he'd have a chance with Mona. It took Ronald to help him garner the courage to pursue. *She loves me. I know she does.* He pounded his head with his fist. *How stupid was I to give in to Peggy's nagging?* Reality set in. It wasn't the nagging that caused him to give in. She'd nagged since their first weekend getaway. He was desperate for money to pay off the gambling debt. If only he could've known Ramona would be coming into so much money, he would've had more than enough to cover his debt and he would've had the only woman he had ever loved. His stomach wrenched. Why go over all the 'what ifs'? What could he do about it now? He didn't have an answer. He only knew he couldn't give up.

Peggy returned with the doughnuts. "Sorry it took so long. They weren't ready when I arrived. Did Frank leave?"

"Yeah, and he was asking about you before he left."

"Why?"

"He's crazy about you, Peggy. Surely, you know that."

She giggled. "Frank is crazy, all right. But not about me."

"You must think I'm blind. I've seen how you two look at one another."

"Joel Gunter, if you think I could ever be interested in Frank Jinright, you don't know me very well."

He had to think of a new angle. She'd never give him up for Frank, and Joel didn't like the idea of giving her up for the likes of Frank Jinright. "You've got a point. I've been thinking about that very thing."

"What very thing, sweetheart?" She picked up the pot and poured two cups of coffee. "That percolator gets coffee entirely too hot. Don't burn yourself." She sat down at her desk and took a sip. "Now, what were you saying?"

"You said I don't know you very well. I've been thinking that we don't really know one another. We might think we do, but we don't."

"Joel, if you're talking about you and Frank, I'll have to agree. He's hard to figure, sometimes."

"I'm not talking about Frank, Peggy. I'm talking about us."

She jerked the cup of hot coffee away from her lips, and a little sloshed on the desk. "Oh, dear, I was telling you to be careful, and look what I've done." She reached for a tissue to wipe the desk. "Now, what were you saying? Something about us?"

"Yes." This was taking much too long to say. He might as well spit it out and get it over with. "Peggy, I've been thinking that our getting married was a mistake."

She dropped the doughnut and napkin that she was holding. "Come again? You're kidding. Aren't you? It's not funny, Joel."

"I'm serious. You're a swell secretary, but you'll have to

admit, we made an impromptu decision to marry when we were both at our most vulnerable."

"Impromptu? You can't be serious. We've discussed marriage for almost four years. I have no idea what you mean or why you'd be saying this. Did Frank say something to make you think there was something going on between us? If he did, it's a lie. He's a flirt, and I'll admit I've enjoyed the attention, but it's you I love."

"If Frank had anything to do with my decision, it was that he helped me see that as a married man, I suddenly began to feel as if I owned you. His flirtations never bothered me before, but until you took my name, I'd never thought of you as property that belonged to me. I don't know how to explain, except to say that when I heard him flirting with you, I felt like a mutt, guarding his bone from a bulldog. There'd be no way for me to stop the big dog from taking what he wanted, without all three of us getting hurt."

Her heart fluttered. "Aww, you're jealous. I don't mind. To be truthful, I feel flattered. I do belong to you. I am yours and you are mine." She held up her left hand, admiring the ring she bought.

His reaction caught her by surprise. "No, you're wrong. You are *not* my property, nor am I yours. That kind of possessive behavior destroys marriages. Lucky for us, we realized it before we had time to become resentful of one another. I'm just saying we can't allow a marriage certificate to destroy the bond between us. We've been together for four years, and it's been great, hasn't it? Why should we ruin a good thing?"

CHAPTER 20

Peggy stood at the window with her hands braced on either side of the frame and sobbed. "I don't know why you're doing this to me, Joel. We had fun in Florida, didn't we? I've never been happier, and I know you weren't pretending. You enjoyed it as much as I did."

"You're right, hon. It was great. But we didn't need a marriage certificate to go to Florida. You know I would've taken you there before now, if you had told me it was something you wanted to do. But I've seen too many great relationships spoiled by a marriage license. We don't want that to happen, do we?" He eased up behind her and kissed her on the back of her neck. "Don't cry, babe. Everything will be just as it was before we signed the marriage certificate. I've told you for years that I wasn't ready to get married, but I let you talk me into it. That was my fault for being weak, not yours."

Feeling his lips on her neck caused her to shiver. She stomped across the room and flopped down in the swivel office chair. Looking up at him, she said, "I certainly didn't have a hard time convincing you, since you were desperate for money to keep that brute from ripping you limb from limb. You were scared stiff. But now, that I've saved your skin, you say you're through with me? Sorry, bud. Nothing doing."

"Okay, so I was scared. The fact remains, I acted on impulse, but it's not as if the mistake can't be corrected. Nothing has to change between us, Peg. You'll still be my secretary, and we'll continue to go on trips together, just as we've done for years."

"No. Joel. I won't give you a divorce."

He ran his hand over the back of his neck. "Don't say that Peggy. What kind of marriage would it be if one of us held on to the other, out of spite?"

"Oh, Joel, you're getting nervous that we might've made a mistake—but we didn't. Can't you see it's the best thing we've ever done for one another? I love you and I'll make you a good wife."

He screamed. "Why can't you get it through your skull. I don't want a wife. I want a secretary."

She swallowed hard, trying to keep her composure. "Joel, this is not like you to raise your voice at me. I'm afraid the stress of losing your money has caused you to have a nervous breakdown. There's no other explanation as to why you'd suddenly want a divorce after being married only thirteen days."

"It hasn't been 'suddenly, Peggy.' I knew the minute I said, 'I do,' that it wasn't right. If you want to get married, find you someone who wants the same thing you do."

"What do you mean if I want to get married. I'm already married."

His teeth gnashed together. "We made a mistake, Peggy."

"No, Joel. We finally did the right thing."

He sucked in a deep breath, and when he reached across the desk and took her hand, she assumed she'd gotten through to him.

"Peg, suppose you're right and it turns out that I *am* having a nervous breakdown. Wouldn't you want to help me?"

"You know I would."

"Then do this for me, because I think you're right. I've been under a tremendous strain that began when Big Ed threatened me. I feel like a milksop having to admit this to you, but the truth is, I was scared stiff, and the insecurities that began then, have festered. I'm an emotional wreck. It isn't your fault, hon, and perhaps these terrifying thoughts aren't real, but right now I feel as if I've put a noose around my neck. I need to be free. I've *got* to be free or else I'm likely to do something crazy. It's constantly on my mind."

"Joel, you're frightening me."

"I'm frightened, too, honey. But when I'm well, and in control of reality, we'll approach the subject of marriage again. You're right, I did have fun on our honeymoon. It was great. And after I'm well, we'll go again. I haven't told you this, but I actually considered taking my life when I realized I'd lost everything."

She thrust her palm over her mouth. "Oh, Joel, are you serious?"

"Very serious. I saw no way out of the situation. I felt cornered—the same way I feel now. Honey, do this for me. Let's go in the morning and sign divorce papers. I'll have my name taken off the deed to the beach cottage and from your bank account. It'll be just like it was before we left for Florida."

"But I don't want it like it was then. I want things the way they were when we were on our honeymoon."

"And in time, they can be. But you can't imagine how it makes a man feel to think he can't support his wife. That's been grating on my nerves, ever since I signed for a joint checking account. I can't take the pressure any longer, Peggy. When I get back to the point that I feel I can handle the stress, we'll approach the subject of marriage again."

"Oh, Joel. I'm trying to understand. Honest, I am. I'm truly sorry that you've been under so much pressure, darling. But if you seriously believe this will help, then I'll have to agree to your terms. But just because we are temporarily dissolving the marriage doesn't mean you have to remove your name from the bank account."

"But I do. Don't you see? If I didn't, I'd still feel dependent upon you. It would always be in the back of my mind that if I couldn't pay a bill with my own money, then yours would be there to bail me out."

"Then allow me to deposit a specific sum into your account,

and we'll call it a loan. Pay it back on your own terms."

He stomped back and forth across the room, then throwing up his hands, he shouted. "How many ways do I have to say it? I don't need, nor do I want your help. I'm already indebted to you for sixteen-hundred. I need nothing more from you than a time to heal. Why can't you understand?"

"I'm trying, darling. Honest, I am." Peggy felt as if her emotions had been pushing against a weak dam. The dam suddenly broke and uncontrollable tears rushed forth like a mighty waterfall. "I'm sorry, Joel. I love you, darling, and I'm worried about you. How do you plan to survive without my help? Your bank account is virtually empty."

Leaning in, he lowered his voice and speaking calmly, said, "Don't do this to me, Peg." He pulled out a handkerchief and handed to her. "Can't you see what you're doing? You're putting it into my head that I can't survive without your help. You keep trying to take care of me, emotionally and financially. I have to get through this situation on my own, or I won't feel like much of a man. You understand, don't you?"

"I think so."

"Good. I'll pay you back the sixteen-hundred dollars I took to Jimbo, as soon as possible. Meet me here at the office early in the morning and we'll take my car to Montgomery and file for the divorce. We don't want the word to get out that the marriage ever took place. I'd hate for folks to think there was something wrong with you, that would've caused me to change my mind about wanting to be married to you. They wouldn't understand. I'm sure you remember that woman who came to us wanting to sue her boyfriend for spreading rumors that she had a sexually transmitted disease. It wasn't true of course, but more people received the word that it was true then those who heard that it wasn't. Her reputation was ruined through no fault of her own, and I'm sure she didn't have many suitors coming around after that. I love you too much, Peg, to allow you to become the subject of vile rumors. So now, do you understand why this needs to be done discreetly?"

"Oh, m'goodness, I do remember the woman. I see your point. Thank you for being considerate. But what do you plan to tell Frank? I guess he's the only one who knows."

"I've thought of that. We'll pretend it was a joke and poke fun at him for falling for our little stunt."

"You really think he'll believe it?"

"Why wouldn't he? We'll get up early in the morning, so we can be back in the office by lunch. We should be as careful to guard your reputation as we were before we left for Florida. Maybe even more so, just in case anyone should suspect you of being my mistress."

Her forehead crunched into a frown. "Is that how you think of me?"

"You know better. I'm just saying that it's what folks might say if they saw your car parked at my house overnight. I'll pack your suitcase after work today and drop it off at your house after dark."

Peggy wanted to remind him of the baby, but in his emotional state, it could be the one thing that could possibly drive him over the edge. Joel couldn't bear the thought of not being able to take care of a wife. What would happen if he remembered that he had more than one dependent who would be counting on him? The fact that he hadn't mentioned the baby was a clear sign that she was right, and he was having a mental breakdown. He had apparently blocked the news from his mind.

Yet, no man could've been happier at the thought of becoming a dad than Joel, when she first told him. It was so cute how he immediately began to choose a name for his child. *His child.* For years, Peggy had dreamed of starting a family with Joel Gunter, but she'd almost given up. She reached down and rubbed her flat belly and tried to imagine how she'd look in a few short months. She was glad she waited until after they were married to tell him she was pregnant. Had she told him earlier, she might always wonder if he felt trapped into marrying her.

As much as the thought pained her of getting a divorce, it was important that she be patient with him. He was a very self-sufficient man and after being stripped financially, his pride had been hurt to the point that he couldn't think straight. He'd always been strong, and there was no reason not to believe that with lots of love and understanding, he'd bounce back from the insecurities and depression that temporarily had him bound. Didn't she vow to love, cherish, and obey? In sickness and in health? Wasn't she still bound to that oath?

"Joel, I'll call Montgomery and set up an appointment for us to sign the divorce papers."

"I don't think an appointment will be necessary."

"Maybe not, but it won't hurt to try."

"Fine. I think Gene Hartselle may be coming by today to discuss a property dispute. When he gets here, tell him I'm checking on it and will get back with him later."

"A property dispute? You haven't mentioned it."

"I forgot."

"Who is the dispute with?"

"I don't remember. It's not important. I've got bigger fish to fry. Just put him off. And while you're at it, here's a number for you to call." He handed her a piece of paper with the name, Dr. Chambers, Birmingham, Alabama and a phone number. "Since we're dissolving the marriage, we need to do the same with that thing you're carrying inside your body."

She placed her hand on her belly, as if to cradle the baby inside her. "That thing? You aren't suggesting—?"

"Not suggesting, Peggy. Insisting. You know the stigma an illegitimate child suffers. Surely, you wouldn't wish that on an innocent child. I know I wouldn't. Do it, Peg."

"Joel, this isn't like you. I wish you'd go see a doctor. There may be something he could give you to relieve some of the anxiety."

His teeth ground together, as he glared at her. "The only thing that is causing me anxiety is your constant nagging. Stay off my back, Peggy and be ready in the morning when I go by to pick you up." He stomped out and slammed the door.

Peggy wanted to wrap her arms around him and tell him everything was going to be all right. Trying to think of how best to help her sweet husband, before he did something drastic, she picked up the phone and made a call to Montgomery. When the receptionist answered, Peggy said, "Yes, this is Peggy Druthers Gunter. I'm Lawyer Wenfroe's great-niece. Could I speak with him please?"

"He's with a client. Would you like for him to return your call?"

Before she could answer, the receptionist said, "Hold on. The client just walked out."

A soft, elderly voice said, "Peggy, is this really you? How are you darlin'?"

"Okay, Uncle Louie. And you?"

"Fair to middlin', but what do you expect from an old man? It's been ages since I've heard from you. Hope no one in the family has died."

"No, sir."

"Good, because I'm next in line. When you get this old and know where you're going after death, the other side begins to look a whole lot more exciting than this side. I'm ready to see your Aunt Tootsie. Oh, m'goodness, how I miss that woman. But that's not why you called, is it?"

"No sir. Uncle Louie, I have a favor to ask. It's an unusual request, but I don't think I'd be asking you to do anything that would break the law."

"Tell me, shug, and I'll be the judge of that."

Peggy poured out her heart, telling him everything except the part about how Joel lost his wealth. She explained that for years, they'd talked of marrying, but kept putting it off. She went through all the details, even confessing she was pregnant when they finally got around to getting married, and although she knew Joel loved her, that he was having a mental breakdown and insisting they dissolve the marriage. She rattled on for ten minutes, telling more than she'd intended to tell, when suddenly she stopped. Her voice broke. "I suppose I sound like the one who is having the breakdown."

Uncle Louie said, "I can't imagine the toll this has taken on you, you being pregnant, and not being able to help him. It sure sounds as if he's having a breakdown, but don't worry about a thing. I'll have papers ready with a lot of small print that he won't take the time to read. No one ever reads the small print when they come in for a divorce. You'll both sign them, but it won't mean diddly squat. Hopefully, it will relieve some of the pressure he's feeling, and when he's able to think straight again, he'll be glad to discover he's still married, and gonna be a papa."

"Thank you, Uncle Louie. Of all my daddy's brothers, you've always been my favorite."

"I appreciate you saying so, sweetie, even though I was his only brother. And of all my nieces, you're my favorite."

"I'm your only niece."

"'Zat right? Maybe that's why you've always been my favorite."

She laughed through the tears. "See you tomorrow. And remember. Don't give it away that we're kin or that we've discussed this."

Peggy hung up, resolved that she'd make things as calm and pleasant for her husband as possible. Since the lack of money was causing him so much anguish, she'd make a trip to the bank, deposit money in his account, and pretend it came from delinquent clients. She'd be so good to him, he'd be begging her to marry him again.

Wasn't there a verse somewhere in the Bible that said something about a woman could win her husband to the Lord, by her conduct? Perhaps she made it up. After all, it had been years since she'd picked up a Bible and the only time she attended church was on Easter each year. Even on those annual visits, she was more interested in showing off her new duds and seeing what all the other ladies were wearing.

Tuesday morning, February 26th, inside the Montgomery County Courthouse, Joel Gunter signed his name on the dotted line, with the intent of dissolving his two-week long marriage to the former Peggy Druthers. He shoved the pen and paper her way. When she glanced up at the elderly lawyer and hesitated, Joel whispered, "Hurry, Peg, and get it over with. I have an appointment after lunch."

Lumbering down the marble steps, she wasn't sure which hurt more—the fact that he was a sick man, or the thought that she'd lied to him—even if she did feel it was for his own good.

CHAPTER 21

The sudden change in Joel's demeaner was evident the minute they got back to the car. "There's a swanky restaurant on the other side of town, called The Guardian. It's a little pricey, but today's a day for celebration. Let's go order the biggest steak they have."

Peggy wanted to be glad that he could've so quickly overcome the extreme anxiety, yet it was difficult not to feel a bit sad that he seemed to consider divorcing her a reason for celebrating.

"I never did thank you, Peg, for collecting from those delinquent accounts. I don't know how you did it, but it sure helped. You're a great secretary. By the way, did I tell you I'll be leaving this afternoon to go locate a client that Frank and I are representing?"

"No, you didn't mention it. But don't forget you have an appointment with Mr. Hartselle at nine o'clock in the morning concerning the property dispute."

"Call and cancel. I can't possibly be back by morning."

"Joel, you put him off last week."

"Yeah, I did, didn't I? Well, tell him I had to leave on urgent business, and I have no idea when I'll be back in the office. Advise him it would be best if he'd find another lawyer to represent him."

"You can't be serious. We need that account."

"Do I sound as if I'm joking?"

"Where are you going?"

"I don't know. That's the thing."

"I assume Frank will be going with you. Who is the client?"

He pounded his fist on the steering wheel. "Would you lay off? We're no longer married, so stop your nagging. Just do as I said and tell him to seek other counsel. I may be gone a couple of days or a couple of weeks. Don't make any new appointments until you hear from me."

Joel drove her back to the office in Eufaula, where her car was parked. "There's no need to go inside. In fact, now that I think about it, there's no need for you to go into work until I get back. Take a vacation."

"A vacation? Alone? Where would I go, Joel?" Peggy was more concerned than ever about his mental state. She had deposited her money into his account, only leaving enough in hers to keep from closing it out. But now, not only was he suggesting she turn away lucrative clients, he was spending her money as if it would last forever. There was no way they could afford to close the office. It was up to her to try to appease clients until Joel came to his senses.

****

Joel stopped at a service station on the way out of town. "Fill it up, Otis."

While the attendant washed the windshield and checked the oil, Joel went inside and bought a pack of peanuts and a grape soda. He laid the money on the counter and sauntered back outside. As he was pulling away, the attendant ran back out, waving him down. "Mr. Joel, you forgot your change."

"Keep it, Otis, I'm in a bit of a hurry."

Recalling the conversation, concerning Deuce's fascination with stories about the fish house, there was no doubt he'd find them there. Whatever the kid wanted, Mona would give her life to make happen. The kid was spoiled. But that would soon change.

Although it wasn't yet Spring, it was unusually warm for the end of February. However, this didn't necessarily signal the end of cold weather. Every February, there'd be a week or two of beautiful warm weather, and the trees would begin to blossom. The farmers would always get in a hurry to plant, then in March, there'd come a freeze. But Joel had a feeling there'd be no freeze this year. It was gonna be nothing but sunshine from now on. With the top down on his convertible, he sang along to Frank Sinatra's latest hit on the radio, "I've Got the World on a String." With the wind in his hair, and the sun warming his shoulders, he belted out the words, "Got the string around my finger, What a world, what a life, I'm in love."

Driving into Jinx Bay, it looked as if time had stood still. The houses all looked just as they did when he was a boy. He pulled up to the Fish House and parked. Looking out across the bay, childhood memories filled his head, although he never understood why Ronald loved the place so much. Joel only went because his parents felt he needed the discipline, and Ronald's Uncle Walter knew how to dish it out.

He walked down the long line in the cannery, expecting to see Mona with strands of hair peeking out from under a bandana and wearing a blood-spattered apron. After working in such an environment for even a short while, he was sure it wouldn't take any encouragement from him to make her understand this was no life for her. He envisioned her looking up and throwing her arms around him. She'd jerk her apron off and with tears streaming down her cheek, she'd say, "Thank goodness, you came. I'm so glad to see you, Joel. Let's go home."

After walking through all three rooms twice, his hopes plummeted. He'd been so sure she was here. But working in the cannery was not the primary reason she would've moved to Jinx Bay. No, it was for Deuce's sake. He was the one who wanted to live there, with the hopes he could one day go out on the fishing boats. But it didn't mean Mona would have to work at the Fish House for that to happen. There were other jobs in town, and he wouldn't stop looking until he found her. A sudden thought crossed his mind and he wondered why it hadn't occurred to him before. If she lived in Jinx Bay, then she would've enrolled Deuce in school. That was it. Find Deuce and he'd find his mother.

The school receptionist was an elderly lady with more wrinkles than a prune. When he first tried to speak, she pushed her palm forward in his face, as if the letter she was typing was urgent and had to be taken care of immediately. Finally, she looked up. "Now, what can I do for you?"

"I've come to see Deuce Jones, ma'am. He's a new student."

"Well, we have a slew of Jones's in this area, but I don't recall a . . . what was that first name, again?"

"Deuce."

"Is that spelled with two O's?"

"No ma'am. D-e-u-c-e."

"What an odd name. Is it Hungarian?"

"Hungarian?" Joel had trouble hiding his frustration. "No ma'am. It's a nickname."

"Well, why didn't you say that to begin with? We don't abide by nicknames. Could you please give me the child's legal name."

Joel scratched his head. Confident that since he was called Deuce, that he would've been named after his grandfather. "That would be Theodore. Theodore Jones."

Her face stretched into a craggy smile. "Now, we're getting somewhere."

Joel cringed when the phone rang. She picked it up and with her hand covering the receiver, she glanced at him and mouthed the words, "Sorry, I need to take this call."

After standing there for over five minutes, waiting for her to finish an apparent private conversation, she hung up and said, "Now, what is it you wanted to know?"

Joel was ready to walk out, when she snapped her fingers, "Oh, I remember, now. I believe you were asking about the new student."

He whirled around. "You're saying he's here?"

"I don't recollect saying such a thing. Jones, you say?"

"Yes ma'am."

"Well, that could be like a needle in a haystack. There are more Jones's in this town than there are cats at the fish house. Unless you can provide his legal name, there's no way for me to know if he's enrolled here."

He wanted to remind her that he had already divulged the information, but why waste any more time. Surely, if Deuce was there, the school receptionist would remember a new kid recently enrolling. He lumbered back to his car and tried to contemplate his next move. "*Mona, Mona, Mona . . . where are you?*"

CHAPTER 22

Deuce stood outside Margo's door, waiting for her to come out to walk to school. As the minutes ticked by, and still no sign of her, he knocked on the door. Still no Margo. Had she left without waiting for him? Knowing he'd be late, he trudged on to school. He thought about how Douglas had been flirting with her lately. Maybe she liked him? Why wouldn't she? Every other girl in school seemed to.

He was late getting to school, but his teacher was writing on the blackboard and didn't seem to notice when he slipped in and quietly sat down at his desk, near the door. He looked over at the empty desk beside him. Where was she? Maybe he didn't wait long enough, and when she did come out, she waited for him, not realizing he'd already left. He watched out the window, hoping to see her.

But what he did see made his muscles tighten into knots. A

convertible pulled up and parked in front of the school. Not just any convertible, but a red one. Squinting, he tried to get a closer look at the driver. That's when he saw Joel Gunter park and step out. He walked down the path leading to the office.

Deuce couldn't breathe. There'd only be one reason Joel would be coming to the school, and that would be to inform them that he and Deuce's mother would be getting married, and he had come to check him out.

I won't go. I'll run away. The teacher was still writing when he quietly slipped out, ran down the hall and didn't stop running until he got to #5. He beat on the door. She had to be there. He couldn't leave without letting her know. When no one came to the door, he slowly opened it, then stepped inside, calling her name.

"Deuce, is that you?"

The cabin looked exactly like his. A front room with a sofa, and a small bedroom. She was in the bedroom. He supposed the sofa was where her father slept. "Is it okay if I come in there?"

"Sure."

He said, "Are you okay?"

"Not really. I'm having one of my headaches."

"I'm sorry. Can I get you an aspirin?"

"We're out and I'm not expecting Papa back before tomorrow, but they don't seem to help, anyway."

"Well, it won't hurt to try. I'll run down to the store and buy a bottle."

"I'd rather have you than the aspirin."

"I won't be gone long." He hurried out the door and ran to the store. He was afraid the old fellow who ran it might question why he wasn't in school, but when he didn't, Deuce wanted to believe it was because he looked old enough to be out of school. He hurried back to Margo's and could hear her moaning in pain as soon as he opened the door. He got a glass of water and told her to take a couple of aspirin.

"Thank you, Deuce. You're very sweet. But I'll only take one. I've heard aspirin can be dangerous if you take too many."

"I've seen Mama take two at the time, but if there's a chance they could be dangerous, I sure don't want you to take more than one. I don't know what I'd do if anything ever happened to you, Margo."

He stuck the bottle in his pocket and found a rag near the kitchen sink, wet it with warm water, then sat on the side of her bed and held the wet rag to her forehead.

"You're sweet, Deuce. My mama used to put a warm cloth on my head when she was alive. No one else has ever done that." She closed her eyes and he assumed she'd dozed off, when she muttered, "Deuce?"

"What do you need, Margo?"

"Need? I suppose it is a need. I need to tell you that I love you."

He swallowed hard. "I love you, too, Margo. I've loved you from the first day I saw you. I never knew I could love anyone as much as I love you."

"Then would you kiss me?"

He moistened his lips and leaned down. It was the first time he'd ever kissed a girl, and it was more wonderful than he could've ever imagined. He wanted to hold her in his arms and never let go.

She whispered, "Thank you. My head is easing off. I don't know whether it was the aspirin or the kiss, but I think I might can go to sleep, now." She slid over. "Would you lie here with me until I fall asleep?"

"Sure. Close your eyes, and when you wake up I'll be gone and I hope your headache will be gone, too." Deuce stretched out on the bed, but there was no way he could relax, knowing she was lying there beside him. As soon as he was sure she was sound asleep, he eased off the bed and sat on the sofa in the front room, waiting for her to wake up, to make sure she was better.

CHAPTER 23

Peggy, who once loved going to church, had stopped going because of sin in her life that she wasn't willing to forsake. Sitting on a pew, while choosing to live a sinful lifestyle, made her feel guilty. Why put herself in such misery? But when a peculiar thought popped into her head, she mouthed the words several times. "By her conduct, a woman can win her husband." She swallowed hard. Where did that come from? Before she could dwell on the question, she recalled exactly where she first heard it.

She was at a youth revival, while sitting around a campfire singing Kumbaya, the night she gave her heart to the Lord. She was impressed at the time, the way the revival preacher talked to them as if they were grown, warning against peculiar things Peggy had never even given thought to. Things he called fornication and 'being unequally yoked.'

How odd that the youth pastor's text, which had no

significance at fifteen, came back to her remembrance as clearly as the night he preached it. And how ironic that it would pop into her mind at this particular time.

A pang of nausea sent her to the bathroom. Perhaps it was morning sickness, but it felt more like pangs of condemnation. Years ago, when Joel first suggested they go away for a weekend, she refused. He wasn't happy with her, but he was patient and understanding. However, it didn't take long before their romantic dinners ended with coffee and dessert at her apartment. One thing led to another, and although there were deep feelings of guilt in the beginning, eventually they were taking weekend trips, which not only seemed right, but exciting.

Peg spent the afternoon making phone calls, and changing appointments that were already on the calendar for the next two weeks. At five o'clock, she watered the plants and was ready to go home when the door opened.

Frank Jinright said, "Hey, beautiful. I hope your ol' man hasn't gone home yet and left you here doing all the work."

She felt a blush paint her face at hearing Frank refer to Joel as 'your ol' man.' "Joel isn't here, Frank, but we've been meaning to tell you. That was all a joke."

"I'm not following you. What was a joke?"

"The thing about us getting married. We had you going, didn't we?"

He stepped back. "You aren't trying to tell me you aren't married."

"That's exactly what I'm saying. We aren't married." She tried to force a smile, but her bottom lip wouldn't stop quivering.

"I don't get it. But why would you have said it, if it isn't true?"

"I suppose we thought it would be funny."

Frank gnawed the inside of his cheek. "Now that you mention it, it is funny. In fact, I find it hilarious."

Peggy couldn't understand how he could call it hilarious with such a straight face. "Good. I'm glad you find it funny. I was hoping you'd see the humor."

"Not the part where you pretended to be married, but the part where I learned that it isn't true. Maybe I'll still have a chance with you."

"You're a born flirt, Frank Jinright. I don't know how Connie puts up with you."

"She has no choice. She's stuck with me. So is Joel planning on coming in the office in the morning, or will he be leaving to find the Jones girl."

"Oh, I think he's probably already left. He said at lunch not to expect him back in the office anytime soon, that he had to contact a client for you." Her brow furrowed. "You say she's a Jones?"

"Yes. Mr. Theo's daughter-in-law."

"He didn't mention her name. I assumed he was helping locate a client for you and that it was someone I wouldn't know. Well, I don't suppose I do. Not really."

Frank rubbed his hand across his mouth. "That's odd, but then

Joel has been acting rather peculiar lately." He shrugged. "I shouldn't have said that. I'm sure it's me." He looked at her and winked. "You certainly think I'm peculiar, don't you, sweetheart?"

Peggy feigned a smile. "I won't answer that." She wanted to tell him that he was right. Joel wasn't himself. It would certainly help if she had someone she could share her fears with. But what if Frank should tell Joel what she said. He'd be furious.

****

Joel was on his way to Frostproof, Florida with his hair blowing in the wind and the sun warming his face. He glanced approvingly at his handsome reflection in the rear view mirror.

A write-up recently appeared in the newspaper about the little town in Florida where fruit growers were desperate for pickers. According to the article, the trees were loaded with fruit, but the workers they'd counted on in the past had migrated further south. Ramona made a point of sharing the article with Joel. But for what reason? Now that he thought about it, it seemed obvious. She'd alluded to two places she could possibly go. Was she hoping he'd prove his love by seeking her out?

He began to think of it as a treasure hunt. She was a treasure, and he wouldn't stop until he found her and took her home. It wasn't as if Frostproof was a large metropolis. How difficult could it be to find her? He'd stop at every grove and wouldn't leave until he found her. Everything was working out perfectly. Everything, except for Peggy, that is, although he tried not to think about it. He knew she loved him, and she'd be hurt when she learned he was marrying someone else. He felt rotten. However, Peg was a beautiful young woman. She'd have lots of suitors. Frank Jinright for one. Joel cringed. *Anyone but Frank.* Why it perturbed him for Frank to flirt with her, he couldn't understand. Maybe it was because of the way Peggy's face lit up whenever he walked into the office.

Frank had been a good friend for years. The fellow had certainly had his troubles. It was in June, just after he graduated college that he received the news his mother and father had died in a house fire in Montgomery. His sister Connie, a high school senior, and his baby sister, Susan were rescued. Frank rented an apartment in Montgomery, and he and Connie were determined to raise the baby. Several years ago, they moved to Eufaula, where Frank opened his own firm. He was a big tease and flirted with all the women, young and old, but Joel had a feeling he wasn't always teasing when he was around Peggy, and that's what got under his skin.

He knew Peg had always assumed Connie was Frank's wife, and Joel wasn't sure why he never told her differently. Or why he never shared with Frank that Peggy thought he was married. Frank once told him he vowed not to marry until after his baby sister was grown and gone. But now that he and his sister had taken Susan to Europe, Joel feared that Frank's joking around with Peggy could turn serious. Just the thought of Frank with Peggy made it hard to breathe. He loved Peggy. He just wasn't *in* love with her. So, why was he so fearful of Frank giving her romantic notions?

He compared Ramona with his expensive new wingtip shoes that he was so proud of, and Peggy with the comfortable, worn slippers that were waiting for him at night when he was ready to put the wingtips away. The comparison caused him to wince. Yet, it was a fair comparison. Ramona was a Jones. In Eufaula, the name carried weight. She was beautiful, and she once belonged to Ronald. He supposed that was the number one reason he had always wanted her as his own.

Peggy, on the other hand, was a Druthers. Old man Druthers was a country preacher who barely made enough to feed his wife and daughter. Peggy told stories of times they only had cornmeal gravy to eat, but she was extremely smart. She worked her way through Massey Draughn Business College, then answered his ad in the newspaper and moved to Eufaula, where she'd been with him for the past four years. He couldn't have found a more efficient, reliable secretary. She did anything he asked of her. Anything. She was young and beautiful. He planned to marry Mona, but was he really ready to let Peggy go? What if he didn't have to let her go? He'd still need a secretary and she'd still need a job. They'd still need to take occasional business trips together, wouldn't they?

CHAPTER 24

Frank hoped Joel could locate Ramona, but not before he had a chance to talk to Ronald, one more time. The man was as stubborn as his father had been. But he had to get through to him. He drove to Jinx Bay and pulled up in front of the little cottage in the woods. Ronald was outside cutting wood. He laid down his ax and walked over to the car.

"Evenin', Frank. It's good to see you, man. But if you're here for the reason I think you're here, you might as well turn around and drive back to Eufaula."

Frank opened the door, got out, and threw his arms around his friend. Then stepping back and staring, his jaw dropped. "Wow! Look at you. You look as if nothing ever happened. I'm happy for you, Ronald. I was afraid if it didn't turn out, you'd blame me, but apparently that doctor is as good as I was told."

"There's still healing taking place, but I can't complain. I appreciate all you did to get me accepted into the study."

"Hey, I just wish Theo was around to see you."

He bit his lip. "So, do I. How is Mona?"

"Actually, that's why I'm here. Joel is looking for her, but I wanted to come here first, before the estate is finalized and try to reason with you, one more time."

"I've told you how I feel."

"But things have changed since the day you got out of the army. Your father went along with your wishes for all those years, and I didn't attempt to change his minds, although I didn't approve. But now, I'm the only one who knows you survived the injuries."

Ronald gave a sarcastic chuckle. "Who said I survived them?"

"Theo loved you so much that there's nothing he wouldn't have done for you. I thought your mother should've been told, but he abided by your wishes."

"I couldn't let Mother see me the way I was, and if she had known the truth, wild horses couldn't have kept her from finding me. I'm just glad Mona didn't know it was me, when she was here."

"Well, she would definitely know you now."

"I was on my way home from the hospital when I drove up and saw the wreck. The surgeon had removed the bandages and applied a coat of Vitamin E oil on the scars, so not only was my face badly swollen, the oil made me look dirty. I could tell it sickened her to look at me. Although the doctor had told me the reconstruction was a success and that I'd look like a new man when the swelling went down, I didn't believe him. Frank, I looked so grotesque that she was actually afraid of me. Do you know how it made me feel to see the horror on her face when she looked at me?"

"Well, she'll feel differently when she sees you now."

"I don't plan for her to see me. The night I took her back to Eufaula, she began to relax and decided that the horribly disfigured man wasn't going to boil her alive. You can't imagine how good it felt having her sitting in the car beside me, talking to me. But if she ever finds out that I've been alive all these years, she'll hate me."

"Why do you think she'd hate you, when she's never stopped loving you."

"That's just it. Because she thought I was dead, she's clung to the memory of the man she fell in love with. But if I had allowed Daddy to tell her I was alive, she would've gone to the hospital, taken one look, applied for a divorce, and would've fallen in love with someone else. Looking back, I know that's what I should've done. I've stolen fifteen years from her by allowing her to hold on to a lie." He shook his head slowly. "I'm dead, Frank. Let me stay dead."

"Ronald, you've got to be sensible. Theo worked hard for all he accumulated. He did it for you. He wanted you to inherit the estate. Go home and claim what is yours."

He shook his head. "Don't you think I want to? I can't. Everyone thinks I'm dead, and that's how it's got to be." He hung his head. "Besides, what right do I have to disrupt Mona's life, now? She's in love with someone else, and I couldn't bear to live in the same town and see them together."

"I think someone has misled you. I've never seen her with another man—well, no one other than her attorney."

Ronald's brow lifted. "He's also the man who has asked her to marry him."

"What? Joel? You can't be serious. Where did you get such a cockeyed notion?"

"From my son."

"Whoa! Your son? Are you now saying that Deuce knows who you are?"

"No, and I plan on keeping it that way. I think he's a little jealous of having to share his mother with someone else, so he isn't too happy about the upcoming marriage. I think he needed someone to talk to."

"He told you that his mother and Joel are planning to marry?"

"Exactly. To be honest, I encouraged it in the beginning. When you told me about the doctor in New Orleans who was performing facial reconstruction, and knowing Mona had never married, I had high hopes of getting my family together. Even though the doctor assured me that the swelling in my face would take time to go away, I looked so horrible, afterward, that I couldn't believe I'd ever look normal again. It was ironic that she and Deuce ran into the deer, just as I was coming back from the hospital. When I saw the way she looked at me as if I were some kind of freak, I knew I had allowed myself to wish for the impossible. She's too beautiful and sweet to continue living alone, so I secretly met with Joel and encouraged him to ask her to marry him. He's always loved her. I've known that since we were kids."

"What? You're saying Joel knows you're alive?" Frank threw up his hands. "Ronald, don't you see how this complicates things? As Theo's attorney, Joel knows the estate goes to you and only goes to Ramona if you aren't living. I don't understand why he didn't tell me you were alive."

Ronald chuckled. "You knew I was alive."

"Yes, but he doesn't know that I know. For crying out loud, who else knows?"

"Relax. He has more reason than either of us to keep Mona from finding out the truth."

Frank sucked in a lungful of air. "As we speak, he's out trying to locate her, but I assumed it was because of his obligation as her attorney. But if it's true what you say about her and Joel, then it's absolutely necessary now, that you come claim what is rightfully yours."

No. "I want her to have it all. She deserves it. Rose Trellis has been their home for almost sixteen years."

"Okay, I don't like to spread bad news, but let me tell you something you apparently don't know. Joel Gunter is a snake-in-the-grass."

"Hey, he can be a braggart, but deep down, he's a good ol' boy."

"Don't kid yourself."

"I don't know what you mean."

"I mean, he's not the same kid you hung out with as a boy. He's a conniving liar."

Ronald shot his palm forward. "Hold on. That's my friend you're badmouthing."

"Friend, my hindfoot! He's a louse. I know for a fact that he's also a compulsive gambler and recently lost everything he owns. He has a sweet little secretary that he's using and abusing. It's sickening. Do you really want to leave Rose Trellis—the place where you grew up and that your mother and father loved—to someone who is likely to gamble it away and leave Ramona and Deuce homeless?"

Ronald's eyes filled with moisture. "Please tell me you're joking."

"I wish I were. But don't you see? Deuce stands to lose his inheritance if Ramona marries Joel. Ronald, it's imperative that you come to the reading of the Will for your son's sake. You can assure him of a future, even if Ramona does choose to marry Joel. If you own it, then Joel can't mess with it, and Deuce will inherit it from you."

Ronald ran his hand over his mouth. "You've just handed me a shocker. Frank, are you sure about all that? Maybe it's just gossip about Joel's gambling habit."

"Not gossip, I assure you."

"But if everything is left to Mona, then he can't touch it, right?"

"Joel is a lawyer, and I guarantee you that as soon as they are married, the deed will be put in both names and the money will be transferred to a joint account. How do you think Theo would feel if he knew you were allowing Joel Gunter to take what he meant for you and Deuce? I can't allow it to happen, Ronald. I'm sorry. Theodore was my friend. He entrusted me with Guardian of the Estate. I can't sit idly by and watch someone steal his beloved grandson's inheritance. I don't know how I'll stop it, but if you don't respect your father's wishes enough to save Rose Trellis, then it's up to me, even if it means exposing you, myself. I'd much rather you be man enough to step up for the benefit of your son."

Ronald paced back and forth across the room. "This is so much to take in. I want to do the right thing, but I'm so confused."

Frank said, "Well, I've said all I can say. If you fail to show up at the reading of the Will, I will present a sworn document that you are alive and well, but due to a recent surgery, we will need a postponement. Ramona deserves to know the truth."

Ronald chewed the inside of his cheek. "You'd do that, wouldn't you?"

"You better believe it. This involves more than just you. I'm doing it for Deuce."

Ronald walked over and looked into a cracked mirror on the wall and ran his hand across his face. "The surgery is healing much better than I ever dreamed possible. I wonder—"

"If you're wondering what your wife will think, I can guarantee you she'll think you're as handsome as the day you left."

"Then why do you look so worried?"

"I do believe you're the first man I've ever told that he was handsome, so I'd appreciate it if you wouldn't make it public." Then as if he'd been holding it back, he guffawed, relieving some of the tension.

"I don't know, Frank. I feel so confused. Deuce tried to tell me things about Joel, but I assumed it was natural for a teenager to resent a man his mother was about to marry. I assumed he'd accept it once it happened. I still find it hard to believe that Joel could be the person you paint him out to be."

"For crying out loud, Ronald. If you can't believe me, then trust your own son to tell you the truth."

CHAPTER 25

Deuce was ready for school thirty minutes early and the time seemed to drag as he waited for seven-thirty—the time he always stopped by for Margo to walk with him. But this morning, he had an uneasy feeling in the pit of his stomach. She acted differently when he walked her home, yesterday.

Normally, he'd wait outside in the afternoons, for her to go inside and fix him a glass of lemonade. She'd bring it out, and they'd sit on the doorsteps, hold hands, and talk until four o'clock, when he'd have to hurry home to get his homework before his mother came home from work. But yesterday, when he walked her to her door, she sounded strange. She didn't ask him to wait, nor did she volunteer to bring out a glass of lemonade.

"Bye, Deuce."

That was it. Just, 'Bye, Deuce.' It had such a final sound to it, as if she were breaking up with him. Was that it? Had he become a bore? Maybe she liked Douglas, who was about the most popular fellow in the whole school. Could he blame her? It had been obvious that Douglas had set his cap for her, but she assured Deuce that she could never be interested in a boy who was so stuck on himself. Maybe she changed her mind.

He trudged down the road to #7, went inside and poured himself a glass of milk. Then plopping down on the sofa, he opened his science book. After holding it in his lap for twenty or thirty minutes, he threw the book across the room. He couldn't concentrate. All he could think of was that the only girl in the world for him had dumped him for someone better looking, richer and more popular. How could he compete with the likes of Douglas Aplin? He couldn't.

****

Ramona had payroll to get out and worked later than usual. She hoped Deuce remembered the ham slices in the ice box and had fried him an egg to go with it. He'd always enjoyed eating breakfast foods for supper, and tonight would've been a pork chops she'd planned to have.

When she drove up, she expected to see the front door open, and her son standing there, ready to scold her for being late, while insisting there was no need in her putting in overtime at the office. He was very mature for his age, and much more responsible than what she gave him credit for. But maybe his maturity was also what caused her angst when he spent so much time alone with Margo. Deuce was a man in every way except the years. But he'd given her no reason to distrust him.

When the door didn't open,' and the porch light didn't come on, she suspected he was perturbed with her for working late, again. Stepping into the cabin, she let out a scream, seeing her son lying on the floor. She ran over, knelt down beside him and tried to wake him. She ran outside screaming for help.

A fisherman in #9 came running out to see what the commotion was about, then followed her inside and picked up Deuce, put him in his truck and they headed to the hospital.

Ramona was stunned when the doctor came out and said they had pumped out his stomach. "Do you have any idea why your son would want to take his life?"

"No. No, no, no. He would never do that."

The doctor's stern expression frightened her.

"Could it be that you haven't been listening to what he's been trying to tell you?"

"You're wrong. We're very close. He tells me everything."

"Everything? Did he tell you he planned to take a bottle of aspirin in hopes of killing himself?"

She burst into tears. "That can't be. I want to see him."

"I don't think that's wise at this time. He's very upset over something, and obviously it isn't something he's ready to share with you, else you'd already be privy to what's troubling him."

"Please, doctor. Please let me see him. You don't understand. He talks to me. He'll tell me why he did this."

"Mrs. Jones, I think you've been living in a dream world,

imagining that you and your son shared everything, but the truth came out tonight, didn't it? He was looking for a way out of life. He's a very troubled young man. Did you two have an argument this morning?"

"No. In fact, he was in a very good mood, laughing and joking around before I left for work."

"I see. How old is Deuce?"

"Fifteen."

"He's a big boy for fifteen."

"Yes. He takes after his father, who was over six-feet tall."

"You said his father, who was—so is he out of the picture?"

"My husband died before Deuce was born."

"I'm sorry."

Ramona swallowed hard. It was the first hint of compassion the man had shown her since bringing Deuce in. She had begun to get the feeling he blamed her for Deuce not wanting to live. But could it be true?

"Why don't you go home and come back in the morning. Give us time to counsel with him."

"If I can't see him tonight, I'll sit here in the waiting room until I can go in. I can't leave, doctor. Surely, you can understand."

He shrugged. "Whatever suits you, but I'm sure you'd be much more comfortable sleeping in your own bed."

"Do you honestly think I could sleep, anywhere?"

"I don't suppose so. I'll ask the nurse to bring you a pillow. Maybe you can stick it between your head and the concrete wall and get a little shut-eye."

He started out, then stopped at the door, turned around and asked, "Do you know if Deuce has a girlfriend?"

She nodded. "There's a sweet little girl who lives a couple of cabins down from ours that has caught his eye. But they're only fifteen so it's nothing serious."

"Are you sure?"

She bristled. "I'm quite sure. Why would you question me?"

"In my years of practice, anytime a teenager gets as desperate as your son, it usually involves someone of the opposite sex."

Her throat felt dry. She slammed her palm to her forehead. "Oh, my goodness. You aren't saying that you think she's—"

"Pregnant? I have no way of knowing. But I hope to find out more from him in the morning when I make my rounds."

The hours drug by, but Ramona didn't close her eyes all night. She kept watching the big round clock on the wall in the waiting room. *Pregnant?* Deuce, a father at fifteen years old? Impossible. Or was it? She couldn't say she hadn't worried about them being alone so much of the time, with no supervision. But at fifteen? They were kids, for goodness sake. She had such high hopes for her only son. He was smart and could be anything he wanted to be. But he was also smart enough to know that at fifteen, any dreams he had for a successful future were doomed if he was about to become a father.

No wonder he wanted to take his life. How could he support a wife, much less a child? It was her fault. He pleaded with her to come home from work at five o'clock, yet too many nights she ignored his pleadings, thinking if she worked hard that she'd get a raise and could move them into a decent house.

She should call Joel. Ronald was right, even though he didn't know Joel. Not only was he in love with her, but he loved Deuce. Joel was one of the most compassionate men she'd ever known, and besides, he was a lawyer. He'd know what to do. He loved Deuce and could afford to take the kids in and help them get a decent start in life, if she agreed to marry him. In fact, she was confident that was exactly what he'd do. Wasn't Deuce's future more important than whether or not she was in love with Joel Gunter? She'd do anything for her son.

Around five o'clock a nurse walked in and made coffee in the percolator sitting on a small table in the corner. Coffee perking had never smelled so good. Ramona asked about Deuce, but all she could get from the nurse was that he had a good night, and the doctor would be making rounds in a couple of hours and would speak with her after he checked him out.

CHAPTER 26

"So, how's the patient this morning?"

Deuce opened his eyes to see a man in a white coat staring down at him. "Where am I?"

"Well, this is not Heaven, if that's where you expected to wake up. I got word that it's full, but that other place is accepting applicants. Lucky for you, St. Peter has put your name on a waiting list."

Tears welled in his eyes. "If you're trying to be funny, it's good you went into medicine instead of comedy. You're lousy at jokes."

"Fair enough. I'll go back to what I do best. Tell me why you pulled such a cockeyed crazy stunt."

"Is that your best shot at 'bedside manner?'"

"Look, kid. I chose the profession I'm in because I want to help people who are suffering. I tend to lose patience with strong, healthy bodies who purposely choose to do harm not only to themselves, but to all those who love them."

Deuce buried his face in his pillow. "But you don't understand."

"You're right. I can't understand how you could be so selfish as to put yourself ahead of those who have loved and sacrificed for you, all your life. Your poor mother is sitting in the waiting room, blaming herself for the stunt you pulled, and I have a feeling she had nothing to do with it. If you had accomplished what you set out to do, she would've mourned the remainder of her life, trying to figure out what she had done to make you not want to be with her."

"It had nothing to do with her."

"So, when were you planning on revealing that to her? In case you haven't heard, the dead don't get an opportunity to explain their actions to those left behind."

"I don't know. I was hurting so bad, I guess I wasn't thinking straight."

"What were you thinking?"

He lifted his shoulders in a shrug.

"It was the girl, wasn't it?"

He shoved himself up with his back braced against the iron headboard. "What do you know about her?"

"Not much. She's pregnant, isn't she?"

Deuce's chin trembled. "She is?"

"You said that like a question. Don't you know the answer?"

"What do you care?"

"I care because I almost lost a patient last night and that tears me up inside when I think about it. You're one lucky kid to still be among the living." At that point, the doctor sat down on the edge of the bed. "I'm sorry if I've come down hard on you, but I'm just trying to get you to understand that taking your life doesn't solve a thing, and only makes life hard on those who love you. Is that what you were going for?"

"No sir."

"Then what was it?"

Deuce poured out his heart to the doctor, crying, unashamedly, as he told about missing having a father, his beloved granddaddy's death, and his mother was considering marrying a man he knew she didn't love.

"You haven't mentioned the baby."

"What baby?"

"Isn't your girlfriend pregnant?"

"No. That's crazy. Why would you think that?"

"I just had a hunch."

Deuce glared into the face of the doctor. "I wish she was pregnant, and I wish the baby was mine. But I've only kissed her twice, and she told me I was the only boy she's ever kissed. She wouldn't lie to me."

The doctor reached over and placed his arms around the distraught teenager. "Oh, kid, don't you see what you almost did? Your plan was to kill a boy to remove his temporary pain. But what you were really about to do was to kill a very successful man, with a loving wife and a couple of bright kids who adore their daddy."

Deuce's eyes squinted. "Are you crazy? I'm not a serial killer. I have no idea who you're talking about."

"But don't you see? You're that man, who almost didn't have a chance to show the world what he had to offer. The adult Deuce wouldn't have had the opportunity to marry the woman of his dreams or have the opportunity to hear a kid look up to him and call him daddy. Is that what you wanted? Because to take the life you have now, regardless of the heartbreak you're going through at this point in your life, let me assure you that you have a wonderful future life—an even more exciting life than you can imagine—waiting for you."

Deuce cut his eyes away. "What makes you think that man will ever be happy?"

"Because God said He knows the plans He has for you, and they're for your good. The plans He has for Deuce Jones are to prosper him and give him a future. Do you really feel you have a right to try and thwart God's plans? The fantastic future that He planned for you while you were still in your Mother's womb?"

"Ok, I'll admit it was a stupid thing to do, but I wasn't thinking straight. All I could think about was that my girl didn't love me anymore and I just wanted to die." His lip quivered. "I suppose the truth is, that I wanted her to be sorry for dumping me."

The doctor rolled his eyes. "At least you're admitting it was stupid. And your girl might've been sorry—for a season. Do you love your mother, Deuce?"

"Yes sir. I love her a lot."

"Well, I can assure you that long after your girlfriend forgot about you, your mother would have you on her broken heart every minute of every day for the remainder of her life. Is that the outcome you hoped for?"

"No sir. But you don't understand. You're wrong about me becoming a man and marrying the woman of my dreams. I'll never love anyone but Margo."

"Did you say, Margo?" His eyes narrowed. "That wouldn't be Margo Lopez, by any chance."

"You know her?"

"I know her quite well. She's a lovely young woman. Margo has been a patient of mine for almost two years. Now, I think I understand. I knew you must've felt you were in a hopeless situation to have done something so drastic. I thought you were afraid of losing your girl to another fellow. Don't give up on her, son, or she'll give up on herself, and that's the last think I want for her. I couldn't guarantee her or her father that the surgery will be successful, but it's a last resort and worth trying."

Deuce's throat tightened. For fear the doctor would not reveal anything more if he discovered Margo hadn't divulged the information, he chose his words carefully. "I suppose the headaches she's been having will go away after surgery?"

"If it's successful, she should be free from those awful

headaches. I'm praying the tumor is operable, but the doctor in New Orleans is the best. She's in good hands. The last thing she needs now is for you to be worrying about her. You need to be strong for Margo's sake. Do you think you can do that?"

He choked. "She won't die, will she?"

"I can't guarantee it. It's in the Lord's hands."

Tears filled his eyes. "I won't ever love anyone else. Ever!"

"I know you feel that way now, but you're young. I hope and pray that Margo makes it, and if it's what you two want, that you can one day marry and live happily ever after. But if the Lord sees fit to take her, then in time you will fall in love again. God is the God of second chances."

"You're wrong about me falling in love again. Once you fall in love—I mean really, really love someone—if they die, then no one can ever take their place. Ever!"

The doctor chuckled. "You sound like the Love Guru. How did you become such an expert on love?"

"You're poking fun at me."

"Not at all. I just find it peculiar that someone so young has such strong opinions on the subject."

"As I told you, my daddy died before I was born, but my mother has never loved anyone else, even though she's pretty and has had lots of opportunities. There's a lawyer who keeps pestering her to marry him, and I'm afraid she might, even though I know she doesn't love him."

"You're right, she is definitely a beautiful woman. But I have a feeling she may love the fellow more than you want to believe. Do you honestly think she waited fifteen years, to say 'yes,' to someone she's not in love with? Maybe you liked feeling that no one could ever take your daddy's place, and when she did find love again, you resented it."

"But I know why she's marrying Joel, and it has nothing to do with love. All my life, we've lived with my grandaddy in the big house where my daddy grew up. But when my granddaddy died, the woman he was married to kicked us out. Daddy Theo planned to send me to college, but now that he's gone, Mama doesn't have the money to send me. I don't care. All I want to do is to become a fisherman, but Mama is all set on me going to college. That's why she's gonna marry the man who was my daddy's best friend, and that's the only reason. He's got plenty of money, and I have a feeling he'd be glad to use some of it, just to get me out of the house. He pretends to like me, but I can see through him."

"Young man, I can certainly see that you've been carrying a heavy burden on your shoulders, but trust me, these things that seem so big at this point in your life, will pass. You have a great big, wonderful future awaiting you. Don't blow it."

"Are you asking me to keep quiet and not tell Mama how I feel about Joel?"

"Not at all. I think she'd want to know. But just as you'll want her to listen to you, you must listen to what she has to say and give her the same consideration you want her to give you. Are you man enough to do that?"

"I think so."

"Well, I have other patients waiting for me to make rounds, and I know your mother is in the waiting room, pacing the floor as she waits for me to let her know that you're going to be just fine." He raised a brow. "You are, aren't you?"

Deuce reached out his hand. "Yes sir. Thanks, doc. I'm sorry I put you through so much trouble last night."

"I'm just glad we got the outcome I was praying for." He took Deuce's hand and shook it. "One last thing. I'm sorry your father didn't live to see what a fine son he had. He would've been so very proud of you."

"Really, sir? You can say that, even after what I did?"

"I can say it for a fact. Not many people know this, but I had a fine seventeen-year-old son who did the same thing you did."

"But he lived. Right?"

He shook his head. "No. That was ten years and three months ago. There's not a day that I don't miss him. When they brought you in the other night, I felt like I was looking down at Adam. If I couldn't save you, it would've been like losing him all over again. He was such a good-looking kid, brilliant, quarterback on his football team, and a bright future ahead of him. But his mother and I were going through a divorce. I moved here from Birmingham. Adam was torn. He couldn't decide whether to come to Florida to be with me or stay in Birmingham with his mother. He loved us both and we both loved him.

The real tragedy is that after his death, his mother and I found we needed one another to share our grief with, since no one else could understand our pain, and we wound up getting back together. Son, promise me that you'll work at getting over this hump in your life, and will go on and live out the wonderful future God has for you."

Deuce's gaze locked with the doctor's. "I'll do it, sir. For you and Adam. I promise."

CHAPTER 27

Joel spent days stopping at every orange grove along the sides of the road, asking people if they'd recently seen a young woman and her teenage son. They looked at him as if he were from another planet. It didn't take him long to stop asking stupid questions. He decided to go to City Hall to find out if Ramona Jones had recently had utilities turned on but was told the migrants generally rented rooms in several shady motels about town and didn't apply for utilities, since they were included.

"But she isn't a migrant. She's a—" Seeing the unconcerned expression on the woman's face, he turned and walked out.

He drove over to nearby Lake Wales, hoping to have better luck, but just outside of town, his car went dead, and he wound up walking a couple of miles to a service station. He was told a fellow who went by the name of Buck was the best mechanic in the county, but that he had several cars waiting for him to work on. The kid pumping gas looked no older than sixteen, yet he seemed to be in charge. He pointed to the concrete building next to the station. "Good luck with getting your car back before the middle of next week. Buck said this morning, he needed to hire another mechanic, but no one around here wants anyone to work on their automobile but him."

Joel walked over and when he didn't see anyone, he called out, "Hey, I'm looking for Buck."

A rough-looking character wearing a pair of greasy overalls wheeled himself out from under a 1936 Ford, covered in rust. "I'm Buck."

Joel started to reach for his hand, but seeing the grease, changed his mind. "Uh, nice to meet you, sir. My name is Joel Gunter, and I'm an attorney from Eufaula, Alabama."

"Yeah?"

"Well, I'm here on business and my car just conked out on me, down the road a piece. I need someone to tow it in, and I need it fixed by the end of the day."

The man chuckled. "Then I'm afraid you've come to the wrong place."

Joel grinned and reached in his pocket. Thumbing through the bills in his wallet, he said, "Oh, I think I'm in the right place. I hear you're the best."

"That's what I'm told. But do you see the four cars parked out in front? They're ahead of you."

"I can't possibly wait for you to finish working on five cars before you get to mine."

"Fine." And with that, he rolled back under the dilapidated piece of junk that he was working on.

Joel tried to convince him that he was in a hurry to locate a client and that he was sure that his need was far greater than the local owners of the other automobiles. "I own a brand-new convertible. I've only had it a few weeks. There can't be anything seriously wrong with it, so it shouldn't take you long to fix it." He waited for Buck to roll back out, but after several minutes, he kicked the tire to let him know that he was losing patience. When there was still no response, he yelled, "How much money will it take to put my car ahead of these others?"

He felt relieved when he heard the wheels rolling back out from under the old car. Buck looked up at him. "Mister, you ain't got that much money."

"I've got more than you might think."

"Like I said, you ain't got that much. You might try calling Sam's Body Shop, near Frostproof, I hear he ain't busy." The way Buck cackled, it appeared he thought he'd cracked a joke.

"Thanks, for nothing." He walked back over to the service station and asked to use the phone. The kid pointed to a pay phone on the corner. There was a phone book hanging from a chain. He looked up Sam's Body Shop and was told they'd send a wrecker to pick it up and could have it ready by closing time, unless there was a major problem.

Joel assured them it couldn't be major. It was a new car. Aggravated that he had just left Frostproof for Lake Wales, yet his car was now being towed back to Frostproof, he inquired about a taxi.

The kid told him the fellow who owned the taxi service had temporarily closed, since his wife was in the hospital. After much cajoling, Joel convinced the kid that he'd make it worth his while if he'd close early and take him to where his car was located.

He agreed, and as they came to the spot where Joel's car conked out on him, he was glad to see that the wrecker had already been and picked it up. It gave him hope that Sam was already working on it, and he'd soon be on his journey to find Ramona.

The kid carried him straight to Sam's shop, but it was obvious when they drove up that the pull-down door was shut and locked. "Well, mister, it looks like we got here too late."

"That's impossible. I told him I was coming. He's got to be here." Joel walked around the block building. Refusing to give up, he beat on the metal door once more.

"Mister, beating on the door ain't gonna change nothing. He ain't here."

Joel lumbered back to the kid's old truck. "Do you know if there's a hotel in this place?"

"There's a motel."

"That'll have to do. Please take me there."

When they reached the motel, Joel got out. The kid said, "What about your clothes?"

"Yeah? What about them?"

"Where are they?"

"In my suitcase." Joel popped his palm against his forehead, then added, "Which is in my car." He opened the door to get out. "Wait here while I see if they have a room available."

The boy gave a hearty laugh. "A room available? From the looks of the parking lot, I'd say you can have your pick. This ain't New York City."

The last thing Joel needed was a smart-alecky kid belittling him. "And when were you last in New York?"

"Maybe I ain't never been, but I've seen pictures, and this ain't it."

"Don't leave until I come back out, or you don't get your money." Joel walked into the office and was greeted amiably by an elderly lady with horn-rimmed glasses and her hair knotted up in a bun.

"I reckon you're the plumber?"

"Plumber? Oh, no ma'am. I'm here to rent a room."

She pushed her spectacles down on her nose and glared at him above the rims. "Why don't you go get your luggage, first, and then I'll get you a key."

"I don't have luggage."

She raised a brow. "That's what I thought. And I don't have a key."

"What d'ya mean?"

"I mean that I have a respectable motel and you fellows need to find you another place to do your cavorting. You won't be doing it in my establishment."

"Ma'am, I'm afraid you have the wrong idea. I'm not here to 'cavort,' whatever it is you mean by that."

"Young man, I wasn't born yesterday. I may be old, but I'm not stupid." She waved him off with her hand. "Now, suppose you leave here before I decide to call the cops."

"Look, ma'am. I'm an attorney. My name is Joel Gunter, and—"

"If you're a lawyer, I'm a ballet dancer. Now get out of here and find you another place to carry on your sinful activities."

"I'll be happy to if you'll tell me where that place might be."

She cut her eyes from left to right as if about to reveal a dark secret. "I feel by telling you, I'm aiding and a bettin' you're up to no good, but they tell me that Ma Rosie has some girls staying at her place. I can't vouch for it, mind you, but I do know she gets more business than I do, and I can't think of another reason for it, unless the rumors are true."

Joel thanked her and got directions to Ma Rosie's. He didn't expect to find the kid still waiting but was pleasantly surprised when he was. It was the only good thing that had happened to him since leaving Eufaula.

As soon as he opened the truck door, the kid looked at him and grinned. "I reckon you want me to take you to Ma Rosie's. Right?"

"How did you know?"

"That was my grandma, and I knew she wouldn't let you have a room, since you didn't have luggage."

"Your grandma?"

"Yes sir."

"Then why didn't you go in with me and tell her?"

"Tell her what? That I met you today, and you told me the same story you told her? Nah, that wouldn't do any good. Grandma has heard lots of excuses in her day and nothing me nor you could tell her would make her take in a stranger with no luggage. You won't have trouble with Ma Rosie. That is, if she has a room available. She seems to have a thriving business."

Joel rolled his eyes. "I'll bet."

The kid drove him across town to four little concrete block buildings. A Neon sign with missing letters, was flashing, "Ma Ros 's Mot l." Joel opened the door, got out, then turned and pointing a finger, commanded, "Don't leave!"

He walked into the office and immediately knew the obese woman with died black hair and lips redder than a fire engine was Ma Rosie. She was arguing with a young girl who looked to be no more than seventeen. The girl was crying and pleading with her not to kick her out.

Ma said, "You lied to me. You said you was eighteen, and your old man called and threatened to shut me down. He said you ain't but sixteen years old. I have a respectable business here. Now git out."

"But I don't have anywhere to go."

Looking up at Joel, Rosie's lips parted. Her teeth reminded him of a picket fence in need of paint, with every other plank missing. She said, "Well, hello, good-looking. I don't recollect ever seeing you here. You a local?"

"No ma'am. But I need a room for the night."

"Well, you've come to the right place. That'll be fifty dollars."

"You're joking. Right?"

"Do I look like a jokester to you?"

He couldn't afford to make her angry. "No ma'am. It just seems fifty dollars is a bit steep."

"Not for the amenities that come with the room." She reached on the wall and took a key that was hanging on a nail. "You want it or not?"

He hesitated, then looking at the young girl with tears in her eyes, he shook his head. "No thanks." Then motioning for the girl to follow him outside, he said, "Where do you live? We'll take you there."

"Can't go back."

"But Rosie said your father didn't want you staying there. I'm sure he wants you to go home."

"You're wrong. First, he's my stepfather, and he's the reason I left. He's a mean, cruel man. I'll never go back."

"Well, I can't just leave you here."

She reminded him of a little scared puppy, the way she looked up at him with those big, sad, blue eyes.

She whimpered. "There's only one other motel in town, but the old lady who runs it will have to think we're married, or she won't let us stay there. I hear she's real religious and don't put up with no hanky-panky."

His jaw dropped. "I think you misunderstood my intentions. Besides, I went there first, and she wouldn't give me a room because I didn't have luggage."

The girl's eyes widened. "Yeah, that's one of the first things I noticed. Some fellows keep an empty suitcase in their car." She looked around. "Where's *your* car?"

"It's in the shop. I got a young guy to drive me here. That's him, sitting in the truck across the street."

Panic streaked across her face. "Oh, no! Please, don't let him see me." She took off running through the woods back of the motel.

"Hey, what's wrong? Come back! Then the kid jumped out of the truck and ran after her.

Joel didn't understand what just happened. He sat in the truck for fifteen minutes waiting, although he didn't suppose he was in a hurry since he had nowhere to go.

He looked up to see the kids coming down the road, hand-in-hand. She slid in the truck between them, neither saying a word. But something about their demeanor told Joel that whatever their problem was, was about to be worked out. He hoped his problem could be solved as quickly.

The kid drove him back to Sam's Body Shop. The metal door was open, and he could see his red convertible inside. He jumped out of the truck, just as the mechanic was pulling the car out front. He saw Joel, and yelled, "It's good as new."

"I came by earlier and you were closed."

"Yeah, sorry about that. Wife called and needed me to pick up my kid. I wasn't gone more than twenty minutes. Sorry, you caught me while I was out."

"Doesn't matter. All that matters is that you have my car running again. Where's the nearest pay phone? I need to call my office."

The guy pointed him to the corner across the street.

When Peggy answered, he said, "I didn't know if you'd be there or not."

Her voice was cool. "I work here."

"Yeah. Uh, about what I said before I left. I'm sorry, sweetheart. You know I've been stressed out, lately. Pay no mind to what I say."

"So, when do you plan to return?"

"That's the thing. I haven't found the client I've been looking for."

"Joel, your client left word for you to call her."

"What? No. I'm sure you're wrong. Besides, I don't believe I mentioned her name."

"You didn't. Frank did."

"I see. So, what did she say?"

"She wants you to call her at this number." He pulled out a pencil and jotted it down. "Thanks, sweetheart."

"One more thing, Joel. I'm your secretary, not your sweetheart. Please refrain from referring to me with such an affectionate term."

"Whatever." He didn't know what got her feathers ruffled, but she'd be over it by the time he got home. He pulled out more change and dialed the number that Peggy gave him. When someone answered saying it was the hospital waiting room, his heart did a cartwheel. He asked for Ramona and heard them call her name. Seconds later, she was on the phone. She told him about Deuce, which didn't surprise him at all. The kid was trying to get Mona's attention, and obviously he succeeded. But what she said next couldn't have been more of a surprise.

"Joel, I've been thinking about it, and if you still want to marry me, I'm willing. Deuce needs a man's guidance. I can't do this alone."

He swallowed hard. "Oh, darling, you don't know how happy you've made me."

"I hate to have to uproot Deuce from school. He loves it here in Jinx Bay, but I'll have to make him understand that it's for his sake that I'm doing this."

"You're in Jinx Bay? But I went there looking for you. I couldn't find you."

"I'm the bookkeeper at the Fish Camp. Deuce will be discharged in the morning, and I'll give a two-week's notice at work."

"It's not necessary that you give such a long notice. Come on back to Eufaula. Tomorrow."

"I can't do that to Boyd—my boss."

"Well, for goodness sake, Mona, two weeks is ridiculous. I need you to come back."

"I'm sorry, Joel. You'll need to wait."

"Fine. Just come as soon as you can. I miss you, honey. I'll get my secretary to call the preacher at the First Church and let him know we'll need the church available for the wedding. Peggy can call the florist and get them to decorate. Oh, sweetheart, you've made me a happy man."

"Hold on, Joel. You're jumping the gun. I don't want a big wedding."

"Oh, it won't be big, but I have important clients, who will be expecting an invitation to a wedding, once they find out we're getting married."

She sucked in a heavy breath. "I wish we didn't have to."

"Honey, I wouldn't ask you to do this, if it wasn't important to me. We'll go on a cruise for our honeymoon. How does that sound?"

"A honeymoon? I'm afraid that's not possible."

"Why not?"

"Deuce has to be in school."

"I'm sure my secretary wouldn't mind him staying with her until we return. She only lives a couple of blocks from the school."

"You don't understand. The kid has been through so much, there's no way I could go away and leave him."

CHAPTER 28

Gussie Jones was waiting outside Joel's office Monday morning when Peggy showed up for work.

Peggy unlocked the door and sighed, knowing this was not going to be a good day. "What can I help you with Mrs. Jones?"

"You can't help me, young woman. I didn't come to see you. I'm here to see Joel. You keep telling me he's not here when I call, but I know he's purposely ignoring my calls."

"You're wrong, ma'am. I've told you he's off on business and I don't know when to expect him back. Maybe I can help, if you'd like to tell me what you need. Please have a seat."

"I'll tell you what I need, but I don't see how you can do anything about it. I need Theodore's will to be executed so that I can put Rose Trellis on the market and get out of this God-forsaken town. I hate it and everyone who lives here. I've never been so ready to leave a place in my life, and Joel is dragging his feet."

"I realize it may seem that way to you, but I assure you that you are the reason Joel is not here."

Gussie's brow furrowed. "I thought as much. I knew he was avoiding me."

"Oh, you misunderstood. He's not avoiding you. He's trying to find the daughter-in-law and grandson to give them notice to show up for the reading of the Will."

"Well, I know Theodore said that grandson of his was to get that old truck, but he has it already, so I see no reason they'd have to be present."

"I don't understand, either, but then I'm only the secretary and not the attorney. I'm sure there's a legal reason for it."

Gussie seemed to calm down, once she was convinced Joel wasn't giving her the runaround. "Well, what you're telling me is exactly what Frank Jinright—he's the executor of the estate—has told me, so I reckon I've got no choice but to wait. It's just that I've heard from my old high school sweetheart. He's recently divorced. To tell the truth I don't know how he lived with that mousy little wife of his for forty-six years. He's wanting me to hurry and sell Rose Trellis and move back to Satsuma, where we grew up."

"It sounds as if the romance may have rekindled. Am I right?"

Gussie grinned. "To tell the truth, it didn't have to be rekindled. The flame never went out. Not that either of us was ever unfaithful, mind you. But I never stopped thinking about him, not for a single day, and he says he's felt the same way about me." She picked her pocketbook up from off the floor and stood. "I'm sorry to have bothered you, young lady. But I'm glad to find out that Joel is working on my case. I just hope he finds that boy and gets him here so we can close this thing out."

"Yes ma'am. I'll relay your message as soon as Joel returns."

****

Ronald was on his way to New Orleans for his final visit. He knew the plastic surgeon would be pleased with the results.

The more he thought about what Frank said about Joel, the more confused he became. It was hard to believe that his lifelong friend could be the shady character Frank painted him out to be. But then Deuce appeared to have the same reaction. Was he sending Mona and Deuce into a web they'd never be free from?

He couldn't take that chance. But would Mona hate him when she discovered he'd been alive for fifteen years without telling her? Could she possibly understand that it was for her sake and for Deuce that he did what he did? Or would she welcome him with open arms and tell him that she never stopped loving him? Was it too much to hope for? Was he only letting himself build things up in his mind? How would Deuce react when he discovered the lie? He seems to idolize the father he's never known. Will the truth be too traumatic for him to comprehend?

Once he arrived at the hospital and the doctor walked in and took a look at him, Ronald knew it wasn't just wishful thinking on his part. He could tell by the doctor's reaction that he couldn't have been more pleased with his work.

He handed Ronald a mirror. "Tell me, sir, have you ever seen a better-looking fellow? Didn't I tell you that once the swelling went down, you'd look like a new man?"

Ronald glared at his reflection. His lip quivered. "But you were wrong, doc. The man looking back at me looks like a fellow that I knew fifteen years ago. It's remarkable."

"Ronald, may I give you a bit of advice?"

"Sure."

"For fifteen years, you've tried to hide because you felt people judged you by the scars they could see. The truth is, the people who matter never judge a person by their outward appearance, but by the heart. From what you've told me about your wife, I believe she would've loved you if you had no face. It wasn't her or your son who rejected you because of the scars you bore, but it was you who pulled away. I've fixed the outward man. It's up to you to help the inward man to see yourself as whole and worthy to be loved.

"You don't understand, doc. Maybe you're right and Mona would've accepted me just as I was. And maybe Deuce could've loved me. It's hard for me to comprehend, since I couldn't love myself, but the truth is, I did pull away and there's no changing the past. And now, my wife is about to marry a fellow who was my best friend, growing up. The thing that hurts most is that I encouraged him to marry her. But I've since learned things about him that make me believe Mona could be making a terrible mistake if she goes through with the wedding—yet, there's nothing I can do about it, now."

"And that hurts you that she could be ruining her life?"

Ronald grimaced. "Naturally."

"Where?"

"What do you mean, where?"

"I'm asking where it hurts you. Your eyes? Your nose? Your lips?"

"Are you kidding?" Thrusting his hand to his heart, he said, "It tears me up inside to think I could be the one sending her into a bad situation."

The doctor continued his peculiar query. "So, the pain has nothing to do with your face. Are you saying it breaks your heart?"

"Yes." Making no attempts to hide his irritation, Ronald said, "Why are you having such a hard time understanding?"

"Oh, I understand perfectly. It's you who needs to understand. The Bible says, 'As a man thinketh in his heart, so is he.' I'm just trying to get a better glimpse into your heart." Ronald, you allowed facial scars to define you, yet, you have the same loving heart that your wife fell in love with. Go home. I have a feeling she'll be as delighted to see you as the father of the Prodigal Son was to see his beloved child return."

CHAPTER 29

Frank walked into Joel's office with a box of doughnuts and handed to Peggy.

She opened the box and swooned. "Aww, my favorite. Thank you. But Joel isn't in, and I don't expect him back today."

"I didn't come to see Joel. I came to see you, Peggy."

"Oh? Then, I hope I can help you."

"I hope you can, too."

"What's up, Frank? You're acting a bit peculiar, even for you."

"If I am, it's because I'm nervous."

"Oh? Does it have anything to do with the case you and Joel are working on together?"

"Not really." He took a seat in Joel's swivel desk chair. "Would you mind making a pot of coffee to go with these doughnuts? I think I may need the nourishment to get up the nerve to say what's on my mind."

"Oh, my. This does sound serious." She walked over, picked up the percolator and proceeded to make coffee.

She thought it odd that Frank wasn't carrying on his usual foolishness. She'd never seen him like this. When the coffee finished perking, she couldn't hold her tongue any longer. "Frank, has something happened to Joel and you're hesitating to tell me?"

His brow furrowed. "No. It has nothing to do with Joel. You really love him, don't you?"

When she didn't answer, he sipped his coffee, took a bite out of a chocolate doughnut, then tossed the remainder in the trash. "I suppose I should go."

"But you haven't told me why you came."

"It wouldn't do any good."

"Frank, you're talking in circles. Please tell me why you're here."

His chest expanded when he drew a deep breath. "I'm here because I'm in love with you, Peg. I love you so much I can't sleep at night. Hilarious, isn't it? Now that I've said what I came to say, I'll leave."

Her mouth gaped open. "Frank, you aren't kidding. Are you?"

"I wish I were. I wish I didn't feel this way. Surely, you've known it for months. I haven't tried to hide it."

"I knew you were flirting with me, but I never took you seriously."

"I know. You can't get past your feelings for Joel, and he

doesn't deserve you, Peggy. I'm not saying that I do. You deserve better than either of us."

"Frank, I haven't taken you seriously because you're a married man. If you weren't, I would've looked at you differently. You're handsome, funny, and kind. But I'm not interested in breaking up marriages."

"What? Who told you that I was married. Was it Joel?"

She rolled her eyes. "I didn't have to hear it from Joel. You've often mentioned your wife. I'm not stupid."

He rubbed the back of his neck. "My wife! And you say I've mentioned her? Pray tell what did I say about her?"

"If you're trying to be funny, you aren't succeeding. You're just acting stupid. You stood here and told me all about you and Connie taking your daughter to Europe to school."

He jerked back. "What? And you thought Connie was my wife?"

"She's not?"

"Of course not."

"Your mistress?"

"Don't be absurd. Connie is my sister. We've raised our little sister Susan, since the death of our parents." Frank told her all about the fire, and that Connie had been in love with a fellow for three years but had waited until Susan graduated before agreeing to marry him. They were planning a spring wedding. "I can't believe Joel hasn't told you my story."

"No. He thinks you're married."

"You're wrong. He knows everything. He just didn't want you to know, since it would interfere with his plans."

The phone rang, and Peggy answered.

"Hi, Peg, It's me. I have a favor to ask."

She listened as Joel spouted off a long rigamarole about how he never meant to fall in love with Mona, but now that he had, he needed for her to call the church and the florist and make arrangements for their wedding.

He said, "This doesn't mean that things will change between you and me, Peg. In fact, I plan to give you a much deserved raise. You've always been there for me when I needed you."

"Joel, you're wrong. Everything between you and me is about to change. I hope your new wife has secretarial skills because you're gonna need a new secretary."

"Aww, honey, I was afraid you'd be upset, but once you learn that I mean what I say about things staying the same between us, you'll realize you have nothing to worry about."

"I already realize I have nothing to worry about, Joel." She hung up and glanced up at Frank.

He said, "I could hear the conversation."

"Do you need a secretary, because I'll be looking for a new job—just as soon as I finish this lemon-filled doughnut."

"Peggy, do you really think Joel will be willing to let you go?"

"He has no choice. I don't know why it's taken me so long."

"If you're expecting me to say that I'm sorry Joel is marrying someone else, you'll be disappointed, because I'm not sorry.

Getting him out of your life is what I've hoped for, but I'm not sure it will ever happen. He won't let you go, even if he does get married. He's an idiot for not loving you the way you should be loved."

"That's where you're wrong, Frank. I'm done."

"Does that mean I have a chance with you?"

"Oh, Frank. I don't deserve you. You don't know what all I've done."

"I think I do, but we all deserve a second chance. I want to be your second chance and I hope you'll be mine."

"No, you think you know, but you don't. Not really. Joel insisted I lie to you and tell you that we didn't marry the week we went away. But we did. Then as soon as we got home, he demanded that we get a divorce, and pretend the whole crazy thing never happened. I assumed he was having a nervous breakdown, since he was acting so loopy."

"It was no breakdown, Peggy. It was a new revelation."

"I don't understand."

Frank told her to pull Theodore's will. She read it over carefully. Her jaw dropped. "So, Mr. Theo's daughter-in-law inherits everything?"

"That's correct. So now, do you understand why Joel is in a hurry to get married? He wants to be married to her when the will is read, so the property will be jointly owned."

Peggy told Frank about the gambling debt. Looking back, she realized he felt it necessary to marry her for her money, but then discovering he'd be getting even more by marrying Ramona Jones, he had to first get the divorce. "Why was I so stupid that I couldn't see him for what he was, Frank?"

"Joel is smooth. He has a lot of people fooled." He looked at his watch. "I have a ten o'clock appointment, so I need to get back to the office. I haven't asked a girl for a date in almost eighteen years, so I'm not sure I know how it's done nowadays, but—"

She thought it cute the way he shifted nervously from one foot to the other. "What time shall I be ready?"

His eyes lit up. "Seven o'clock?"

"I'll be looking forward to it."

"Connie will be giddy when she discovers I have a date. She's tried for years to get me to ask a lady out."

"Why haven't you?"

"I was waiting for someone like you." Deep dimples sank into his cheeks when his lip curled. "Gotta go. See you tonight."

CHAPTER 30

Ronald stopped by the hospital cafeteria in New Orleans to eat lunch before getting on the road. He looked across the room and saw a fisherman that worked on one of his boats, sitting there with his daughter.

"Hey, Carlos, I hope you're just here for Margo's checkup. Nothing wrong, I hope."

The big man stood and held out his hand. He attempted to hide the tears welling in his eyes. "Much prayer, needed, Bossman. My little girl's tumor is giving her big trouble. Operation scheduled in the morning. You pray for her, yes?"

"You bet I'll pray for her."

Ronald walked over to his table, picked up his tray and took it over to sit with Carlos and Margo.

Margo said, "Mr. Skip, you sure look a lot different than you did before. I wish I could have the same doctor you had. I can see he's very good."

Ronald placed his hand on top of hers. "My doctor is good in his field, but yours is good in his. I know Dr. Rodolph, and he's considered one of the top surgeons in the United States."

Carlos said, "Bossman, I won't ever be able to thank you for all you've done for us. I would never have been able to afford the doctor bills."

"I'm glad I could help."

"You going home, now?"

"I was, but I think I'll stick around and keep you company tomorrow until this beautiful daughter of yours comes out of surgery."

Carlos grabbed his hand and squeezed. "You're a good man, Skipper."

"And you're a hard worker, Carlos. I'm blessed to have you on my team."

"Ah, but fishing don't seem like work. I love what I do. And Margo likes living in Jinx Bay, don't you, precious?"

"I do. More than ever, now."

Skip grinned. "Do I detect a blush on those pretty cheeks? A boy couldn't be the reason for you loving it more than ever, could it?"

Carlos said, "You guessed it. My Margo is in love. But I think he's a good boy."

"Does his father work at the Fish Camp?"

"No. I don't think he has a father." Then snapping his fingers,

Carlos said, "Oh, I remember now. You know the kid. He was with Margo one day when she went to meet me at the dock. You told me, 'He a good kid.'"

Margo said, "His name is Deuce. His mother is the bookkeeper at the camp, and he goes to my school."

Skip nodded. "Yes, I think I remember seeing you with the boy. So, you like him?"

She grinned. "I like him a lot. Mr. Skip, if I don't . . . well, if I happen not to . . ." She glanced at her father, then seeing the moisture in his eyes, she placed her hand on top of his.

Carlos said, "Go ahead, baby. Say whatever it is you want Bossman to know."

"I just want Deuce to know that I've never felt this way toward any boy, and that if I don't make it through the surgery, that I don't want him to grieve because I'm gone but tell him I want him to be glad that he allowed me to know what real love feels like."

Skip said, "I have no reason to doubt that the tumor will be removed and that you'll come through the surgery just fine. But if it gives you a sense of peace to know that should it become necessary, then I will deliver your message. I promise. But I have a strong feeling, you'll be going home and telling him in person, whatever you want him to hear."

"Thank you." She turned to her father. "Papa, would you please get me the pencil and paper out of the drawer?" Carlos opened the drawer and handed it to her. The two men watched as she wrote something on the paper, then handed to Skip. "It's not that I didn't trust you to remember what I said, but I wouldn't want Deuce to think you were making up something to make him feel better. I want him to know that the words are coming from me."

****

The doctor released Deuce to go home, but Ramona decided it was too soon to break the news to her son that she planned to marry Joel and they'd be moving back to Alabama. Now that he and his little girlfriend had apparently broken up, she was sure it would make it much easier for him to leave.

On the way home, he said, "Mama, did I tell you that I found out the truth?"

"The truth?"

"About Margo."

"I believe you did. I'm sorry, she broke up with you, sweetheart, but you'll fall in love lots of times before you're grown."

His forehead creased into a frown. "Did you? Fall in love lots of times, I mean?"

He knew the answer. "You're right. I didn't. But I'm the exception to the rule. I found my true love before I ever dated another guy, but as a rule, kids fall in love dozens of times."

"Not me. But that's what I'm trying to tell you. She didn't break up with me. My doctor said she is a patient of his, and that her father has taken her to New Orleans to the hospital."

"Oh, my goodness. Whatever for?"

"He says she has a tumor in her head that's causing the headaches. According to him, she'll be having surgery to remove it, and then the headaches will go away. It was the tumor that was causing her to act strange. I thought it was me. I hope she doesn't have to stay long. And Mama, please don't tell her what I did. It was a stupid thing to do, and she'd feel responsible if she finds out I did it because of her."

"Deuce. You are right. It was a very stupid thing for you to do. Please promise me that you'll never do such a horrible thing again. Can you imagine how devastated I would be if anything ever happened to you?"

"I understand. I was only thinking about how I felt at the time. I'm glad you came home and found me when you did. I don't want to die, Mama. I really don't."

As soon as they pulled onto Cannery Road, He opened the door to the car while it was still moving.

His mother yelled, "What are you doing?"

He jumped out and ran toward the door to #5. Ramona stopped the car and watched him slowly turn back around. With a wry grin, he said, "I forgot. She's in New Orleans. I know you need to go on to work, so I'll walk to the house."

Ramona drove to the office. She walked in and saw Boyd sitting at her desk.

He reared back in the swivel chair. "Well, come in, sweet lady. Are you ever a sight for sore eyes. I trust you got Deuce home, and everything is gonna be okay?"

"Deuce will be fine, but I'm not sure I will be. I had quite a scare. I would never have imagined him wanting to kill himself, but he thinks he's in love, and love can make a person do strange things."

"Ain't that the truth. I'm just glad everything turned out okay. But I can only imagine how frightening it must've been."

"More than anyone can imagine, unless they've been through it. And that's why I need to tell you something that won't be easy for me to say."

He pursed his lips. "I don't know that I want to hear it. I don't like the way you sound."

"Boyd, I appreciate you giving me this job. But I feel it will be in Deuce's best interest if we pack up and head back to Eufaula."

"I hate to hear that, Ramona. Do you mind sharing with me your reason for leaving? I suppose it's for the sake of your son. It's hard changing schools at his age. I'm sure he'll be glad to get back home to his friends and familiar places."

"No, in fact I dread telling him that we're leaving. He thinks he's in love, so I'm sure you can imagine how leaving is gonna complicate things. But if I stay, I'm afraid things will become even more complicated. It frightens me to think of trying to raise a teenage boy alone. I feel if we'd had a man around, perhaps Deuce would've opened up and told him how he felt—things that a boy might not be able to talk about with his mother. So, I plan to marry a man in Eufaula."

"Well, congratulations. I didn't know there was a man in your life. That's wonderful. I never felt you belonged in this place. I'll sure miss the ray of sunshine you bring into this room. I'll have a hard time replacing you, Ramona. You're the best bookkeeper I've ever had."

The next morning, Deuce was up and dressed for school, without having to be called.

He sat down at the breakfast table and Ramona was surprised to see he had such a hearty appetite.

"The pancakes are delicious, Mama." He gulped the mild down from the quart bottle. "I expect Margo should be getting ready for surgery about now, wouldn't you think?"

"Seems likely. Doctors normally want to get an early start. You seem to be in good spirits."

"I'm glad she's getting help. The headaches were so bad they were making her throw up. I just wish I could be there for her. How long do you think it will be before they'll release her to come home?"

"I have no idea, son. I'd think it's a rather delicate surgery, so they may keep her for a good while."

His face revealed his disappointment. "I suppose you're right. I sure hope they give her enough pain medicine, so she won't suffer, but I don't imagine any pain could be worse than what she went through earlier. I don't know where I got the crazy notion she was breaking up with me. I know now, she didn't want me around to see how bad she hurt. I wish I had been more understanding."

"Honey, I think you're right about her not wanting you to see her in such pain."

"Mama, I know we don't have much money, but do you think you could let me have enough to buy her some flowers when she comes home?"

"Of course. Now, I need to get to work, and you need to get to school, so hurry and finish your breakfast. I've written you an excuse to give your teacher, telling why you were absent."

His jaw dropped. "You didn't! Did you? Oh, Mama, I don't want anyone to know."

"Honey, I only said you were sick. I didn't go into detail."

He blew out a lungful of air. "Thank goodness." He grabbed the paper, folded it, and stuck it in his pocket.

****

At four o'clock, Boyd walked into the office, and said, "Ramona, would you please call J.W. at the Funeral Home and ask him to prepare to go to the hospital in New Orleans."

"Did someone die?"

"Yeah. I don't know if you've ever met Carlos Lopez, but—"

"Lopez? You don't mean . . ." She gasped for air. "No. No, it can't be. Please tell me it isn't his daughter."

"I wish I could say that it isn't. The doctor just called me and said the tumor was too close to the brain. He said he wouldn't have taken a chance on operating, except that she could only have lived a few weeks at the most without it. He felt it was worth the risk, but she died four hours into the surgery. So you've met Margo?"

She nodded. "She's the girl my son is in love with. The reason he tried to take his life."

"Forget making the call. I'll do it. You need to get home and be with your son, so you can tell him before he hears it from someone else. It won't take long for the word to get around the camp. Everyone was crazy about that kid. She grew up here and would get so excited when she'd see her daddy coming in on the boat. She'll be missed. This is gonna be so hard for Carlos. He adored her."

CHAPTER 31

Deuce ran out to the truck as soon as he heard his mama drive up. "Why are you home so early? You didn't get fired, did you?"

"No, sweetheart. It's worse than that. Come on inside. I need to talk to you."

"What's happened, Mama?"

"Sit down on the sofa. I have some sad news." Ramona broke into sobs. "Oh, Deuce, I wish I didn't have to tell you this."

"Please, Mama. Whatever it is, you and I will work it out together. Like we always do. I'm here for you."

Hearing her son wanting to console her, when she didn't have the courage or the words to console him broke her heart. "Deuce, there's no easy way to say this, but "Margo didn't make it."

His eyes came together in a fixed frown. "What do you mean she didn't make it? They didn't operate today?"

"They did, but honey, I've just learned that she didn't live through it, but according to the doctor, she couldn't have survived without it."

His reaction was not what she expected. She thought he'd go to pieces hearing the news. Instead, he sat there as if to be taking it all in. "Deuce, say something."

"What can I say, Mama? She's gone. Nothing I can say will bring her back."

His voice was low and subdued. "I think I'll take a walk. I need time to think."

"Deuce, please, don't go. I'm afraid for you."

He turned around and wrapped his arms around her. "I don't plan to pull another stunt like the one I just pulled. Don't worry, Mama. I'll be okay. I need to get alone for a while. Would you mind if I took the truck and drove around until I can absorb what I've just been told?"

She wanted to say no. She wanted to keep an eye on him and not let him out of her sight, but her better judgment told her it was best to give him that space. "Sure, hon. Take the truck."

"Thanks. I love you, Mama."

Ramona couldn't catch her breath for crying. "I love you, too, my sweet Deuce. Please come back to me."

He took his thumb and lifted her head until their gaze locked. "I made you a promise. I won't break it."

She watched him walk out the door, but the minute she heard the truck crank, she questioned her wisdom. It was getting dark outside, and she didn't like the thought of him driving at night. She should've been firm. Ramona now understood, more than ever, that Deuce needed a man's guidance. Joel would be good for him. He'd be good for them both.

Deuce drove straight to Skip's house and was disappointed when he realized the car was gone. Driving away, he saw Skip walking down the road.

He yelled, "Hey, Deuce. I was praying you'd come. Don't leave."

"Praying? You act as if you were expecting me, but that's impossible. I don't even know why I'm here, except I felt if I couldn't talk to someone my heart would explode."

Skip wrapped his arms around his son. "I gather from your demeanor that you've already heard the tragic news."

Deuce nodded and broke down. "I loved her so much, Skip. No one will ever know how much. I know you probably think we were too young to know what real love is, but I'll never feel the same toward another girl. I didn't know I was coming here until I turned down the road. I needed someone to help me clear my head. Someone besides Mama. Not that she doesn't listen. She does. But she gets too emotional when she knows I'm hurting and instead of hearing what I'm trying to tell her, she's spending her time babying me."

"I understand. There are things you need to say, and I was close by."

"No, it's not just that you were close by. Aww, shucks, I can't explain something that I don't understand myself. But it's almost

271

as if instead of me driving my truck here, it drove me here. Why did God have to take her from me, Skip? Why?"

"Deuce, I wish I had all the answers for you, but I don't. But I do know that God loves you and that He has a plan for your life. Don't give up. I was there at the river when Margo was baptized. There's no doubt in my mind that she's happier now than she's ever been. I know from hearing Carlos speak of her mother, that they're together. So, although I know the separation is terribly hard on you, just remember, it doesn't have to be permanent. One day, you can be with her again." Then he said, "Oh, I have something very important to give you. I almost forgot."

"What is it?"

Skip reached in his pocket and pulled out the paper that Margo had given him.

Deuce slowly unfolded it, and read it aloud: *My dearest Deuce, I had a most peculiar dream the other night, and I can't explain, but I really don't think I'll be going home to Jinx Bay again. So, if I'm right, and I don't make it through the surgery, I don't want you to grieve for me. God put you in my life so that I could know what true love feels like. That was my prayer the day the doctor first told me I had cancer, two years ago. He heard my prayer. I'll be going into surgery in a few minutes, and if I should die before I wake, I'll be with my precious Lord and my sweet Mama. But if I make it through surgery, I'll be with you and Papa. I love you all, so very much. As the apostle Paul once said, to live is Christ, but to die is gain. I feel the same way. I love you, and I'm so glad God chose you for me.*

Margo.

Deuce folded the paper and stuck it in his pocket. "I'm hungry. I have enough money for a couple of burgers. Would you like to go to Lulu's with me?"

"Sure. I could eat something. I haven't eaten since breakfast. Will your mother be worried about you?"

"I don't think so. I told her I needed time to sort out my feelings, but we can go see if she'd like to go with us if you want to."

Skip shook his head. "Not tonight. Let's let it be a male thing."

"Yeah. I like that."

As they sat eating their burgers, Skip said, "Deuce, if you should need someone to talk to, I understand what it's like to lose the one you love."

"I had a feeling you understood. I'm sorry for your loss. Did you grieve for her?"

"Every hour of every day since she's been gone."

"I'm trying not to grieve, since it was Margo's last request, but—" He bit his quivering lip. "But it's just so hard. So very hard. Ya know?" Then, answering his own question, he said, "I'm sorry. Of course, you know."

After finishing their meal, Deuce said, "It's dark. Mama will be getting frantic."

Skip drove him back to pick up his truck. Deuce got in, stuck his head out the window and said, "Now I know why I needed to come here. You had Margo's letter, and I needed to hear what she wanted to tell me. Do you think God led me here?"

"I don't know. What do you think?"

"I think he did."

Skip rubbed his hand across his mouth. "You're looking at me strangely. Do I have food on my face?"

"No sir, but I didn't want to mention it, but I gotta know. What happened to you, Skip?"

"What do you mean?"

"You had really bad . . . uh . . . I mean, you look—"

"Different? I understand what you're trying to say, Deuce. I was badly injured many years ago and wound up badly scarred. Then, two years ago, a friend told me about a doctor in New Orleans who had a new technique for facial reconstruction. I guess he needed a guinea pig, and my buddy talked me into letting him try out his skills on me. So, for two years, I've been going through extensive surgeries. I had just finished the last one the night you and your mama had the wreck."

"Agreeing to let someone cut on your face must've been scary."

"Nah, the way I figured it, I had nothing to lose. In fact, because of the way I looked, I had already lost everything."

"I guess you're referring to your girl."

"Yes, but I lost even more. I decided that if allowing the doctor to practice his new technique on me could possibly help other wounded soldiers in the years to come, then perhaps my life would have meant something."

"Are you saying you got your face blown off in the war?"

The corner of Skip's lip curled. "Not exactly blown off, but rearranged, that's for sure."

"I hope you don't mind me staring, but you look so different. In fact, you remind me of someone, but I can't recall who it is."

"You'd better get on home, kiddo."

Deuce tried all the way home to remember why Skip looked so familiar. When he walked in the door, he could see that his mama was trying hard to pretend she hadn't worried. "Sorry, I stayed so long, Mama."

She put her arms around his neck. "Honey, I can't imagine how hard this has been for you. But I'm so proud of how you're handling it. If you need to talk, I'm here for you."

"Thanks. I had someone to talk with. I went to see Skip."

"I suppose it should hurt me that you didn't come to me, but actually, I'm glad you went to Skip."

"You are? Why? Is there something you know about him that you haven't told me?"

She shook her head, dismissively. "Now what would I know that you don't know? I'm just saying that I hate that you haven't had a male influence since your Granddaddy died, and you were accustomed to having Daddy Theo around to give you guidance."

"How do you feel about Skip?"

"I feel he's a good, gentle man. I know I was suspicious of him in the beginning, but that was before I really got to know him."

"You didn't like him because of those awful scars. Isn't that right?"

"That sounds so heartless, Deuce."

"But isn't it the truth?"

She hesitated to answer. Was it the truth? She didn't like to think of herself as being cold and unsympathetic to someone left disfigured by a horrible accident, and even worse was knowing that it was how her son viewed her. But wouldn't any woman have been frightened by having a scary looking man pick them up and carry them to a shack in the middle of nowhere? "Deuce, don't you see? Once I got to know him, I liked him. I liked him a lot."

"You did?"

"Yes. Why are you questioning me?"

"Just thinking about how I'd feel if my face was scarred and someone I liked a lot was frightened of me."

"I didn't say he liked me a lot. I said I liked him."

"But he does. I mean, he did like you. I could tell."

"Well, I'm not so sure either of us were comfortable in the beginning, but I think we both calmed down a bit on the trip, after we became better acquainted. But enough of this chatter. I have several items I need to rinse out before going to bed, so I'd better get busy, or they won't have time to dry before morning."

Ramona was out on the porch washing out a few

undergarments, when Deuce walked out.

"Mama, there is something I'd like to ask you."

"Anything, sweetheart."

"Do you still keep that picture of my daddy under your pillow every night?"

Her eyes narrowed. "I do, but I've been thinking about that lately. I think it's time I gave it to you."

"Why would you do that?"

"Maybe it's time I moved on."

"You're gonna marry Joel, aren't you?"

"Honey, let's don't go into that now. You have enough on your mind without adding to it."

"I know you are. That's the only reason you want to get rid of my daddy's picture."

"Deuce, I didn't say I wanted to get rid of it."

"You didn't have to. For as long as I can remember, you've pulled it out every night before going to sleep and kissed it. Now, you want to give it away, because you know Joel would tear it up and throw the pieces in the garbage."

"Honey, you are so wrong about Joel. He and Ronald were very close. He loved your father, but to be fair to him, if I did marry him—and I said if—I can understand it might be hurtful for his wife to be kissing a picture of his best friend before they go to sleep at night." She chuckled, as if she were teasing. But was she?

"I want it." He walked back in the house, jerked the pillow off her bed, then flopped down on the couch with the picture and stared at the handsome man in his new army uniform. After several minutes, he broke down in sobs.

His mother slid near him and pulled his head over to her shoulder. "Go ahead and get it out, Deuce. I understand."

"No, mama. You don't understand and neither do I. The man in this picture is my daddy."

She glanced down at the 8x10 photo of the handsome soldier. "Yes, he is. I miss him, Deuce. I'll always miss him."

"But I know where he is."

"Yes, we do, sweetheart. He's with your precious Margo."

"You're wrong, Mama. He isn't."

"Deuce! Why would you say such a thing?"

"Because Margo is in Heaven and Daddy is not."

"Son, I know you're hurting, but that's an awful thing to say about your father." Ramona didn't know whether to scold him or hug him. Perhaps it was normal teenage behavior for a kid to lash out and want to hate his father for not being there for him. "Deuce, honey, let me assure you that when he died, your daddy heard the Father say, 'Well done, my good and faithful servant.' I know that I know that I know that Ronald is in Heaven. He surrendered his life to the Lord, even before we were married. He told me all about it. His salvation is secure and one day we can be with him."

"I've already been with him. Mama, I'm trying to tell you that he's alive and I know where he is."

Ramona bit her bottom lip. Was losing Margo causing this irrational behavior? She sucked in a deep breath. In a low, calm voice, she said, "No, Deuce. Your grief is affecting your thinking, son. Your daddy died before you were even born."

"No, Mama. I know you believe that, but I just talked to him this evening. He doesn't know that I know who he is. I had to be sure, first. But now, I am."

It was as if a lit cannon in her head suddenly exploded. She jumped up and covered her ears. "Deuce Jones, stop it. I can't take any more of your nonsense."

"You don't have to believe me, but I know the truth. Goodnight, Mama."

****

The following morning, neither Deuce nor Ramona mentioned the incident of the night before, although an elephant sitting between them at the table couldn't have been more obvious than the cause of their contention.

Even if she had to keep him home from school another day, she couldn't allow him to leave the house in such a frame of mind. She was the mother, for crying out loud. It was up to her to set ground rules. To allow Deuce to continue fabricating scenarios that felt comfortable to him would only lead to deeper emotional problems.

He took the last swallow of milk, then jumped up from the table and mumbled, "Enjoyed my breakfast."

"If you're calling a bite of toast and a glass of milk, breakfast, then perhaps you did. You haven't touched your scrambled eggs. Why don't you sit back down and eat."

"I've had plenty. I don't wanna be late for school."

"Deuce, this is not a suggestion. I'm telling you to sit back down."

"Why? I told you I don't want the eggs."

"I have something important to tell you."

He groaned and plopped back down in his chair. "What?"

"I don't think it will come as a surprise to you, but Joel and I are getting married. I know that's not what you want to hear, and I'm sure you don't understand, but it's for your sake as well as mine."

He yelled, "Well, don't do me any favors. I didn't choose him. You did."

She had to be firm. For too long, she had skirted around the issue. "Exactly. And my mind is made up. I've already accepted his proposal. We'll be moving back to Eufaula, as soon as I work out my notice at work."

"You can't get married. You already have a husband."

Ramona's throat tightened. "I had a husband, but he's dead, Deuce. You know he is, so stop the nonsense."

When he jumped up from the table, she said, "I'm not through, yet. Sit back down."

"There's nothing more to say, Mama. You've made it plain. You plan to marry Joel. Well, I'll make it plain, too. I won't be going with you. I plan to live with my daddy, if he'll have me."

CHAPTER 32

Peggy closed the office and left for Montgomery after receiving a phone call that her beloved Uncle Louie was in the hospital and had asked for her. She arrived at the hospital and hurried down the hall and took the elevator to the third floor, then knocked lightly on #314.

A sharply dressed elderly man eased the door open and said, "You must be Peggy."

"Yes." She peeked around him and saw her precious uncle lying under an oxygen tent.

The man ushered her in, and said, "Louie, she's here."

He opened his eyes. "Hi, sugar. Sorry to interrupt your day, but I needed to see you."

She reached for his hand. "You can interrupt my day anytime you like, Uncle Louie. Nothing is more important to me than you. What can I do for you?"

The short, pudgy fellow who let her in said, "Louie, perhaps you should not try to talk too much. Would you like for me to tell her why you asked her here?"

"Please."

"Mrs. Granger, I am not only Louie's attorney, but I'm a lifelong friend."

Peggy thought it ironic that hearing him call her Mrs. Granger caused her to cringe, when for four years she had dreamed of having Joel's last name.

He said, "Louie and I grew up together and were roommates at the University, many, many years ago. My name is—"

She interrupted. "You're Shorty, aren't you? Uncle Louie has told me all about the capers you two got into growing up. So nice to finally meet you, Mr. Appleton."

He chuckled. "Call me, Shorty, please. I've heard a lot about you, also, and now that I meet you, I know there was no exaggeration."

"How long has Uncle Louie been sick?"

"He hasn't been well for several years, but he didn't want me to tell you. However, the doctor told him this morning that if he had anything he needed to tell his family, it would be best to call them in. Being you're the only family he has left, I called you immediately."

"I'm glad you did."

"Louie has shared with me the unethical stunt he cooked up to prevent the divorce. Although I won't go into all that was wrong with such an unscrupulous act by an accomplished attorney, the good news is that he later realized the absurdity of his actions. And with your permission, we've come up with a way to remedy his lack of judgment, if you will agree to our proposal."

She looked down at the frail man lying on the bed. "I'm sorry that I involved you, Uncle Louie. I knew there was nothing you wouldn't do for me, but I never should've asked. I wish now the divorce was real. I've been so foolish."

Louie said, "Shorty, fix it."

"Sure, Buddy. It's as good as done."

Peggy's brow lifted. "Fix it? Fix what?"

"I've had legal divorce papers drawn up. Louie has already signed everything. All you have to do is sign and give them to Joel for his signature. Tell him there was a problem filing the initial divorce papers, and we need his signature on these. He'll assume the papers were sent to him at the office."

"This sounds like the answer to prayer, but how did you know I'd want to sign divorce papers?"

"We didn't. But Louie said after meeting your husband, he was leery of the man. His gut told him to withdraw the bogus divorce papers at that time. However, against his better judgment, he continued with the hoax. He fretted over his actions for days, but when the doctor told him his clock was about to run out, Louie asked me to do a little investigating. The things we uncovered about Joel Gunter were even worse than Louie had suspected. He didn't want to have to tell you what a louse you're married to, but he felt an obligation to let you know what we discovered, but it appears you've already discovered it for yourself."

"Yes."

"So, are you saying you are willing to sign legally binding divorce papers?"

"Not only willing, but eager. I thought Joel was having a mental breakdown and would come to his senses and regret signing divorce papers, knowing we have a baby on the way. But I'm the one who needed to come to her senses. It took me far too long, but once I realized how he was using me, I didn't know how I'd tell him the divorce was a farce without getting Uncle Louie in trouble. Joel is money-hungry and would not only have sued Uncle Louie for all he owns, but he would've destroyed his good name."

"That's not something you have to worry about. I've taken care of it." He flipped to the last page and pointed to a line at the bottom. Are you ready to sign your name?

"And that's all I have to do to dissolve the marriage?"

"Almost."

After signing, she hugged Shorty, then reached for Uncle Louie's bony hand. "Uncle Louie?" She turned and looked at Shorty about the time the door opened, and two nurses rushed in.

Peggy stepped back and whispered, "He's gone."

Shorty took her by the hand and walked her out to the hall. "I've just lost the best friend a fellow could ever wish for. But his prayer was answered. He asked the Lord to allow him to live until you arrived. Thank you for coming so swiftly." They stepped aside when Louie's body was rolled away with a sheet covering his face.

Shorty said, "Let's walk outside and sit on the bench near the water fountain. I have some things to discuss with you."

Peggy blinked hard in an attempt to keep the tears that were gathering in her eyes from spilling onto her face. "I loved him so much. He was my daddy's only brother. They were both good men. Uncle Louie went into law, and daddy became a preacher. Daddy was proud of his older brother. We didn't have much, since daddy was paid mostly in syrup and eggs, but there was a lot of love in our family, and that was worth more to me than money."

Shorty pulled out his handkerchief and wiped Peggy's cheek, then handed it to her. "Louie accumulated a vast amount of wealth through the years, and although he called himself being frugal, I teased him that the word was cheap and not frugal. He guarded his pennies."

"Really? Judging from the little house he lived in, and the old car he drove, I always felt he must've accumulated a ton of debts, due to Aunt Tootsie's automobile accident years ago, which left her crippled. I never wanted to ask."

"The reason Louie had Joel Gunter investigated was because he wanted to make sure that as your husband, he wouldn't steal all your money."

She laughed. "Sweet Uncle Louie. Where did he think I got money from, working as a secretary?"

"I don't think you understand what I'm trying to tell you. Your uncle has left ten percent of his accumulated wealth to his church and the balance to you."

Peggy found it difficult to speak. Then sucking in a lungful of air, she said, "I can't seem to take in what you're saying. I don't know which is harder to believe—that Uncle Louie had money or that he left it to me."

"Well, you can believe both." Shorty reached into his briefcase. "I have the papers with his signature, and now I need mine and yours on the dotted line on the last page." He handed her a number of pages, all stapled together. "You can take time and read them all if you like, but if you trust me and your Uncle Louie, then you can just initial the first eleven pages."

She nodded, picked up the pen and began initialing each page.

Shorty asked if she wanted to make funeral arrangements or if she wanted him to do so.

"Since you live here and have been close to him through the years, would you mind?"

"It will be my privilege. I'll contact you with details." He walked her to her car, then said, "You haven't asked when you'll receive possession of your Uncle's assets."

"I haven't thought about it. It's still hard to believe."

"Well, his request was that nothing be changed into your name until after the divorce is final, but after that happens, everything will be transferred to you. He wanted to be assured that the money he saved for you didn't go to someone else."

Peggy got back to the office and was surprised to find Joel

there.

He said, "Where have you been?"

"I had business to attend to."

"Well, I needed you here."

She pulled papers from her shoulder bag and slipped them in her desk while he was on the phone. When he hung up, she made sure he saw her reach in and pull them out. She handed them to him and said, "Sign this."

He took the pen from her. "What am I signing?"

"It seems there was an error on the divorce papers we signed, and they needed our signature on these."

"Well, of all the incompetent nincompoops. Don't they know the trouble that could've caused? What if I should've married again, not knowing that I was still married to you?"

"Joel, sign your name underneath mine, and I'll get them into the proper hands, so you won't have to worry about Ramona charging you with bigamy."

"Oh, honey, I hope I didn't hurt your feelings. I was just saying—"

"I understood, Joel. No need to explain." She reached in her desk and pulled out a letter and handed to him.

He read it, then looked up and let out a sarcastic chortle. "Another letter of resignation? Sweetheart, how many of these have you written in the past four years? Let's stop the games. You need a job and I need a secretary. I realize things haven't turned out the way we planned, but we're both adults. You and I have a bond that can never be broken." The skin around his eyes tightened as he ripped up the letter. "Now, would you please get Frank on the phone for me?"

"I'll do better than that. I'm meeting him for coffee at the café in a few minutes. What would you like for me to tell him?"

"Not on my time, you aren't."

"Your time? I don't have time for you, Joel. The letter you tore up gave a week's notice, but since it no longer exists, I take it that I'm not bound to the stipulations."

She picked up her shoulder bag and the percolator and slammed the door behind her.

CHAPTER 33

Frank was waiting when Peggy arrived at the café. He stood, pulled out her chair and sucked in a deep breath of air. "How did it go?"

"As of ten minutes ago, I am now unemployed."

Smiling, he said, "That's what I was hoping to hear. How did it take it?"

"He didn't." She told Frank about meeting with Shorty, the death of her Uncle Louie, and the divorce papers.

"And Joel signed them without questioning you?"

"Oh, I gave him a short explanation, but he didn't seem to care. All he was interested in was making sure that he was divorced. He has big plans."

"I know he does. Now that he's found out that Theodore's daughter-in-law is about to inherit a windfall, he won't be able to get to the alter fast enough. He's hoping to marry her before the reading of the will, so that she'll deposit the money into a joint account."

"Well, I could care less what he does, but I do feel sorry for her. She's no more suspecting of his malicious nature than I was for years. Now, looking back, I can't understand how I could've been so blind."

Frank said, "I can't let him do this. She has a son."

"I don't know how you can stop him. He's slick."

"Maybe not as slick as he thinks he is. Peggy, I'd love to spend all day sitting here, looking across the table at your beautiful face, but I have an urgent errand to run. Do you mind?"

"I understand. I don't need to be wasting time. I plan to finish my coffee, but then I have a few resumes I need to deliver. I can't believe Joel practically drained my banking account, but to be rid of him was worth every penny he's taken from me."

He said, "I'll be gone overnight, but I'll call you tomorrow after I return."

She didn't ask questions, although she felt that somehow, someway, he wanted to save the Jones girl from falling into the same trap she almost fell into. It wasn't until after Frank left that she realized how absurd it was for her to fret over a single penny that Joel took from her. With so many other things to think about, the fact that she'd soon have more money than she'd ever had in her life, completely slipped her mind until now. Sweet Uncle Louie. Her heart was touched when Shorty told her that he had lived such a meager life, in order that he could leave her well fixed. But what would she do with so much money? All she had ever cared about was having enough to take care of her needs.

She thought about what Frank said, and knew he was right. Joel would do whatever it took to get access to the Jones girl's fortune. How ironic that if Shorty had not drawn up the divorce papers and if Joel hadn't signed them, he could've had access to Uncle Louie's money. The thought caused her to cringe. But apparently, Uncle Louie took special care to make sure it didn't happen.

****

Frank drove to Jinx Bay and went first to the boats. When he didn't see Ronald there, he drove to his cabin.

Hearing the car drive up, Ronald walked out on the porch. "Hey, what a surprise! To what do I owe this pleasure?"

Frank met him halfway and shook his hand. "If I were to say I was just passing through, would you believe me?"

Ronald laughed. "No, but if that's your best line, it'll suffice. Come on in, you're just in time. I was about to cook a steak, and I happen to have an extra. I hope you haven't had supper."

"As a matter of fact, I haven't, but I wouldn't pass up one of your steaks, even if I'd just got up from the table."

They walked inside, and Ronald plopped two steaks in two separate pans and had them both sizzling at the same time. "Frank, if you've come to try to talk me into going back for the reading of the will, you can think up another subject. That subject is closed."

"Not yet, friend. That's why I'm here."

"Well, I hope the steak will make it worth your trip, because I have no intention of taking Rose Trellis from Mona and Deuce."

"Just listen to what I have to say with an open mind, Ronald, and I think you'll see things differently."

As they sat at the kitchen table, Frank told Ronald all the things he'd learned about Joel's crooked shenanigans and the dirty way he had treated his secretary. "I'm telling you, not only as the Guardian of your father's estate, but as your friend, if you still have any feelings for your wife and son, you'll show up next Friday, or they'll be ruined. Joel has an addiction to gambling, and he's not as good as he thinks he is. It won't take long for everything that your father worked for to be in the hands of a few greedy men."

Ronald stood and walked over to the window. "I hear what you're saying, and I want to stop him. But I'm afraid."

"What do you have to be afraid of?"

"Isn't it obvious? When Mona discovers I'm still alive, she'll hate me."

"Look at it this way. If you knowingly allow her to lose the only real home she's ever known, to a lying crook, and she finds out you're alive and could've stopped him, she'll hate you, anyway. And eventually, she will find out."

Ronald thought about Frank's words. For fifteen years, he'd stayed hidden, knowing the chance of Mona ever recognizing him, even if their paths crossed, was improbable. But could he, in good conscience, remain out of the picture if Joel attempted to steal from Mona or Deuce what was rightfully theirs? He didn't want any part of the Estate, but he couldn't allow Joel Gunter to gamble it away.

Frank waited. Finally, he said, "What about it? Will you do it?"

"I'll be there. I know she'll hate me, but I have to save Rose Trellis for her and Deuce. I'll accept the terms of the will and keep it in my name, with it to go to Deuce at my death. That way, when Mona marries Joel, they'll be able to live there, but with it in Deuce's name, Joel can never sell it, or even borrow money on it. Am I right?"

Frank let out a loud sigh. "One-hundred percent. That's exactly what I was going to advise. Thank goodness, you finally came to your senses. I can go on back now."

"It's late. Why not stay here? I sleep on the sofa as many times as I sleep in the bed. You're welcome to spend the night."

"Thanks, but I want to be home before morning, to have coffee with my girl."

Ronald's lip curled. "Your girl? I know that's a joke. After all these years, I can't see you settling on one, when you have them all swooning over you."

"No joke. I started to say that I've found what I've been looking for, but that's not right. I didn't know such sweetness and beauty was available to me. God just sent her to me."

"Anyone I know?"

"I don't think so, although I just spoke of her minutes ago."

"Hold on. The only females I recall you mentioning were Mona and Joel's secretary. Are you saying . . . You? And Mona? Is that why you want me to keep Joel from getting his hands on Rose Trellis? You want it?"

"Don't be ridiculous. I'm in love with Peggy—Joel's secretary. Or at least she was his secretary until today. I think she's finally seen him for what he is."

"Well, I'm proud for you, Frank. Man wasn't meant to be alone. No one knows that better than I."

CHAPTER 34

Friday morning, Joel arrived in Jinx Bay to drive Ramona and Deuce to the reading of the Will in Eufaula.

When he walked up to the door of #7, he could hear the argument taking place inside. "Hey, what's going on?"

Ramona said, "Deuce doesn't want to ride with us. He's insisting he drive his truck."

Joel's brow meshed together. "Is that all? So, what's the problem?"

"He doesn't have a license. It's one thing for him to drive around town here, but I can't let him drive all the way to Eufaula."

"Honey, how many times have you told me how trustworthy he is? So, why are you having trouble trusting him, now? He loves that truck, and he's a good driver. I say let him drive it back. It's mostly country roads, anyway."

Deuce knew the only reason Joel sided with him was to get rid of him, but it suited him fine.

Ramona bit her lip. "I don't know. I'm not comfortable with this."

Deuce walked over and kissed her on the cheek. "Joel trusts me, Mama. Why can't you?"

"Fine. Just make sure you follow us all the way."

Joel said, "Deuce, do you know how to get to Eufaula?"

"Yes sir. But I have a map in the glove compartment of my truck, so even if I didn't know the way, I'm capable of reading a map."

Joel put his arm around Ramona. "Honey, we need to give him space. Now, if you have everything you need, we should go. I don't want to be late." He walked her to his convertible and opened her door. As they drove away, she turned and looked back at the truck, still parked in the yard.

"He went back into the cottage."

Joel chuckled. "Relax, sweetheart. He just wants to find out if you really trust him as you said. I'm sure he'll leave as soon as we're out of sight."

"Thank you for being so reassuring. This is why I needed to marry you."

He frowned. "I was hoping it was because you loved me. You do, don't you?"

"I'm very fond of you, Joel. You know that." She glanced in the side mirror, hoping to see a green truck.

****

It was almost midnight when Frank arrived back in Eufaula.

He called Peggy, hoping she hadn't fallen asleep. When she answered, he said, "Hi." He suddenly felt like a tongue-tied teenager, calling his girl for the first time.

"Hi, Frank. I was hoping you'd get back tonight. There's something very important that I need to tell you."

"I hope it's what I want to hear."

There was silence on the other end. His pulse raced. Just as he feared. She was still in love with Joel. How stupid of him to get his hopes up.

She said, "I know it's late, but could you possibly come over. I'd like to ride around as I share something with you that I should've told you before now."

He knew why she wanted to ride around. She wouldn't have to face him when she broke the news. She knew how much he loved her.

"I'm on my way." Before he could get out to walk her to the car, she was waiting for him. She opened her own door and slid inside. "Thanks for coming, but I have to get this off my mind."

He sucked in a lungful of air. "I'm listening."

"Frank, I'm pregnant." When he didn't respond, she said, "It's Joel's baby."

"Did you think I'd even suspect that it could be anyone else's?"

"I guess not. But I should've told you before now. I know you were hoping there could be something between you and me. So, did I. But it's a secret I can't hide. I am so sorry."

"Sorry you're pregnant?"

"I can't say that I'm sorry I'm pregnant. I love this baby growing inside of me, already. I'm just sorry that it's Joel's and not yours."

"Do you mean that, Peg?"

"Of course, I mean it." She began to cry.

"But you're divorced. Right?"

She nodded.

"Then we'd better get to the Court House as soon as possible. We're about to have a baby."

"Oh, Frank. How I wish! But Joel already knows I'm having his child, though I'm sure he'll deny it, now that he's getting married."

"No, Peggy. We're having our child."

"What are you saying?"

"I'm saying I want you to choose our baby's first name, but I get to choose the last name and I choose Jinright."

"Oh, Frank, I don't know what to say."

"Save it until in the morning, and then say, "I do.""

She slid over and kissed him. "I love you, Frank. I thought I knew what love was, but I was mistaking sympathy for love. I felt Joel needed me and I tried to meet his every need, even when it went against everything I knew to be decent and honest. How could I have been so naïve?"

"All that is in the past, sweetheart, and that's where we'll leave it. I'm looking forward to spending the rest of my life with you. Can you be ready in the morning around nine o'clock?"

"You bet! I'll be ready as soon as the sun comes up."

"I hate that I'll have to marry and run tomorrow, but I have to be at the reading of the Jones Will at two o'clock. There could be fur-flying when things don't go according to everyone's expectations, but as soon as I can, I'll get away."

"I understand. Do you plan to tell Joel? About us, I mean?"

"I owe Joel nothing except a big thank you for finally exposing his corruptness, allowing you to see his true colors."

****

Deuce drove straight to Skip's cottage, but seeing his car gone, he drove on over to the Fish Camp. He spotted him stepping from the wharf onto a boat. He ran, yelling his name, hoping to get to him before the boat left the dock.

Skip waved, then stepped off and ran toward his son. "What's wrong? Where's your mama?"

Deuce couldn't hold back the tears. Apologizing, he said, "I guess you think I'm a big baby. I was afraid you'd leave before I could talk to you."

"I wasn't going anywhere. I just stepped on board to talk to my men."

"Your men?"

"On my boat."

Deuce dried his eyes. "Your *boat?* The Momo?"

"Yep."

"Whoa! You're the. . . skipper?"

"That's what they call me. I own the Fish Camp. One day, it'll be yours, if you want it. I miss fishing, but the doctor didn't want me exposed to too much sunlight. However, I have a feeling you didn't come here to talk about me. What's going on? Where is Mona?"

"She's with Joel. They're on their way to Eufaula. My grandfather's will is gonna be read today, and then they're getting married. But I won't ever live in the same house with that man."

"I'm sorry you feel that way. I wish there was something I could do."

"Do you, Daddy?"

Skip felt the blood drain from his face. "What did you call me?"

"Daddy. You are my daddy, aren't you?"

"How did you find out?"

"You look like the picture Mama keeps under her pillow at night."

Skip threw his arms around his son in a hug. "Oh, Deuce! I've wanted to do this for so long, but we need to hurry."

His jaw jutted forward. "If you're planning to take me to live with Mama and Joel, you can forget it. I'll run away. Don't you want me?"

"Want you? You can't imagine. When you walked up, I was giving my guys their instructions before they take off. Then I planned to get on the road and head to Rose Trellis."

"Rose Trellis? For real?"

"For real. Get in the car. We have no time to waste."

"Are you gonna stop Joel from marrying Mama? That's why you're going, isn't it?"

"Stop them? No, son. Mona is a grown woman. If Joel is what she wants, I have no right to stop her. I have another reason for being there today."

"Do you still love my mama?"

"I'll never stop loving your Mama. Now, no more questions. Just trust me."

Deuce rolled down his window, stuck his head out and let the warm, Spring breeze blow in his face. He had fifteen years' worth of questions, but they'd keep. For the time being, he was going to bask in the moment of being in the presence of his daddy.

When they arrived at Rose Trellis, Ronald pulled up to the door and told Deuce to go in and not to mention how he got there. Mona and Joel would assume he came on his truck.

He walked into the huge room, glanced around, then walked over and sat beside her mother. He pretended not to notice Joel sitting on the other side of her.

The way Gussie looked him over, Deuce assumed she didn't approve of him wearing pegged dungarees to her important event. With a scowl, she said, "Well, it's about time you got here. I can't believe your mama allowed you to drive that old truck all the way from Florida. Why I bet you ain't even got a drivers' license."

Joel whispered to Ramona, assuring her that although they'd

get a judge to marry them at the Court House after the will was read, he promised to see to it that she'd have a big wedding as soon as they could get it planned. "I'm thinking in the gardens. What do you think?"

"I don't want a big wedding, Joel. Let's just get it over with." She bit her lip. "I didn't mean for it come out like that. I simply meant I've been married before. I don't plan on wearing a white dress and veil and pretend to be a blushing new bride."

"Whatever, darling. I'll sell my family's old homeplace, and we'll live here at Rose Trellis. I'm sure that's what you want, and I want nothing more than to make you happy."

Ramona raised a brow. "If that's your idea of a joke, it isn't very funny. You know how that woman feels about me. Deuce and I left because of her. If you think she's gonna let the three of us move in with her now, you don't know her very well. Besides, she plans to sell the estate."

He had a peculiar look on his face. "Oh, but I have a surprise for you, my darling."

Ramona cringed. If he planned to buy Rose Trellis from Gussie, she'd have to stop him. It was the first home—the only home—that she and Ronald shared. It wouldn't seem right to be married to her husband's best friend and living in the house that should've been Ronald's.

Gussie hollered. "Well, what are we waiting on? I've got places to be."

Joel apologized and said, "Sorry, Gussie. You're right. It looks as if we're all here."

Frank looked out the window and saw Ronald coming up the walk. "Hold on. I think there's one more."

The confused look on Joel's face revealed that he was not aware that anyone else had a reason for being present. He cleared his throat. "Not meaning to dispute you, but according to my count, I believe we're all here. I agree with Gussie. It's time to begin." He looked down at the leather binder on the desk, holding the Will, and pushed it over toward Frank. Clearing his throat, he said, "Ladies and Gentlemen, we have requested your presence here today, to make known Theodore Alexander Jones's wishes as put forth in his Last Will and Testament. I was privileged to serve as Mr. Jones's attorney, and Mr. Franklin Jinright was appointed as the Guardian of the Estate. At this time, I'll ask Mr. Jinright to read the Will in its entirety."

Frank picked it up, then walked over toward the door.

Deuce reached over and took his mama by her hand and squeezed. She looked at him and winked. "I suppose this is your way of saying you forgive me?"

He shrugged. "Forgive you? For what?"

"For marrying Joel?"

He couldn't breathe. "You haven't . . .? Oh, mama! You didn't. Did you?"

"Not yet, but the three of us will go to the Court House together, after this is over. I don't know why it was even necessary for us to be here. Gussie had no objections to you having the truck."

He bit his lip. "I know why we're here and it has nothing to do with the truck."

Frank opened the door, and Ronald walked in. "Good afternoon, everyone. Hope I didn't keep you waiting."

Gussie pulled out her spectacles. "Who are you?"

"I'm Ronald Maxwell Jones, ma'am. Son of your former husband."

She groveled. "What are you trying to pull? That's impossible. You're dead."

"Forgive me for disappointing you." He glanced over at Mona, who was leaving her seat. She walked over and stood facing him. Their gaze locked. Then glaring into his eyes, she began crying and beating on his chest. "Why? Why, didn't you let me know you were alive?"

Joel looked at Frank. "You're responsible for him showing up here. Aren't you?"

"You're right. What a travesty it would've been if two attorneys had allowed the estate to go into the wrong hands, when we both knew the truth." He glanced over at Ronald, who now had his arms wrapped around Ramona. Both were sobbing.

Deuce's glad heart felt as if it would burst wide open, when he heard his father say, "Don't cry, Momo." Not knowing why the funny little name made his mama's face light up, didn't matter. Just seeing his mother cradled in his father's arms, reminded him of something his grandfather once told him. Although his mama never believed him when he said his daddy appeared in his dreams, Daddy Theo had acted as if he understood. He said, "Hold on to your dreams, Deuce, even when things look impossible. For with God, all things are possible." Did Daddy Theo have the same dream?

Frank said, "Uh . . . if I may ask everyone to take a seat, I think it's time to make Theodore's wishes known."

After reading twelve detailed pages, which left no room for speculation, Frank stuck the will back into his briefcase. I thank you all for coming."

Gasps could be heard, but it appeared everyone—or most everyone—was too surprised to speak.

Frank sprinted across the floor with a broad smile and an outstretched hand. "Welcome home, Mr. and Mrs. Ronald Alexander Jones—and Deuce."

EPILOGUE

Gussie Jones stormed out of the room, making threats and uttering words that would shock a sailor. Joel was too stunned for words. Everything he ever wanted had slowly slipped away before his eyes. The only thing that had ever remained stable in his life was Peggy, and he couldn't blame her if she never spoke to him again. But she would. He knew it, just as sure as his name was Joel Gunter. He didn't deserve such a special woman, but this time, he'd treat her right.

Trudging down the marble steps of the home that should've been his, he looked across the street and saw sweet Peggy sitting in her car, waiting for him. Good ol' faithful, Peg. He yelled and waved. "Coming, sweetheart!"

Shielding his eyes from the sun with his hand, he thought he saw Frank Jinright opening the door on the passenger side of Peggy's car and crawl in. He squinted, then felt the blood rush to his head. It was Frank, all right.

Up until now, Joel had been patient with Frank's obvious

obsession with Peg, but it was time to put a stop to it. And he would. He'd let Peggy know he was ready for her to become Mrs. Joel Gunter. Not just ready, but eager. He'd explain that Ramona was never what he wanted—it was the breakdown causing him to have such crazy thoughts. They'd plan a real wedding, then go back to their beach cottage and on to the Everglades for a real honeymoon. He was sure that would please her.

After waiting for traffic to pass, he ran across the street, just as Peggy's car cranked and pulled away from the curb. Joel ran after it, waving his arms and yelling her name.

It was not until after she and Frank drove away that he saw the crude, bold letters on the back window, written in white shoe polish. "Just Married!"

KAY CHANDLER BOOKS

JINX BAY SERIES

    CANNERY ROAD – Book 1

VINEGAR BEND SERIES

    Chalkboard Preacher from Vinegar Bend – Book 1
    Drawing Conclusions -Book 2
    A Clean Slate – Book 3
    2 x 2- Book 4
    No Crib for a Bed Book 5
    While Mortals Sleep Book 6

SWITCHED SERIES:

    Lunacy – Book 1
    Unwed – Book 2
    Mercy – Book 3

GRAVE ENCOUNTER SERIES

    When the Tide Ebbs – Book 1
    When the Tide Rushes In – Book 2
    When the Tide Turns – Book 3

THE KEEPER SERIES

    The Keeper – Book 1
    The Prey – Book 2
    The Destined – Book 3

HOMECOMING SERIES:

    Sweet Lavender –-Book 1
    Unforgettable – Novella - 2
    Gonna Sit Right Down – Novella- 3
    Hello Walls – Novella - 4

PLOW HAND –-Stand-alone
A GIRL CALLED ALABAMA –- Stand-alone
SWAMP ANGEL-Stand-alone